THE
PHOENIX
APPROACH

THE PHOENIX APPROACH

The Contrarian Investor's Guide to Profiting from Out-of-Favor, Distressed, and Bankrupt Companies

William J. Grace, Jr.

Bantam Books
Toronto • New York • London • Sydney

THE PHOENIX APPROACH
A Bantam Book / February 1984

Chart on page 148 reprinted by permission of *Barron's,*
© Dow Jones & Company, Inc. 1982. All rights reserved.
Chart on pages 152–55 reprinted by permission of
Financial World.
The article "Buy a Company Nothing Down, Easy
Payments" Report Number 83-271 from *Investment Strategy
Perspectives* reprinted by permission of Oppenheimer &
Co., Inc. Copyright © 1983 by Oppenheimer & Co., Inc.
All rights reserved.

Library of Congress Cataloging in Publication Data

Grace, William J.
    The phoenix approach.

    1. Investments—United States—Handbooks, manuals,
etc. I. Title.
HG4921.G7   1984   362.6'78   83-22455
ISBN 0-553-05046-X

ISBN 0-553-05046-X

Published simultaneously in the United States and Canada

PRINTED IN THE UNITED STATES OF AMERICA

DC   0 9 8 7 6 5 4 3 2 1

Author's Note

All opinions expressed in this book are entirely those of the author himself and are not to be viewed as representative of any institution that he may be associated with.

Similarly, the title of the book, which refers to the magnificent desert bird that rose from its ashes in Egyptian mythology, implies no connection whatsoever with any other entity that happens to make use of the Phoenix name. The financial community has often employed the word as a symbol of rebirth and immortality.

Any investment advice can be dangerous to your financial health, even when taken as prescribed. Be sure to supplement the strategy found in this book with current information on the specific companies that interest you. Be particularly careful when dealing with troubled companies; uncommon hazards lurk in every corner. With this warning, the author and publisher must disclaim any liability for losses that could be incurred by readers of this book. Actual investment decisions are always your own.

Acknowledgments

On the balance sheet of any book is a tug-of-war between various assets and liabilities which eventually determine its net result. Among the liabilities of this book were the special time constraints of an ever-changing financial world and the personal discipline required of a weekend writer.

Fortunately for me, the book has also had some invaluable assets from the beginning. Perhaps the greatest of these advantages can be found in the wonderful and talented people that I have been associated with during the book's development. I wish to thank a few of them:

Valerie Ruebush, who made it possible for me to immerse myself in this project, helped in every phase of the book and was the key to its fast completion.

Robert Garfield, financial columnist for *U.S.A. Today*, added spice to the final draft of the manuscript. I blame all hyperbole on him.

Wayne Nelson, friend and colleague, has continued to share the trials of full-time brokering and part-time writing with me. Allen Model has shared his constant flow of creative ideas over the past year, including a number of important suggestions for this book. I value our friendship and have learned much from him.

Data Resources, Inc. provided tables and graphs for each of my first two books. The Work Place, in Washington, typed each manuscript. Paula Sewell, my long-time assistant, has been essential in keeping my business running efficiently despite the considerable demands on my time over the past two years.

My agent, Rafe Sagalyn, and editor, Peter Guzzardi, have been enthusiastic believers in *The Phoenix Approach* from the very beginning. Without them, the project would never have begun.

I also thank those who have had an indirect influence on this book. These are the real achievers in the professions of money management and financial writing. In the first field—one in which even mediocrity is often rewarded —it is encouraging to find people like John Templeton, whose thirty-year investment record is living proof that a sensible, consistent strategy really can work. And in the field of financial writing—one cluttered with reckless schemes—it is refreshing to discover the works of truly responsible and creative people, such as David Dreman, Charles Rolo, Andy Tobias, and a handful of others. I have learned from each.

Contents

Introduction: The Investor's Guide to Bottom-Fishing

Who isn't a bargain hunter these days?

I don't know about you, but I've stood in a supermarket aisle for minutes at a time deciding which brand of paper towels to buy. I've stood there making minute calculations while examining the various sized and colored packages. All for the difference between $1.19 and 89¢.

You've probably done it, too—if not for paper towels, then for toothpaste or some other item. It's part of America's ever-present search for value. But why do so many people behave differently in the stock market than they do in the supermarket? If you're careful not to waste money on overpriced paper towels—or soup or bread or toothpaste—why would you pay $20 a share too much for an overpriced stock? As an investment advisor, I have always been amazed by how quickly and thoughtlessly most people make decisions that involve a great deal of money, sometimes their entire life savings. A tip from their neighbor, a one-minute conversation with their broker, and whoosh—$20,000 gets shifted from one investment to another. And these are the very same people, of course, who carefully calculate in the supermarket and who spend weeks consulting consumer reports before buying a $600 TV set.

What most investors are missing is a *strategy*—that invisible, impalpable theory which separates the sound investor from the crapshooter; that boring, unrelenting set of guidelines, unaffected by hot tips, erratic markets or passions of the heart; that maker of fortunes.

Of course, there's nothing magic about strategy. Even in possession of one, you must know two things:

1) That it will work. Can you demonstrate, based on underlying theory and market history, that it will be profitable?

2) That you will stick with it. Think of Ted Williams' batting stance. Think of Hank Aaron's. Babe Ruth's. Pete Rose's. If you're a baseball fan, you can probably imitate those stances, because they were the same from the beginning to the end of each player's illustrious career. Now, picture Bob Uecker's stance. Having trouble? He was in the major leagues for six years, but he also had six different batting stances. His lifetime batting average was .200.

This is a book about a *strategy*. The strategy is about *bargain hunting* on Wall Street.

On the heels of one of the most dramatic bull markets in history, many investors entering the stock market are putting their money into grossly overvalued stocks. At the same time, they're ignoring undervalued securities with long-term growth potentials better than those of the soundest blue-chippers or the most speculative high-fliers. These are the stocks of out-of-favor companies, to which Wall Street has turned a cold shoulder, and of distressed companies, which are losing money now but are very likely to bounce back.

Stocks like these have always been around, in good times and bad, through economic sickness and health, in bear markets and in bull. In August of 1982, as the Great Bull Market was just starting through the gate, two years of deep recession had left the market awash in such bargains. Investors who got in that market early learned in the most dramatic fashion possible that good, solid companies don't stay down for long. Even some of the sickliest tended to re-emerge, Phoenix-like, from the ashes of financial distress. And as those Phoenix companies rose, propelled by the bull market, fortunes were made again and again.

Needless to say, bull markets like that don't come along too often. But the fact is, the very same principle that made the biggest fortunes for '82–'83 Bull Market investors can be applied every trading day of every year. The very nature of the market dictates that there are always undervalued stocks, and they're usually not nearly as risky as you might think.

These are not ordinary times for the Phoenix Approach. Conditions now are virtually ideal. Remember that the country is still recovering from one of the worst financial periods in its history. Some 225 publicly traded corporations have filed for protection under Chapter 11 of the Bankruptcy Code since 1980. In 1982 and 1983 alone, there were over 50,000 total corporate failures. Thousands of others suffered severely, registering huge losses. Not to be too mercenary about it, but the fact is that the recession created investment opportunities the likes of which this country hasn't seen since the 1930s. The Great Bull Market had a highly visible effect on popular stocks, but its harvest has yet to be reaped in out-of-favor and distressed stocks; many of them remain ignored. They will emerge gradually, as other, overpriced stocks fall back to earth. The Phoenix Approach explores one of the great stock market opportunities of the 1980s.

This book concentrates on the selection of investment opportunities among companies in various degrees of trouble: from cyclical difficulties to bankruptcy proceedings. It is based on an extension of the "contrarian" theory, which contends that the market usually overreacts to both good and bad news. Adverse publicity and fearful market psychology usually drive the prices of securities down much further than the real situation warrants. In many cases, for example, distressed companies will be selling for less than the intrinsic value of their underlying assets. The longer term capital appreciation potential of many of these companies is substantial, sometimes dramatic. The contrarian theory dictates that we should act in opposition to most investors: buy stocks that are currently out-of-favor and sell stocks that are universally *in* favor. The theory holds that a market movement which is expected by a consensus is unlikely to materialize because the anticipation itself will alter prices long before the consensus is formed. The contrarian sells when he finds that just about everyone is finally bullish, and buys when everyone is throwing in the towel at any price.

By extending that theory to its logical limit, you come to what I call "super-contrarianism," the surprising conclusion that the *best* buys are sometimes in the stocks and bonds of very troubled or even bankrupt companies. And, in fact, there has always been a highly specialized marketplace for distressed securities. Wall Street even has a name for playing that market. It's called *bottom fishing,* and there are those who've prospered mightily doing it. One such investor is William Simon—Wall Street veteran, cabinet official, entrepreneur—whose "leveraged buyouts" of whole companies at bargain prices have made investment news recently. Another is a man named Warren Buffett. He bought one third of the shares of GEICO (about which you will read more) a few years ago when the company was troubled and its stock was selling for only a few dollars a share. Granted, it took a certain amount of foresight and a great deal of capital to buy seven million shares of GEICO at $6.50 per share. But any Phoenix investor could have bought then too, and could have reaped the rewards as GEICO rose back up to its original heady price of $60 a share.

If you're not sure of what to think of an investment strategy that claims so grand a name as the Phoenix Approach, that's fine. You may prefer to think of it the way Wall Street does. Call it bottom fishing. But call it that with pride. Do it with the satisfaction of knowing that you're likely to fare much better than most investors. Think of battered companies as wrecks on the ocean floor, and think of their securities as plump bottom fish that swim around the wrecks. Now imagine most of Wall Street as fleet fishermen, all of whom cruise to the same location to harvest the same schools of surface fish. Over time, none of the fleet fishermen does any better than any other. And because they're all fishing in the same places for the same species, they wind up depleting their mutual resources. The fleet as a group ultimately cannot prosper. Meanwhile, the bottom fisher hauls in the big ones in solitude.

It seems that everybody's got investment ideas these days. For the first time in twenty years, stock tips are being exchanged in elevators and office lunchrooms. One scheme, then another, gets media coverage. Your neighbor is making a killing buying fertilizer futures. You can hardly go to a party without hearing about one brilliant investment gambit or another.

Given that the bull market which began in August of 1982 has been so consistently strong, it would have been difficult for those cocktail-party financeers *not* to have made money during the past two years; but if they behave like most investors, they'll give back much of their profits without the benefit of an explosive market. These fleet investors do have courage and heart and brains. What they don't have, as the Wizard of Oz would point out, is *strategy*. This book is going to offer you a strategy.

The Phoenix Approach provides both the experienced investor and the novice with a demonstrably sound, enduring set of investment principles. As you will see, the history of the market proves that the stocks of out-of-favor companies perform considerably better over time than popular ones. In exploring that lightly-traveled corner of the marketplace, the Phoenix Approach helps you discover the most important, and the most elusive, ingre-

dient of successful investing: real value. This strategy is
by no means a get-rich-quick scheme; the objective is
long-term asset growth and the gradual creation of personal wealth. And it works.

I

From the Brink of Disaster

1

Four Case Histories

For every piece of Horatio Alger rags-to-riches fiction, corporate America has dozens of real-life counterparts. If you think the make-believe stuff is inspiring, the honest-to-goodness corporate comebacks will send chills up your spine.

Think about Chrysler Corporation. What, no goosebumps? Then one thing is certain. Way back in 1982, when Lee Iacocca was begging Uncle Sam for loan guarantees, and Chrysler stock was selling for $3 a share, you didn't call your broker and buy some. If you had, your gain as of mid-1983 would have been over 1,000%.

Every industry has its Chryslers. Aerospace has Lockheed; communications, MCI; transportation, Penn Central; insurance, GEICO; financial, Orion; retailing, Toys 'R' Us. Each, at one time or another, was in severe distress. True, there are a lot of defunct companies in the obituaries of Wall Street, but the number of comebacks from critical financial trouble is surprising. The Phoenix investor knows that these recoveries have created some of the greatest wealth in America.

The company in Chapter 11 bankruptcy today might be rising, Phoenix-like, tomorrow. Sometimes such revivals are dramatic and well publicized, à la Chrysler. More often, though, they are accomplished gradually, unevenly, and with little fanfare. These little-known turnarounds provide the greatest opportunities of all. That's why the Phoenix investor, or bottom fisher, doesn't follow the big commercial fleet; he's dedicated to the art of fishing alone.

In this chapter, I'll take a look at the declines and recoveries of four highly successful companies. Each was unique in the cause of its trouble and the means of its return to profitability. The first two are among my favorite success stories; both are Washington-based companies that once came perilously close to bankruptcy, only to be guided back to prosperity by remarkable leaders. The second two firms are even more astounding. Each rebounded from the depths of actual bankruptcy to become —as the financial journalists are fond of saying—"wildly successful." Phoenix investors who hooked them at the bottom were wildly successful too.

• MCI COMMUNICATIONS •

You could say that MCI was asking for trouble from the very start. If William G. McGowan, the company's founder and chairman, had walked into my office in 1972 and said, "I'm taking on AT&T," I'd have escorted him to the rubber room. Not that he didn't have an intriguing idea. McGowan wanted to build his own long-distance telephone network, bypassing the AT&T long-lines system but connecting his lines into local Bell systems, so that people could use their existing phones to make MCI long-distance calls at a cut rate.

When a frustrated MCI filed a civil antitrust suit against Ma Bell in 1974, it looked like David taking on Goliath— the small newcomer was sure to be crushed. Then, in the same year, the Justice Department filed its own suit against AT&T, charging it with unfair, monopolistic practices in the equipment and long-distance segments of the phone industry. That made MCI's quest look less futile, but the company still lost $39 million that year. By 1976, MCI stock was selling for a whopping 44¢ per share, adjusted for splits. But things were happening.

While the company was managing to lose that $39 million on only $7 million of revenues, and was $100 million in debt, McGowan introduced something called Execunet Service, similar to AT&T's own long-distance service.

It was a bold trespass into Ma Bell's long-lines business. Instead of continuing to operate separate intercity tie lines for each corporate customer, McGowan wanted to do what AT&T does: use a computerized switching network and service many customers on the same line. MCI petitioned the Federal Communications Commission, which took due note of AT&T's lack of enthusiasm about the proposal. MCI set up the service pending approval, but in June, 1975, the FCC nixed the whole idea.

MCI headed right back to federal court. Three years and $27 million of additional losses later, MCI won. The FCC was overruled, MCI was ready to step into the long-lines business, and a corporate success story was well on its way. William McGowan, whose personal holdings in the company are now worth over $100 million, had proven his right to compete with the world's biggest corporation in a business where no one had ever dared to trespass. His boldness has changed the face of the gigantic telecommunications industry itself. The stock price was still only $3, but it began moving up quickly. By 1983, shares were selling at $57. Phoenix investors who paid $440 for 1,000 shares of the distressed stock in 1976 finally saw a profit of $56,560—a tidy 12,000% return on investment—although at that level the now-popular stock was overpriced, and it fell considerably in value by late 1983.

MCI, incorporated in 1968, today is a billion-dollar company with a strong foothold in three areas of telecommunications: domestic long distance, international services, and personal communications. For years a struggling company often on the verge of disaster, now it is one of the most actively traded stocks in America.

• GEICO •

Are we talking corporate comebacks? Let's talk GEICO. In 1976, after two years of hard knocks in the rough-and-tumble insurance business, GEICO was selling for $2 a share. As you'll see in a minute, management was not doing anything to make the Street exactly giddy with optimism about the company's future. But the true bottom fisher heeded basic contrarian sense: billion-dollar insurance companies do not just curl up and die. Verily, the bottom fishers once again were rewarded. Today GEICO trades in the $60s.

Just as MCI's idea of going head-to-head with AT&T seemed to most people a bit irrational in the early 1970s, GEICO's founding in the 1930s was an equally bold move in the insurance industry of the time.

Leo Goodwin began Government Employees Insurance Co. on the premise that government workers are a lesser risk than the population in general. The innovation that would catapult his company was not in risk selection, however. It was in marketing. He had the brilliant idea of selling automobile insurance directly to the customer by mail order. What he saved by not paying sales agents their 10 to 20% commissions was realized by customers as a savings.

It worked. A thriving GEICO went public in 1948 and, over the next twenty years, proved a phenomenal success for both customers and investors. Customers got good service and a discount rate that tended to hook them for life. Shareholders watched their stock skyrocket from 21¢ (adjusted for splits) per share in 1948 to more than $60 at its peak in 1972, as GEICO became one of the nation's largest auto insurers. Many Washingtonians became wealthy by investing in their pet local company. The $10,000 investor in the late 1940s had more than $3 million by the early 1970s. (How's that for Washington cocktail conversation?)

Then things began to unravel.

The early 1970s were not kind to property-casualty companies, and GEICO fared worse than most. The cause of its problems was a near-fatal triple whammy: severe inflation, the introduction of no-fault insurance, and a management team too slow to respond.

Insurance claims grew vastly more expensive as inflation began raging in 1973, and no-fault made a bad situation worse. Instead of reducing litigation by eliminating lawsuits for small claims, it encouraged injured policy holders to run up their medical expenses to exceed the $200-to-$500 thresholds. GEICO had almost half of its business in no-fault states. Making matters worse, a moratorium on auto insurance rate increases was imposed during the early stages of the energy crisis in 1974.

But when the moratorium was lifted, did GEICO do the obvious and raise rates? No. Management probably figured to get an edge on the competition by keeping prices stable. GEICO got a lot of business all right, but when all those new customers began filing claims—based on steadily inflating health and repair costs—the insurer took a bath. The operating results of 1974 and 1975 were disastrous. In 1975, the company lost a staggering $126 million. Its all-important policyholders' surplus (the capital reserves an insurance company holds to back up its policies) shrank to $49 million against premiums of $660 million. (The industry's safety guidelines call for a 3:1 ratio. GEICO's was 14:1.) The company was on the edge of collapse.

That's when the "smart money" bailed out and the Phoenix investors climbed aboard. In early 1976, trading in the company's stock was suspended for two months. When it finally opened, trading began at $2.12 a share. Then came a management shake-up—the hiring of Travel-

ers Corp. Executive Vice President John J. Byrne—and
the institution of Operation Bootstrap.

First, Byrne slashed away at payroll and boosted rates
wherever possible. Then he said, "So long, New Jersey," a
no-fault state in which the company had suffered extensive losses. GEICO simply stopped doing business there.
Then he went to his competitors and asked for help. He
figured they'd bend over backwards to prevent GEICO's
failure, which might have sent the whole industry into a
tailspin. He figured right. Not only did twenty-seven companies reinsure much of GEICO's risk, some of them also
bought into the company in the form of newly issued
convertible preferred stock.

By 1977, GEICO was back in the black, and it has
increased its profits each year since. Its surplus has grown
nearly tenfold to $451 million; its return on shareholders'
equity has been around 40% for three years running;
and its stock price has climbed from $2 all the way back
to its old peak of $60.

The glory goes to Byrne; the rewards, to the Phoenix
investor.

• PENN CENTRAL •

The match was not exactly made in heaven (it was
more like the Northeast Corridor), but at least there was
reason for cautious optimism when the great Pennsylva-
nia and New York Central railroads merged in 1968 to
form the colossal Penn Central.

Yes, both were unwieldy, troubled companies; both
were fettered by beaten-up equipment, deteriorating right-
of-ways, diminishing traffic, and burdensome government
regulation. The merger, however, promised reduction of
duplicative facilities, services, routes, and manpower. The
Penn Central would be leaner, meaner, and profitable.

Except it wasn't. Everything that hurt the railroads
separately hurt the combined company more. Add to

those problems hard feelings and rivalries in top management, mismatched computer systems, and rising business costs, and the picture became clear. Penn Central was headed for the biggest corporate train wreck in history. In 1970, with creditors' claims exceeding $4 billion, Penn Central filed for bankruptcy.

It was one of the most complicated reorganization efforts ever, a proposition that led most investors to do what they usually do in the face of adversity: run. The stock, which had traded at a high of $72, dropped to $9. More significantly, bond prices plummeted. A $1,000 bond could be picked up for $100. The "smart money" didn't mind selling at a 90% discount. Ten percent of $1,000, they figured, was better than 100% of nothing. (When the old Boston and Providence Railroad reorganized, it was forty years before bondholders got any money. And what did they get, a nickel on the dollar?) If some investor was misguided enough to shell out even $100 for a Penn Central bond that probably never would be honored, that was his problem.

What then transpired was one of the more heroic—and peculiar—comebacks in corporate history. Take away those annoying railroads, it turned out, and what you had was the heart of a magnificent conglomerate: acre after acre of prime real estate for asset strength and lots of diverse enterprises as potential profit centers.

By 1978, the reorganization was complete. Consolidated Rail Corp. (Conrail) had taken over the Penn Central rail system and that solid conglomerate was emerging. True, prebankruptcy security-holders fared poorly. The reorganization diluted stockholders' holdings to virtually nothing in a 1-for-25 reverse split. But post-bankruptcy investors did well, particularly bond investors. Secured bondholders walked away with most of the newly distributed equity, plus cash—a return of about $800 on a $1000 face value bond. Unsecured bondholders got stock plus a stake in what was called the Valuation Case—the eventual settlement with Conrail for the cash value of the rail system.

After five years of negotiation, the government paid Penn Central $2.5 billion for its old rail system, which Conrail had taken over, giving unsecured bondholders a return of roughly $500 on a $1000 face value bond. Phoenix investors who bought their bonds for only $100 in 1970 realized a 500% return on investment.

Meanwhile, the new Penn Central has been busy disposing of many of its 8,000 pieces of real estate (including such grand hotels as the Biltmore, Roosevelt, Barclay, and Commodore) and expanding its other enterprises. The modern Penn Central is in such varied businesses as telecommunications and oil-rig manufacturing. With the help of a vast tax-loss carry-forward of $1.5 billion, the company will be operating tax free until 1993.

Revenues now exceed $3 billion, and profits for the first half of 1983 alone amounted to $100 million.

Even the Phoenix investors who bought Penn Central stock in the early '70s at $9 per share now have a $40 per share piece of a prosperous, growing firm—and a lot to talk about with friends who bought popular Polaroid at $150 about the same time. That blue-chipper now trades for $28.

• TOYS 'R' US •

"Wait a minute," you may be saying. "Toys 'R' Us? Since when has that company ever been in trouble?"

Answer: never.

From the time Charles Lazarus got into the toy business in the late 1940s, his sales and profits have grown dramatically each year. Today, the chain of retail toy stores is 144 stores strong, accounting for annual sales of more than $1 billion.

So what has Toys 'R' Us got to do with bottom fishing? Everything.

After returning from the Army in 1948, at the age of twenty-four, Charles Lazarus started selling children's furniture in his father's bicycle repair shop in Washington, D.C. Soon after he got started, he found that his customers were asking for toys to go along with the cribs and playpens that they were for their children. The young shopkeeper began stocking an assortment of toys, and quickly realized that toy buying was a repeating business, while furniture buying tended to be a one-time purchase. Lazarus now says that he knew toys were a good business when he realized that they broke.

There was little competition in the retail toy industry in the 1950s. Lazarus quickly built his business through a combination of disciplined uniformity and unusual market insight (he bought the first Barbie doll in 1952). He was a perfectionist who confronted obstacles with unyielding determination. This determination, he says today, is easy to explain: he was poor and he wanted to be rich. By anyone's measurement, Lazarus' business has been a success. His little toy shop in his father's house has evolved into a billion dollar company called Toys 'R' Us, which Lazarus, now 59, still runs with an iron hand today. His personal stake in the company—one of the best run and most profitable retail chains of any kind in the country—is about $100 million.

The road to success for Toys 'R' Us, however, has not been without adversity. Even more dramatic than its record of meteoric growth is its re-birth from the clutches of bankruptcy over the past five years.

From 1966, when Lazarus sold out to Interstate Stores, to 1974, when Interstate filed for bankruptcy, Toys 'R' Us was about the only profitable asset of a corporation that seemed unable to do anything right. In 1975, Interstate sold for 12¢ a share. This despite the efforts of Lazarus himself, who had stayed on to manage the toy business and—for all of the parent company's ineptitude—was building his division into a toy-retailing giant.

This is where the bottom fishing comes in. In the same

way that Penn Central was a great company once it got
out of the railroad business, so did Interstate have enormous potential once it got out of its mainstay, department
stores, and concentrated on toys. The Phoenix investors
recognized this, and so did Charles Lazarus.

It was Lazarus who sold his four-store chain to Interstate and still retained management control as division
president, and who, in 1976, took control of the reorgan-
izing parent company and sold off all but a few department stores.

It was Lazarus who changed the parent's name to Toys
'R' Us, the psychological value of which was immeasurable.

It was Lazarus who coined the clever name Toys 'R' Us
in the first place. (Toys 'R' Us—Laz 'R' Us. Get it?)

And it was Lazarus who, as any self-respecting Lazarus
would, led the bankrupt company back from the dead.

By 1978, all of the creditors were paid off. In full. The
stock has split in each of the past four years. Phoenix
investors who bought the bankrupt Interstate's stock at
12¢, and hold it now at $48, have earned a remarkable
38,000% return on their investment. (A $10,000 invest-
ment at the bottom is now worth $4 million.)

WARNINGS

Does a 38,000% return on investment have you all
worked up? It's fine if it does, but there are a number of
things you should know:

1. One would be straining accepted notions of probability to expect ever to buy a stock at the nadir of its market
value and sell it at its zenith. If *I* could do that, I'd be
doing it, instead of spending my nights and weekends
explaining my secrets to you. This book is not a thirty-day
course in how to become a millionaire. What it is, though,
is a look at one investment strategy that really does work
over long periods of time.

2. This book could be dangerous to your financial health. Any investment guide can be harmful if the reader plunges headlong into unfamiliar waters, especially without a life jacket. And where the debt and equity markets are concerned, nobody should be in the water without one. The jacket consists of a balanced portfolio: savings, life insurance, an IRA, sources of credit, and, for most people, home ownership. All should be in place before you begin dabbling. (See Chapter 12 for details.)

3. What makes Phoenix investing work are peculiarities of the stock and bond markets. Though they are based on the simple fact that investors overreact to bad news, the details of the investment strategy are not simple at all. What's more, for the Phoenix concept to make any sense, you have to understand what the rest of the market is all about. You can't be a super-contrarian if you don't know what behavior you're going to act contrary to. So the beginning of this book is about standard, predictable, bluer-than-blue-chip institutional investing. Pay close attention to how these people behave. Not only do their actions cue you in on what to do in the market (whatever they're not doing), but their behavior is precisely what causes the market conditions that make Phoenix investing attractive in the first place.

II

Searching for
Value

2

The Traditional View

Welcome to the world of securities analysis, a curious world indeed. It is a land of highly trained, highly paid experts who, among them, somehow have defied the laws of probability, and managed over the years to be wrong more than half of the time. Still, it is a world wherein the utmost of self-confidence is exhibited by its two kinds of inhabitants.

In the majority are the *fundamental analysts*. They study factors that have to do with corporate earnings, dividends, and assets, as well as the state of various industries and the economy in general. Then there are the *technical analysts* who base their research on factors that influence supply and demand in the stock market: price and volume patterns as recorded on charts, and a variety of statistical "indicators" used as ingredients in forecasts. Neither species has developed what it would take to dominate the other: a perfect system. By the market's very nature that would be impossible. If everyone wanted to do the same thing, there would be no market, for a price is simply the result of a tug-of-war between investor opinions.

Still, much of the information in these systems, particularly fundamental analysis, will be essential to the Phoenix investor in examining and evaluating opportunities in the unpopular sector of the marketplace.

● THE FUNDAMENTAL APPROACH ●

Fundamental security analysis is what motivates most of us when making investment decisions on stocks. This is the traditional wisdom of the best brains on Wall Street. It's the thinking that has been used by both institutional and knowledgeable individual investors for the last fifty years. Mutual fund and pension fund managers think fundamentally and, most likely, so does your broker. The fundamental analyst himself holds the unique distinction and power of being the main transmitter of information and opinion to most investors in the stock market.

Fundamental analysis is the method of estimating the real value of a stock by analyzing what the underlying company *owns* and what it *earns*. Measurements taken in this approach include price-earnings ratios and future growth potential, as well as book value and return-on-equity. The basis of this entire school of thought is the belief that intelligent research can reveal information about a company that has somehow been overlooked by other research being done on the same company. The fundamentalist hopes to discover high-potential companies that have gone unnoticed by the investment community, and to have a better perception than most of his competitors of well-analyzed companies. Eventually, this logic follows, everyone will come to have the same perception of any given stock, and its market price will then reflect its true value.

Benjamin Graham (1894–1976) is considered the father of fundamental security analysis. A classics scholar by education, Graham became a successful investment manager as well as the best-known theorist of his time while teaching at Columbia University. His epic text, *Security*

Analysis, first appeared in 1934 and is still widely used today. Graham's theory of stock valuations (which became known as the "standard method of valuation") was simply that a company's market value should be a direct reflection of its fundamentals: dividends, earnings, and assets.

Graham's principles seem quite restrictive compared to today's sophisticated theories. His guidelines for both earnings and asset criteria are stringent: (1) PE ratios (which we'll learn about next) are attractive only when they are 40% below the going average (7:1 when the average was 11:1 at the time); (2) a company's current liabilities and long-term debt (combined) must be less than the company's current assets (see Chapter 11 on interpreting financial reports). Graham measures a company's value not only by what it earns, but also by its financial strength as determined by what it owns and what it owes.

Graham's fundamental approach introduced the idea of an analytical search for value by using both quantitative and projected measurements of a company's earning power and asset value. All security analysis since then has borne his influence, and, as Phoenix investors, we will apply many of Graham's concepts to our appraisal of companies that we consider to be recovery candidates.

PRICE-EARNINGS RATIOS

The principal tool that the fundamentalist—or almost any investor, for that matter—uses in determining stock values is the *price-earnings ratio*, commonly called the PE. This is simply a figure which represents the relationship between a stock's current price and its earnings per share. If a $10 share of stock is backed by $1 of net annual profit, it is said to be selling at ten times earnings or at a 10:1 PE.

Everything else being equal, one would think that a low-PE stock is always a better bargain than a high-PE stock. *The real question about a company's earnings, though, is not its past or current profits, but its potential for future earn-*

ings growth. The reason that one company's "valuation" is thirty (30:1 PE) and another's is only five is usually not because the low-PE stock is undiscovered, but because it is not expected to have the future earnings growth of the high-PE stock. The price of a stock in the open market-place is a reflection of total investor demand for a dollar's worth of that company's earnings. In the case of the high-PE stock price, the marketplace is willing to pay thirty dollars for every dollar of current earnings only because it feels that the company has the potential for rapid growth and increased earnings. This company may be expected to increase its earnings by 25% a year for the foreseeable future, for example, while the low-PE stock's future earnings may be expected to be flat or even decreasing.

The problem with future earnings estimates, of course, is that they are only educated guesses (the key word being "guess"). Smart security analysts are often well off the mark in their estimates, particularly for earnings a year or two in advance. Other factors that determine a stock's price and PE (also called its "multiple" or "valuation") are the industry that the company is in, its management, what its balance sheet looks like, and, of course, the general state of the stock market and the economy.

Price-earnings ratios tend to have cyclical patterns in cyclical industries. In highly volatile industries—such as airlines, equipment manufacturing, and construction—PE ratios tend to be low during good times (because of expected declines in future earnings) and high during bad times (because of expected increases in future earnings).

Over the past fifty years, the average PE for all U.S. stocks has been around 14:1. This average has expanded to almost 22:1 during the optimistic "go-go" years of the early 1960s, and contracted well below 10:1 during the early 1950s and in the severe recessions of 1974 and 1982. With hindsight, it's easy to see where the opportunities were for both buying and selling by looking at the PE trends. Each of the lowest PE periods was

Standard & Poor's—Industrials Price/Earnings Ratio

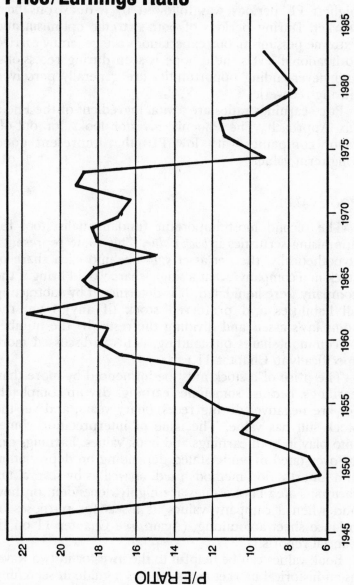

followed by a dramatic bull market, and each of the highest PE periods was followed by a disastrous bear market. During periods of both extreme optimism and extreme pessimism, our expectations are generally carried to irrational levels: little hope is seen during recessions, and never-ending opportunities are generally perceived during recoveries.

Price-earnings ratios are a vital ingredient of the Phoenix Approach. The Phoenix investor looks for out-of-favor companies with low PEs that represent good long-term value.

BOOK VALUE

The second most important fundamentalist tool for appraising securities is *book value*. This value represents, hypothetically, the net asset value behind each share of stock in a company: what a single share would bring if the company were liquidated. It is determined by subtracting all liabilities and preferred stock (if any) from the company's assets and dividing the result by the number of common shares outstanding. (This is discussed more specifically in Chapter 11.)

The price of a stock must be influenced by more than earnings, because sometimes earnings dry up completely (or are negative) during recessionary years, and yet the stock still has value. The issue of interpretation comes into play in both earnings and book values. Earnings can be overstated or understated depending on depreciation and amortization methods used, as well as by several tax factors; stated book values are highly dependent on how and when a company values its assets for purposes of balance sheet accounting. (Again, see Chapter 11 on financial reports.)

Book values can be helpful to the investor in two ways: as an historical market trend, and as a guide in searching for individual undervalued companies. After times of abnormally low price/book value averages, the market has

Standard & Poor's—Industrials
Stock Prices as a % of Book Value

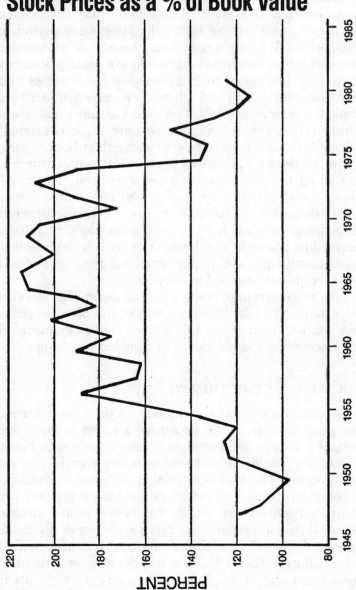

Courtesy Data Resources, Inc.

generally made sizable and sustained rallies. (Bull markets occurred after 1949, 1974, 1978, and 1982. Long declines came after the high price/book value period in the 1960s.) We might conclude, based on book value patterns alone, that individual stocks are underpriced any time they fall below their underlying book values and that they are overpriced when they exceed underlying book values by about 50%. This theory assumes that, given a relatively healthy economic environment, stocks should normally sell at prices somewhat above their book values.

But all theories are based on an ideal, and, if there is one thing the stock market is *not*, it is ideal. There will always be stocks that are priced well below their stated asset value. Many of these are stocks of cyclically battered companies, such as the distressed ones you'll eventually be reading about in this book. The trick is determining which companies are undervalued bargains and which ones are just as troubled as they look.

Like price-earnings ratios, asset valuation also plays an important role in the Phoenix scenario. In upcoming chapters you will learn of several techniques of asset appraisal for discovering hidden values in troubled companies.

THE PRESENT VALUE THEORY

Dividends are another valuation factor that influence the price of a stock. Some stocks, such as utilities, are bought primarily as income-generating investments. Here, a company's record of dividend increases over the years is an important factor in determining the price of its stock. A company that has increased its dividend every year for the past twenty years usually has better future income potential than a company that rarely increases its dividend. Even with growth stocks, the ultimate determination of value is the company's ability to pay the investor dividends, since the value of owning any business depends upon how much money the owners can eventually take out of it. *Think of the value of your stock in much the same way that you would think of the value of owning an interest in the neighbor-hood grocery store. Its only real value lies in how much money it eventually pays out to you or some future owner.* The actual intrinsic value of a stock, according to the *present value theory,* is simply a reflection of all its future dividend payments.

A more precise "present value" of a common stock is the sum of all its future dividends plus its future price when sold, discounted by current interest rates (to reflect a competitive no-risk return on your money). There is little question about this valuation. The difficulty comes in determining those future values: future dividend payments depend on earnings, and future market prices depend on a multitude of ingredients. To make the present value formula meaningful, an analyst would have to have very accurate estimates of a company's future sales, profit margins, and competition. But then, the job of the fundamental analyst is to determine current intrinsic value, and to predict future prices, by using just such predictions.

Dividend payments are very important to the Phoenix investor. Not only is the cash flow important over long holding periods, but the history of the stock market tells us that high-dividend stocks, as a group, have outperformed low-dividend stocks, as a group, over time.

• THE TECHNICAL VIEW •

While the fundamentalist believes that stock movements are rational, and that every stock actually has a specific value that can be discovered through intelligent analysis, the technician takes a slightly different view. Pure *technical analysis* says that all fundamental information is irrelevant.

The technical analyst views the market as all-seeing and all-knowing. He says that all of that silly stuff like earnings and capitalization and long-term debt has already been reflected in a stock's price. Price movements, he believes, are determined by just two things: supply and demand in the market.

The technical analyst tracks the price movements of both individual companies and of the stock market itself. His theory is based on the premise that stock prices have a tendency to form patterns. So the technician's job is to look for trends and figure out what they suggest. His principal tool is the chart, which offers an accurate visual display of the history of the stock being analyzed. Although charts date back to the turn of the century with Charles Dow's original theory, the technical approach has burgeoned in the computer age. By and large, it is a post-war phenomenon.

There is a minor flaw in the technical approach, however: no one has ever proven that stock prices really do have any pattern at all. And though the technician may believe his work is more science than art, the fact is that competing technicians often interpret the same signals in very different ways.

This isn't to say you should ignore the charts. The stock market itself may have no memory, but human nature is human nature, and people do tend to repeat themselves. The market, after all, is one of the best barometers of the collective human emotions of fear and greed. The continuous tug-of-war between supply and demand is reflected in price and volume data—what the technicians call the real language of the market. The exact reasons that actually motivate each buyer and each seller are irrelevant, because that information has already been reflected in the price and volume (how many shares traded). Remember, the technician reminds us, that *for every single intelligent investor who concludes that this is the exact time to buy, there is another, equally intelligent, investor who has decided that this is the exact time to sell the same stock at the same price.* That's what makes a market, and the results make up the technician's data with which he measures the pulse of the market.

There are two elements of technical analysis: *charts,*

which track the price and volume of either a specific stock or a market average (such as a ten-year price history graph of IBM or the Dow Jones Average) and *market indicators,* which are quantitative measurements of the market and various economic data (such as the weekly change in the money supply). Both of these approaches attempt to predict future prices by focusing on that all-important supply and demand.

THE DOW THEORY

Charles Dow, publisher of *The Wall Street Journal* at the turn of the century, is considered by many to be the founder of technical analysis with his famous Dow Theory. (Ironically, Dow was first a fundamentalist who felt that earnings were the most important ingredient in price determination.)

The Dow Theory is an attempt to forecast the direction of the market by using the movements of both the Dow Jones Transportation Average and Dow Jones Industrial Average (both of which were invented by Charles Dow). Dow's theory is an analogy between the movements of the stock market and the movements of the sea; we are told that he had a lifelong fascination with the ocean tides. The market's daily changes, which Dow called "minor trends" and likened to ripples in the water, are too short term to be meaningful. "Intermediate trends" or "secondary movements" of a few weeks to a month, however, are significant. These he compared to the sea's waves. The longer term market patterns, extending from a few months to a year, Dow named "primary trends" and likened to the tides of the sea. The primary trends are the most important in defining a bull or bear market. A new trend is considered confirmed when both the Industrial and Transportation Averages break into unusually high or low levels at the same time.

Charles Dow, who was also the cofounder of Dow Jones & Co., died at an early age in 1902. Most of what is known as the Dow Theory today was actually developed by Dow's successor at *The Wall Street Journal*, William P. Hamilton, who later gained great fame when he accurately predicted the worst stock market crash in history (in which it lost more than 85% of its value) in his October 25, 1929, editorial, "A Turn of the Tide."

CHARTING

The basis of modern technical analysis is that stocks and stock market averages, like Newton's heavenly bodies, tend to continue moving in the same direction until their courses are altered.

The way the technical analyst keeps track of price movements is by using a chart, which you might think of as a photograph of price history. There are as many kinds of charts as there are investors with hunches, but the most commonly used is the *bar chart*, which illustrates both price and volume over time.

Charts tell us that the market does repeat itself often, as the same patterns emerge for both market averages and individual stocks. Since the market develops certain expectations of each stock, based on its own past record of performance, price ranges and patterns become self-perpetuating. The chartist calls the level to which a stock has dropped repeatedly—only to rebound back up—a *support level*. This is considered a floor price; of course, the more widely the floor is perceived, the more likely it is to continue. The level to which a stock rises repeatedly—only to come back down again—is called a *resistance level*. This is seen as the ceiling price. The prices within which a stock has developed a pattern of support and resistance are called its *channel* or *trading range*. The stock is said to have "successfully tested" these floor and ceiling levels if it reaches either one and shies away once again. The prudent investor should at least be aware of a stock's recent trading range before making a buy or sell decision.

If trends and patterns were always consistent, investing

Reversal Patterns

Bullish Formations	Bearish Formations

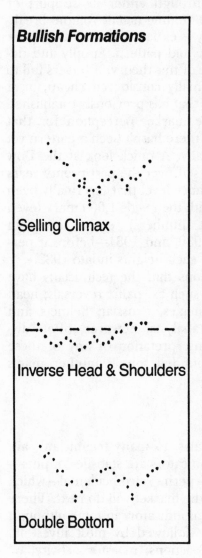

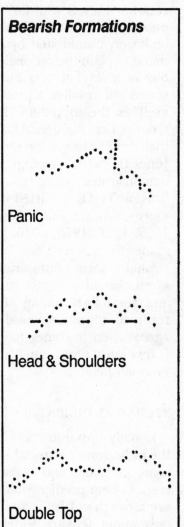

Bullish Formations

Selling Climax

Inverse Head & Shoulders

Double Bottom

Bearish Formations

Panic

Head & Shoulders

Double Top

would be easy. But the chartists know that every stock will eventually break out of its pattern. When a stock (or market average) breaks through either its support or resistance levels with large volume (small volume breakouts don't count), the analysts expect it to go even higher or lower, uninhibited by its old pattern. Supply and demand explain the rationale of this theory: if buyers fail to buy at a level that is normally considered cheap, or if sellers fail to sell at a price that has previously established itself as the top, then the market perception for that security has changed. And there hasn't been a pattern yet that didn't change eventually. A quick look at the Dow Jones Industrial Average itself over the past twenty years demonstrates a clear resistance level that has finally been broken. The Dow flirted with the magic 1,000 mark (even more resistant than most numbers) several times—in 1966, 1968, 1973, 1976, 1980, and 1981—before it permanently erased its fear of such heights in late 1982.

Charts form configurations that the technicians have given charming names to, such as: panic reversals, head and shoulders, selling climaxes, Prussian helmets and rounded tops. Technical analysts, however, often disagree when it comes to interpretation of any of these formations. One man's rounded top is another man's Prussian helmet.

TECHNICAL INDICATORS

Equally important as charts, to many technicians, are the indicators. Technical indicators are statistical inputs—some germane and some perhaps coincidental—which seem to help predict what the market will do next. There are more than fifty technical indicators in total, although only about ten are widely followed by most investors. Indicators include market actions, investor activity, or business and economic statistics. The following is a sampling of some of the most important:

Index of Leading Economic Indicators. The Commerce Department, through its Bureau of Economic Analysis, announces an index of twelve economic statistics that is supposed to give us a clue to coming business conditions in the country. The stock market happens to be one of the components of the index. Others have to do with employment levels, business contracts, and corporate liquidity. Even though the Bureau often changes its mind on reported findings, this indicator is widely followed as a foreseer of coming economic trends.

Money Supply. The Federal Reserve announces the money supply, which is simply a measurement of all the money circulating in the economy, every Friday after the stock market closes. Many investors anxiously await this announcement each week because the Fed's reaction to the money supply figures can have a major impact on both the stock and bond markets.

The Fed, which is responsible for managing the country's supply of money and credit, will usually tighten (reduce) the money supply if it is expanding too fast and loosen (increase) it if it is expanding too slowly. It does this primarily through its "open-market operations" (buying and selling treasury securities) which regulate the amount of cash flowing through the nation's monetary system. Wall Street generally reacts *favorably* when the Fed *buys* securities from the nation's banks, which adds money to the system and puts downward pressure on interest rates. Correspondingly, the investment community generally reacts *adversely* when the Fed finds it necessary to *sell* its treasury securities. This tremendous power of the Federal Reserve, combined with its control over bank *reserve requirements* and the *discount rate* (the interest rate at which banks borrow money from the Fed), makes Fed watching the most popular spectator sport on Wall Street.

Moving Averages. The moving average, an important trend indicator to the technical analysts, is the specific time segment with which they measure a stock's movement. Its purpose is to capture a more significant trend perspective than what individual daily prices would indicate. Moving averages, we might say in the nautical view of Charles Dow, look beyond the ripples and waves to see which way the tide is really running.

To track a simple thirty-day moving average, the investor graphs the average closing prices of a stock based on the past thirty days' input. Every day a new average is calculated, adding input from a thirty-first day (the current day) and throwing out the first day. This constant updating gives the investor some perspective of the stock's real trend over that measurement of time. A buy signal is indicated when a declining average reverses itself and starts an upward trend.

Volume Indicator. The volume of turnover behind price changes is often ignored by the average investor. But to the market technician, volume is often even more important than price since it is the ultimate indicator of supply and demand. A stock may rise in price one day by a full point, but on very light volume, and then fall in price by just a fraction of a point the next day, but in very heavy trading. Even though the price has increased over the two days, the net flow of money has actually been out of the stock instead of into it: There has been more supply than demand.

Advance-Decline Indicator. All market indices, especially the popular Dow Jones Industrials (which tracks just thirty stocks), tell us less than the whole story of what the entire market is doing. The number of all stocks advancing compared to those declining, however, gives us a much more accurate reading of the market's "breadth." Technicians consider this information, which is listed in many newspapers every day, to be the best indicator of the market's real direction.

Short-Selling Indicators. A reliable indicator of supply and demand is the total number of "short shares" (shares that have been borrowed and sold in hope that they can be bought back later at a lower price) on the New York Stock Exchange, as announced by the NYSE each month. Even though short-selling represents a negative attitude about the market, the shares that have already been sold short must eventually be bought back and therefore represent built-in demand or purchasing power. (Unlike most investors who own and hold shares "long" in their accounts, the short seller *borrows* the shares that he sells and therefore must eventually buy them back.)

The technician tracks total short selling through an indicator called the *short-interest ratio*, which measures the relationship between the total short interest (number of shares) and the average daily volume on the NYSE (all shares traded). This ratio tells us just how much shorting is being done relative to total market activity. A high short-interest ratio (when total short interest exceeds average daily NYSE volume) is a bullish sign; a low ratio is bearish.

Besides measuring supply and demand, monitoring short selling is also used as an important indicator of investor "sentiment": how various types of investors feel about the market at a given time. There are two investor groups that the technician is particularly interested in tracking: the "odd-lotters" (small investors who trade in less than a hundred shares), who are usually wrong, and the "specialists" (traders on the floor of the exchange), who are usually right.

The *odd-lot short-sales ratio* is known as a "negative indicator." The theory, which is surprisingly accurate, says that whenever the most unsophisticated investors (odd-lotters) start doing an increasing amount of sophisticated speculating (short selling), it's time for the wise investor to do just the opposite. This ratio, which measures the amount of odd-lot shorting being done compared to total odd-lot activity, has been one of the most consistent forecasters of major market trends for the past fifty years.

An equally accurate indicator is the *specialist short-sales ratio*. Since the specialist actually creates and maintains the market for stocks traded on the floor of the NYSE, he is rightfully considered the most knowledgeable market participant. When specialist shorting makes up a large proportion (60%) of the total shorting activity, we have a bearish signal for the near future; a ratio of 45% or less is a bullish signal. A range of 45%–60% is normal for specialists since they are required to do a certain amount of shorting just to maintain a liquid market. Both the odd-lot and specialist short-sales ratios are reported in *The Wall Street Journal.*

Other technical indicators. Technicians monitor several other statistics to get more input for their forecasting caldrons. The personal investment habits of corporate executives and other insiders who must report their activity to the Securities and Exchange Commission (SEC) are interesting to know. The amount of cash held by mutual funds is watched; a high percentage represents eventual demand. The relationship between the NYSE's total value and the Gross National Product is an indicator, with a low percentage NYSE-to-GNP (40%) signaling bargains and a high percentage (70%) signaling warnings. (These figures are reported weekly in *Barron's* and *The Wall Street Journal.*)

Ironically, a consensus of advisory letter sentiment is, like the odd-lot short ratio, a negative indicator. Past performance tells us that the majority of advisory letters and services are wrong, so the opposite of their collective opinion is used as yet another technical ingredient. (More on the collective opinion of experts in Chapter 3.)

There are dozens of other market indicators and market theories: some perhaps useful, others no doubt frivolous. It is true, for example, that the stock market's performance in the month of January has foretold the remainder of the year every time but once since 1950, lending credence to the "January barometer theory." Even the "Super Bowl theory" has been accurate; whenever the NFC wins, the market goes up for the succeeding year. These theories, however, have no economic or market significance, and they are easy to formulate given the advantages of hindsight. There is no doubt that we could find many other concurrences among good or bad market years when looking back on them. But the probability of repetition is no greater than the flip of a coin—unless widespread belief in the concurrence itself becomes an influence.

3

The Contrarian View

Most people think that contrarianism is the view that the *majority* is always wrong. But that's not quite it; majority opinions, after all, are what move the market. The true contrarian looks for *consensus* opinions—when almost everyone sees something the same way. These opinions, at least when found on Wall Street, are relatively reliable signals to do just the opposite.

The poor record of institutional investment managers, as a group, is often cited as evidence of the irrationality of group behavior in the stock market. Despite the intelligence and talents of the individuals who are given responsibility for managing billions of dollars, their collective behavior is quite different from what you might think. Institutional portfolio managers have always had a tendency to seek each other's company in making decisions. That's one reason that the institutions tend to concentrate on a relatively small group of the largest, and supposedly safest, companies—even when those companies are often over-priced.

The theory of contrariness and group psychology is not new. Modern-day market contrarians cite two nineteenth-century books as influences on their theory: Charles

Mackay's *Extraordinary Popular Elusions and the Madness of Crowds* (1841), and Gustave Le Bon's *The Crowd* (1895). The first to connect crowd psychology and the modern stock market was Humphrey Neill, a very successful investor himself, in his 1954 book, *The Art of Contrary Thinking*.

In this rambling, conversational little book, Neill tells us that we are often swayed by popular opinions and that when masses of people are so influenced, they act irrationally. "The 'crowd' thinks with its heart (that is, is influenced by emotions) while an individual thinks with his brain." He says that contrary thinking can be useful in almost any endeavor. "The act of contrary thinking consists in training your mind to ruminate in directions opposite to general public opinions; but weigh your conclusions in the light of current events and current manifestations of human behavior." The modern-day market contrarian can use this theory to profit from the consistency of the institution's errors.

Neill recommended questioning any viewpoint that is universally accepted because popular consensus is so often untimely. The human characteristics of fear and greed often get in the way of objective judgment when a crowd is swayed.

Neill cites several examples of group opinions that were drastically wrong about the stock market in the twentieth century: from the popular view in 1929 that "stocks are now at what looks like a permanently high plateau" (Yale Economist Irving Fisher, just a few days before the crash), to the widely expected post-WWII depression that never came. Since the time of Neill's book we can find numerous occasions of consensus blunders, including the opinion in the late 1960s that the economy had seen its last recession, and the absurdly high prices that the institutions drove some stocks up to in 1973. (Many of the popular "nifty fifty" stocks—including Eastman Kodak, Avon, IBM, and Walt Disney—crashed to just a fraction of their 1973 prices by 1974.)

FUN WITH MANIAS

Neill provides even more frivolous examples of group action gone mad by reaching back to some of history's greatest investment manias: the "South Sea Bubble" in England, John Law's "Mississippi Scheme" in France (when the market price of a single company was run up so high that it was valued at eighty times all the gold and silver in France), Boston's Ponzi Scheme, the 1920s Florida land boom mania, and the famous "tulip mania" in seventeenth-century Holland. These are all similar examples of irrational group perception that distorted value to an absurd level. Mackay's recounting of tulip mania is a particularly revealing example of irrational group behavior when the primary motivation of the group is greed.

> Tulips were introduced to Europe in the mid-1500s by Turkish traders. Over the next fifty years the flowers grew in popularity, becoming quite fashionable among the upper classes in most northern European countries. Climate and soil conditions being superb in Holland, the region between Amsterdam and The Hague became the center of the tulip growing business by the early 1600s.
>
> The economics of the prospering Dutch tulip business were reasonable for the first quarter of the century. Demand rose steadily as interest in the botanical beauties spread. During this time the expanding industry functioned normally and rationally: buyers were simply collectors and the sellers were simply producers.
>
> In the 1620s, however, the producers started experimenting with the tulip bulbs, cultivating more and more exquisite mutations of the original species. Tulip growing was becoming a new horticultural study that attracted a lot of attention. Prices started rising for the rarer varieties of

bulbs, but the demand continued to come from collectors as opposed to investors.

By 1633, the investment potential of buying tulip bulbs, and the business potential of tulip horticulture, were well known. Suddenly tulips became a craze, and according to Humphrey Neill, "In 1634, one of the most extraordinary public manias in all recorded history took place in Holland." Over the next three years "tulip mania" completely engulfed the nation. Investors from all over Europe and other parts of the world flocked to Holland to invest in tulips at any price. Virtually every Dutch citizen, rich or poor, dabbled in tulips.

Prices went through the roof. Extraordinary amounts were paid for specific bulbs. A single Admiral Liefkens bulb went for $6,600, and you couldn't touch a Semper Augustus bulb for less than $8,000. Hundred-dollar bulbs were soon selling for a thousand dollars, and amateur growers who got in early made small fortunes with their tulip gardens. Many people actually sold their homes to purchase a few bulbs.

Then came the seventeenth-century mutual fund: tulip bulbs packaged in assortments.

As money poured in from all over the world, tulip bulbs started trading on the sophisticated Amsterdam Stock Exchange, and a commodities futures market was started up specifically to trade bulbs. More and more Dutch common people sold everything—including their homes and land—to participate in the new promise of riches.

The crash came in 1637 when, reportedly, a single dealer failed to resell a bulb. Panic struck and everyone tried to sell at the same time. As in all irrational markets, the fall came faster than the rise. The entire Dutch economy was ravaged and took years to recover.

Holland's tulip mania is an interesting study in value perception. Despite the absence of any intrinsic value at all, the tulip craze shaped its own reality. Eight thousand dollars for a bulb seems reasonable if other bulbs have already sold for that much or more. In every greed-motivated investment craze, people are blinded by the apparent easiness of riches. The foolishness of the Dutch mania continues in this century, from the late 1920s stock market to the late 1970s gold market. In each case, the individual investor is swept away by the sentiments of the crowd despite his individual good sense.

The stock market, in recent years, gives us many examples of irrational action. New issues were the craze around 1960; the price of Control Data, for example, rocketed up 120 times its offering price in just a few years. In the late 1970s, gambling stocks (the ultimate speculator's stock group) were the craze; Resorts International went from $8 a share to $108 in just nine months, only to lose 85% of its value over the next few years. In 1981, Apple Computer went public at 100 times earnings and yet could fill only one out of every hundred orders to buy the stock on the offering. Shortly before, Genentech had gone public at 800 times earnings and could fill only one out of a thousand orders for its stock. (On the offering day the stock jumped from $35 to $89, only to slide back down to the original price over the next few months.) And unlike the Dutch tulip traders, those who have lost fortunes in stocks don't even have any pretty flowers to show for it.

The prospect of instant wealth is irresistible, even for the rational person who knows that value has been completely distorted. *But real value does eventually establish itself.* Just as companies with unrecognized potential finally become popular, so it is that the real fundamentals of overpriced companies usually pull their stock prices down to earth. In each of the recent periods of stock mania mentioned above, investors finally came to their senses. Just as the rare Semper Augustus bulb eventually lost 99% of its market price, so too did General Electric and

General Motors lose about 95% of their values shortly after their 1929 heights. (At least in this case, real conditions—not just perceptions—had changed drastically.)

After the 1960 market craze, such favorites as Lionel and Texas Instruments lost most of their value. After the late-1960s rally, the darling of the institutions, National Student Marketing, dropped in price from $140 a share to $4 in less than a year (just after it had been voted the clear favorite in a poll of two thousand portfolio managers). Again, institutional favorites crashed after huge gains in the early 1970s—Disney free-falling from $119 to $16 and Polaroid from $149 to $14. So too did the Great Bull Market of 1982–83 produce the usual number of vastly over-priced stocks, many of them new issues and high-tech companies. The summer of 1983, one year into the bull market, took a heavy toll. Digital Switch, a one-product OTC company which had sky-rocketed up from $15 to $148 in one year, gave up half its value. Apple Computer again made an about-face, losing 70% of its value during that same time. Even our Phoenix example, MCI, had become overly popular by this time, forcing it to give half its price back to the marketplace.

ANOTHER LOOK AT TRADITIONAL ANALYSIS

Objective academic studies over the years have not been flattering to Wall Street's long-accepted methods of security analysis or to its long-revered club of institutional money managers. In short, these studies point up dangerous shortcomings in both fundamental and technical analysis the way they are used by most investors, and virtually confirm the poor performance record of some of the best brains on Wall Street. Let's look at some of the problems of securities analysis first:

A. As for the *fundamental research* analysts and their sophisticated methodology, the main ingredient in their formulas remains conjecture about future earnings. It is

• TULIP MANIA IN 1983 •

THE 89 HIGHEST PE STOCKS ON THE NYSE
AS OF 6/30/83

STOCK SYMBOL	COMPANY	INDUSTRY	STOCK PRICE 6/30/83 IN DOLLARS	EARNINGS PER SHARE FOR PAST 4 QUARTERS IN DOLLARS	PRICE-EARNINGS RATIO
MMR	MOORE MCCORMACK RESOURCES	*transportation*	27.00	0.01	2,700.00
KLM	KLM ROYAL DUTCH AIRLINES	*airline*	59.75	0.03	1,991.66
MSY	MODULAR COMPUTER SYSTEMS	*computer*	14.00	0.01	1,400.00
SYB	SYBRON CORP	*health products*	28.50	0.03	950.00
SMC	SMITH (A.O.) CORP	*automotive*	27.75	0.03	925.00
M	MANAGEMENT ASSISTANCE	*computer*	14.62	0.06	243.75
BDK	BLACK & DECKER MFG CO	*electrical tools*	21.87	0.10	218.75
ZAL	ZALE CORP	*jewelry*	30.12	0.14	215.17
APC	ALPHA PORTLAND INDS	*construction*	21.87	0.11	198.86
CIW	CAMERON IRON WORKS	*oil*	21.50	0.11	195.45
MLT	MITEL CORP	*communication*	18.25	0.10	182.50
SPY	SPECTRA-PHYSICS	*laser*	34.00	0.19	178.94
SGN	SIGNAL COS	*aerospace*	38.62	0.27	143.05
UCT	UNITED CABLE TELEVISION	*cable tv*	22.50	0.16	140.62
DAY	DAYCO CORP	*chemical*	13.37	0.10	133.75
DI	DRESSER INDUSTRIES INC	*energy*	23.50	0.19	123.68
NRT	NORTON CO	*energy*	41.00	0.34	120.58

TYM	TYMSHARE INC	computer	19.75	0.17	116.17
REC	RECOGNITION EQUIPMENT INC	computer	13.75	0.12	114.58
HVE	HIGH VOLTAGE ENGINEERING	electronic	12.50	0.11	113.63
ZE	ZENITH RADIO CORP	electronic	26.12	0.25	104.50
GDC	GENERAL DATACOMM INDS INC	computer	25.87	0.25	103.50
WLY	WLY CORP	computer	13.75	0.14	98.21
SAL	SELIGMAN & LATZ INC	beauty	15.62	0.16	97.65
LFE	LFE CORP	electronic	16.62	0.18	92.36
AR	ASARCO INC	metal	39.12	0.44	88.92
BRY	BEATRICE FOODS CO	food	27.12	0.31	87.50
WLE	WHEELING & LAKE ERIE RY CO	railroad	63.00	0.74	85.13
OIL	TRITON ENERGY CORP	oil	15.00	0.18	83.33
WBB	WEBB (DEL E.) CORP	publishing	24.00	0.29	82.75
ROL	ROLLINS INC	energy	16.00	0.20	80.00
AMA	AMFAC INC	food	27.62	0.35	78.92
HZN	HORIZON CORP	real estate	10.25	0.13	78.84
AHM	AHMANSON (H.F.) & CO	insurance	31.50	0.40	78.75
HT	HUGHES TOOL CO	oil	20.87	0.27	77.31
AMR	AMR COMP-DEL	airline	37.62	0.50	75.25
NIC	NICOLET INSTRUMENT	electronic	17.75	0.24	73.95
LEN	LENNAR CORP	construction	27.75	0.38	73.02
GP	GEORGIA-PACIFIC CORP	wood products	26.25	0.36	72.91
AMD	ADVANCED MICRO DEVICES	electronic	64.50	0.91	70.64
DOC	DR PEPPER CO	soft drink	15.50	0.22	70.45
NBI	NBI INC	computer	31.62	0.45	70.27
LPX	LOUISIANA-PACIFIC CORP	wood products	33.12	0.49	67.60
MMO	MONARCH MACHINE TOOL CO	tools	24.87	0.38	65.46

STOCK SYMBOL	COMPANY	INDUSTRY	STOCK PRICE 6/30/83 IN DOLLARS	EARNINGS PER SHARE FOR PAST 4 QUARTERS IN DOLLARS	PRICE-EARNINGS RATIO
EEE	ENSOURCE INC	energy	3.25	0.05	65.00
NWT	NORTHWEST INDUSTRIES	chemical	43.12	0.67	64.36
PPR	PANTRY PRIDE INC	supermarket	6.37	0.10	63.75
BKY	BERKEY PHOTO INC	photography	7.00	0.11	63.63
HWL	HOWELL CORP	energy	13.75	0.22	62.50
DPT	DATAPOINT CORP	computer	21.75	0.35	62.14
NWA	NORTHWEST AIRLINES INC	airline	51.25	0.83	61.74
CHG	CHICAGO MILWAUKEE CORP	food	91.75	1.50	61.16
WSN	WESTERN CO OF NORTH AMERICA	oil	7.87	0.13	60.57
TER	TERADYNE INC	electronic	63.50	1.06	59.90
KZ	KYSOR INDUSTRIAL CORP	automotive	13.12	0.22	59.65
AX	AXIA INC	metal products	22.50	0.38	59.21
GEN	GENRAD INC	electronic	44.00	0.78	56.41
AVX	AVX CORP	electronic	42.87	0.79	54.27
MKC	MARION LABORATORIES	pharmaceutical	41.75	0.78	53.52
ACF	ACF INDS	transportation	34.50	0.66	52.27
KGM	KERR GLASS MFG	glass	15.00	0.29	51.72
ADI	ANALOG DEVICES	electronic	34.12	0.66	51.47
BHC	BROCK HOTEL CORP	hotel	9.25	0.18	51.38
DGN	DATA GENERAL CORP	computer	56.50	1.10	51.36
ARO	ARO CORP	tools	20.12	0.40	50.31

TIX	TIMEPLEX INC	*computer*	27.75	0.56	49.55
HBJ	HARCOURT BRACE JOVANOVICH	*publishing*	27.25	0.55	49.54
STG	STEEGO CORP	*automotive*	4.87	0.10	48.75
CUL	CULLINANE DATABASE SYS INC	*computer*	39.37	0.81	48.61
CBE	COOPER INDUSTRIES INC	*tools*	36.00	0.75	48.00
TLR	TELERATE INC	*computer*	20.00	0.42	47.61
ACE	ACME ELECTRIC CORP	*electronic*	13.37	0.28	47.59
WMB	WILLIAMS COS	*various*	24.75	0.52	47.59
SRT	ST REGIS CORP	*wood products*	29.37	0.62	47.37
ICN	ICN PHARMACEUTICALS INC	*pharmaceutical*	13.12	0.28	46.87
KOL	KOLLMORGEN CORP	*electronic*	34.00	0.73	46.57
SII	SMITH INTERNATIONAL INC	*drills*	25.37	0.55	46.13
CVN	COMPUTERVISION CORP	*automation*	48.00	1.06	45.28
GRB	GERBER SCIENTIFIC INC	*computer*	32.00	0.71	45.07
HMW	HMW INDUSTRIES INC	*silverware*	28.25	0.64	44.14
WY	WEYERHAEUSER CO	*wood products*	37.87	0.87	43.53
CYR	CRAY RESEARCH	*computer*	51.00	1.19	42.85
ENT	CANADIAN PACIFIC ENTERPRISES	*various*	20.12	0.47	42.81
STX	STEWART-WARNER CORP	*electronic*	28.12	0.66	42.61
MAI	M/A-COM INC	*communication*	32.75	0.78	41.98
ESL	ESTERLINE CORP	*electronic*	32.62	0.78	41.82
SKY	SKYLINE CORP	*transportation*	28.75	0.70	41.07
GOI	GEARHART INDUSTRIES INC	*oil*	22.00	0.54	40.74

such an unexact science that an analyst is considered on target if he is within twenty percent of actual earnings. Twenty percent. Better hope your bank teller measures better than that. And your druggist.

The economic basis of fundamentalist market timing is logical enough. Analysts look at information that would seem to signal a market movement, such as changes in inflation rates, corporate profits, interest rates, or other factors that would affect the prospects of a particular company.

The problem is that everyone else is looking at the same data.

One explanation of the lack of success of many of those who adhere to these seemingly rational and intelligent methods can be found in what is known as the *efficient-market hypothesis*. This notion states that a stock's current price is, in fact, an exact reflection of its true value. This idea must be most disheartening to the market analyst, whose job it is to search for unrecognized value. And yet it is his very opinion that becomes the ultimate factor in the stock's price. The efficient-market theory says that the prices of most stocks (relatively obscure companies being the exception) are a reflection of all that is known about the company, in much the same way that the stock market itself is a reflection of all that is known about the state of the economy.

This hypothesis, obviously not a popular theory in Wall Street's venerable research departments, is based on a paradox: it can be true only if the securities industry believes it not to be true. The market's very efficiency depends on the continuing efforts and opinions of competing analysts, which are then synthesized to produce an accurately reflective price. That is particularly true when applied to the 500 or so most highly monitored companies —the large capitalization companies traded on the NYSE, whose every twitch and rumble is scrutinized by every institutional money manager and research department on the Street. But what of the thousands of other companies that are actively traded but not widely monitored? The efficient-market theory does not apply here. There is too much information about those firms that most people on Wall Street know too little about.

B. The school of *technical analysis* has fared no better than the fundamental school in objective evaluations of its reliability. Several studies indicate that the technicians' trends and patterns seem to indicate little more than recorded history, and that the market's future direction has no proven relationship to its past.

An extensive study undertaken in the 1960s supports the suspicion that no technician's system is really dependable. ("Spectral Analysis of New York Stock Market Prices" by Oskar Morgenstern and Clive Granger, Kyklos, 1963.) Price movements were carefully researched, covering a period of forty years, to determine any correlation between technicians' expectations and actual results. None was found. From their work, and the work of others about the same time, came the now-popular "random-walk" theory, which states that past prices have no bearing on future prices. (The 1960s researchers got the name from the work of French mathematician Louis Bachelier who, in 1900, had compared the random movements of certain particles under his microscope to the price behavior of stocks.)

THE ART OF CONTRARIAN THINKING

The concept of contrarianism, as it applies to investment strategy, is based on the well-documented theory that the market usually overreacts to both good news and bad news. Price trends in the marketplace often extend to irrational levels because of wide popularity or unpopularity.

Basically, the contrarian believes that consensus expectations are usually wrong. By the time a great majority concur on the market's next move (or a single stock's next direction), chances are that most of the potential buyers have already bought or potential sellers have already sold. *The true contrarian is not tempted by fast-moving stocks that have already increased in price dramatically, knowing that the good news has already been figured into their prices and that any bad news could be particularly damaging.* Conversely, most out-of-favor stocks are relatively insensitive to further bad news, but can react quickly to any better developments.

THE HERD INSTINCT AMONG WALL STREET'S FINEST

*"Worldly wisdom teaches that it is better
for reputations to fail conventionally
than to succeed unconventionally."*
J. M. KEYNES

Most small investors think that the big guys on Wall Street control the market and always have the inside edge. That should be true, but it isn't.

The world of portfolio management—the guardians of pension funds, mutual funds, insurance companies, bank trust departments, and university endowment funds—is intensely competitive. Money managers are continually under the gun, with fickle clients ready to switch their huge portfolios from one manager to the next at the drop of a bad quarterly report. Despite the accusations of many individual investors, the big boys hardly act in pre-planned collusion to control the market. What they do, though, is perpetually follow each other's lead, for fear of being left behind. They think of it as safety in numbers. The bottom fisher should think of this as opportunity.

The contrarian believes that professional investors make such predictable blunders that the astute individual investor can take advantage of institutional behavior. Like the foolish Dutch tulip buyers, institutional managers are hopeless victims of group persuasion. Burdened with an overload of information (believing that more input produces better output), portfolio managers always keep their eyes on the competition. They are all fighting over the same relatively few stocks; only about five hundred companies are even considered by most institutions. The very nature of their jobs usually compels these people to go along with the crowd. If the market (or a certain stock group) starts moving, it's just too risky not to participate. The portfolio manager has got just three choices in a stock market rally: (1) If he goes along and is wrong, he's no worse off than everyone else. His performance will still be average. (2) If he stays put and the market gets away from him, he loses clients and maybe his job. (3) If he moves with the market, but picks unpopular stocks, he's on his own. No one will blame him for losing money in IBM, especially if all his peers make the same mistake. But losing money in a little-known or out-of-favor stock could be the end of him.

So much for the professionals' edge in the market. I wish I had a share of GEICO for every disgruntled investor who says that if he'd done just the opposite of what he was advised to do over the years, he would have made a fortune. Almost every objective survey of portfolio management and institutional research analysis supports the suspicion that the industry itself has consistently underperformed the market averages. There have been a total of over fifty legitimate surveys over the last half century which measured such performance. The studies have been conducted and reported in a fair and systematic way by such credible publications as *Business Week, Trusts and Estates, Institutional Investor* and *Financial World,* and have measured periods ranging from one year to over twenty years. The collective result of all surveys for all time periods is startling: professional advice has been wrong over 75% of the time. Consider the following:

A. *Investment advisory letters* are considered such bad advice by the industry itself, in fact, that their collective opinion is actually used as a *negative* indicator by virtually all security analysts. There is actually a near-perfect correlation between advisory letter sentiment and actual market performance. The closer the market gets to the top, the more bullish the overall advisory sentiment gets; the closer to a bottom, the more bearish the sentiment gets. This correlation is even confirmed by investment letter advertising: a preponderance of bullish ads at the top and bearish ads at the bottom.

B. *Mutual fund managers*, as a group, have performed miserably over the years. Like the advisory letters, the mutual funds have been awarded the dubious honor of being used as a reliable negative indicator. A high percentage of cash held by the mutual funds, for example, is considered a bullish sign. Just when they should be loading up on stocks for the next up-cycle, most of the funds are busy liquidating stocks to build up their cash reserves. Several credible surveys, similar to the ones cited above, shows up that only about 40% of all mutual funds have even matched the market averages.

C. Have the *bank trust departments, insurance companies,* or *pension funds* fared any better? Well, no. Very conclusive surveys indicate that only about 20% of the nation's pension funds, for example, have outperformed the market averages over the years.

Let's be charitable about the experts' performance and attribute it to that peculiar psychology of group behavior. In the world of portfolio management, it's just plain safer to fish with the fleet. And safety is important to investment managers, many of whose careers hinge on what's known as the 12/24 rule: If they are underperforming the market by twelve percent after just twenty-four months, they are replaced. For them, the safest way to avoid underperforming the market is to become part of the market by investing the same way as everyone else.

THE PHOENIX APPROACH

Should we simply ignore all the opinions of Wall Street? Does the industry's poor performance record make the very basis of its research—fundamental analysis—invalid? Not by any means. The Phoenix Approach uses basic, Benjamin Graham fundamentals within the realm of contrarianism. Many of the upcoming tests we will use to appraise unpopular and distressed companies are the same ones that any security analyst might use. The difference between us and them lies in our perception of the field of choices. We fish deeper, and we fish alone.

So here's a definition of the Phoenix investor: he is a "contrarian fundamentalist." And here's what the Phoenix investor *does*: he buys low and he sells high. Don't laugh. *That advice is so basic it has become the joke of the investment game. Yet most people are so blinded by fear and greed that they somehow manage to do just the opposite.* As we've just seen, even the most sophisticated institutional investors get more and more bullish and confident as the market soars, and more and more bearish as it plummets.

The Phoenix Approach tells us this is a foolish trap to fall into. It tells us that we must often go against the grain of our emotions. It says: *just when things look the worst, buy, and just when they look the best, sell.* Many investors sell out right at the bottom of the market, really believing that things will never get better, while attempting to salvage what they still have. Others get caught up with the enthusiasm of a good market, stepping in after finally being convinced that the market will brave new heights.

The key ingredient to the Phoenix idea of acting oppositely to the general sentiment has to do with *expectation*. News that is widely expected (about either a particular stock or the market itself) seldom has much effect on price. But *unexpected* news can have a big effect. Consequently, the Phoenix investor always asks himself whether good news or bad news is more expected in any given situation.

The Phoenix investor looks for opportunities way ahead of the crowd. He searches among unpopular or ignored companies for real value that will be recognized in the future. Next to individualism, patience is this investor's greatest virtue. Sometimes it takes years for true value to be realized in the form of profits.

But make no mistake about it: the Phoenix Approach has really always been the strategy by which great fortunes have been made in this country. How many people do you know who've made money over long periods of time by trading in and out of popular stocks?

John Maynard Keynes is a good example of a lifelong contrarian fundamentalist. He started buying extremely out-of-favor issues during the Depression, and, with a strategy that he stuck with, ended up multiplying his money some sixty-five fold to today's equivalent of $10 million.

The smart money is always bottom fishing, never chasing the crowd. When the Belzberg family bought 363,000 shares of Bache in 1979 for $8.25 a share, many people thought that troubled brokerage house was an endangered species. But the Belzbergs sold their shares to Prudential a few years later for $32 a share. It's not just a matter of knowing when to buy; the smart money always seems to know when to get out, too (whenever the crowd starts getting in). Denver oil magnate Marvin Davis sold his exploratory leases for $630 million in December, 1980, just two weeks before the very peak of the energy boom. Most people at the time were finally convinced that oil prices would continue to rise for years to come. *The Phoenix investor always asks where the smart money is going.*

In the next two chapters you will learn what to look for when bottom fishing for out-of-favor and distressed companies. Then I'll tell you exactly how to put a Phoenix portfolio together. But before going on, let's take a closer look at what the Phoenix investor is, and what he isn't.

THE PHOENIX APPROACH

THE FLEET FISHER	THE BOTTOM FISHER
Profile: Has a short-term outlook; wants a quick fix; trades a lot, switches objectives; has *no real strategy.* Most investors are fleet fishers, including most institutions with their committees of experts.	*Profile:* Is a position-taker with a long-term view; is an independent, contrarian fundamentalist. Is an asset-buyer. Has a *definite strategy* and sticks with it. The smart money fishes the bottom.
Buys popular stocks.	Buys unpopular stocks.
Buys mostly high-PE stocks.	Buys mostly low PEs, the exception being companies that are just starting to make money again after being in the red.
Buys stocks even after they've made big advances; generally bails out after a big drop.	Lets the high-fliers go; is more interested in the one that just dropped way down.
Buys on good news, sells on bad news.	Buys on bad news, sells on good news.
Goes after every craze; new issues, high-techs, whatever is hot.	More apt to sell short during the mature stages of any craze.
Shies away from trouble, such as companies in the red, or in Chapter 11.	Eagerly explores the distress and bankruptcy markets for undervalued securities.
Looks for "sure things".	More apt to sell a "sure thing" short; sells any stock that makes the cover of *Newsweek* (on good news).
Buys what everyone else is buying, especially the institutions.	Buys what the institutions are selling, knowing their historical record.
Often buys stocks despite lack of real value.	Buys only real, measurable value.
Buys on tips and rumors.	Almost never buys on tips and rumors.

Trades a lot.	Has a longer term view; trades little.
Buy and sell decisions are often based on complicated technical timing data.	Considers the charts mostly because of their impact on other investors; considers some technical indicators for the same reason.
Market attitude is that of a gambler.	Market attitude is that of a person buying a business, such as the corner grocery store.
Often lets emotions defy fundamental principles.	Is an old-fashioned Ben Graham fundamentalist; is very objective about value.
Often buys "concepts".	Looks for real value such as unrecognized assets and earning power; checks concept stocks carefully.
Buys on far-reaching projections of continued earnings growth.	Is skeptical of long-term earnings estimates, knowing their historical record of accuracy.

4

•————————————————————•

The Phoenix Approach to the Out-of-Favor Market

After long periods of economic prosperity it is difficult to find undervalued securities. But today, because of the devastating recession of 1980–82, the opportunities are greater than ever before. Recovery candidates come in three forms: out-of-favor stocks (as determined by their low price-earnings valuations), distressed companies (that are currently losing money), and companies that are actually trading in the state of bankruptcy.

Unlike most stock market strategies, the Phoenix Approach is not dependent on luck or exact timing, and does not require the expense of frequent trading in and out. The Phoenix investor does not depend on sustained performances of the overall market, and, by concentrating on securities that are already depressed, is less susceptible to general market downturns. Furthermore, this approach, particularly when applied to distressed and bankruptcy issues, is relatively quantitative; valuations can sometimes be measured with surprising accuracy.

That's what the Phoenix Approach is. Here's what it isn't: easy. It requires careful selection, occasional monitoring, and a lot of patience. The objective is long-term cyclical recovery, based on identifiable, intrinsic value. If you accept the premise that the market usually overreacts to distress and bad news, then the opportunities are plentiful today for eventual market recognition of value.

THE LOW-PE THEORY

One of the most thorough and clever exposés of the shortcomings of traditional investment methodology is *The New Contrarian Investment Strategy* (Random House, 1982) by David Dreman. After fully delineating the failures of other theories, Dreman presents an excellent case for a simple and sensible approach to out-of-favor stocks based on price-earnings ratios. What follows is the essence of his views on being contrary by using low PEs.

Dreman proposes not only shunning the stocks that institutions favor, but actually buying the very stocks that the professionals ignore. Such stocks are easily identifiable because they sell at low PEs: investors are willing to pay very little for a dollar's worth of these companies' earnings. While one dollar of earnings (per year) might be "valued" at forty or fifty dollars (on the stock market) in a very popular company, the same amount of earnings can often be purchased in a downtrodden company for as little as five or six dollars. And yet there is abundant evidence that low-PE stocks, in general, have far outperformed high-PE stocks over time. Here we find Wall Street's greatest irony: *it is the very companies that are expected to perform poorly in the market (as indicated by what investors are willing to pay for their current earnings) that end up outperforming the averages, and the companies that are expected to do so well in the market that end up performing poorly.* We are speaking in terms of relative prices, of course: The prices of the popular companies start off at a disadvantage in this competition because they are much higher relative to their current earnings than are the unpopular companies.

Dreman cites several studies that have compared actual performances of high-PE versus low-PE stocks. A comprehensive study by Francis Nicholson reported in *Financial Analysts Journal* (Jan–Feb 1968), covering a twenty-five-year period, for example, shows us that lowest-quintile-PE stocks outperformed highest-quintile-PE stocks considerably in one-year measurements (16% appreciation versus 3% appreciation). The differences in three-year and five-year measurements were equally impressive (55% versus 21% and 90% versus 46%). A later survey by Paul Miller, Jr. (reported in Drexel & Co., Philadelphia, monthly review, 1966) gives us similar results, with the lowest-PE stocks appreciating by over 18% annually for a sixteen-year period versus less than 8% for the highest-PE.

More recent studies through the 1970s show the same results. One study shows that $10,000 invested in 1968 in the lowest-PE stocks (bottom 10%), with quarterly revisions made in the portfolio to stay with only the lowest-PEs, would have grown to over $32,000 by the middle of 1977. A similar strategy based on highest-PE stocks for the same time period would have reduced the $10,000 down to $7,700. The studies cited and conducted by Dreman covered several market cycles. The better performance of low-PE stocks does not seem to depend on starting or stopping points in any of the surveys. All evidence points to the superior performance of investing in out-of-favor stocks and holding them for the long term, or trading them for even more out-of-favor stocks over time. The very stocks that are thought to have the least potential in the marketplace (based on how investors value their current earnings) consistently do the best.

Conventional investment advice tells us that some stocks are good for growth while others are good for income, but the two objectives can never be expected in the same investment. As David Dreman points out, a close look at actual price history clearly demonstrates just the opposite. As you would expect, low-PE stocks yield more percentage income in general (because their prices are lower relative to what they are earning and able to pay out). But what is surprising, and contrary to most conventional investment wisdom, is that *there is also a direct correlation between yield and growth: the highest yielding stocks have consistently shown the most appreciation over the years in both good and bad markets.* Once again, real value eventually asserts itself. (Remember the "present value" theory? A company's intrinsic worth is simply the sum total of all its future dividends.)

How can any investment strategy be so simple? If there is conclusive proof that out-of-favor stocks outperform popular ones, why don't the big boys on Wall Street just use low PEs as their main investment criterion? Dreman explains that the great catch that makes his PE theory workable is the fact that the vast majority of the investment community still thinks it can outsmart the averages and accurately predict which companies will perform better than the rest. This undying belief, which, after all, is the very basis of all security analysis, is what creates popular companies to begin with. Popularity breeds more popularity as the herd instinct takes hold on Wall Street, sending those PE ratios up higher and higher.

As we have seen earlier, however, earnings estimates by analysts are full of flaws; overall industry estimates historically are off by an average of 20%, and in some years have averaged worse than 40% off the mark. Yet it is accuracy, ironically, that is the basis of any belief that research efforts can predict high performers. The low-PE theory states that if future earnings of companies are mostly unknowable anyway, then low-PE companies would have a distinct advantage because of their lower relative prices. *Dreman concludes that since it is almost impossible to predict a company's future earnings, there should be a relatively narrow range of PE differentials among all stocks. But since there is instead a very wide range of PEs, a workable strategy based on this criterion alone exists.*

If anything is predictable about popular versus unpopular companies, in fact, it may just be that their fortunes are more apt to change course than continue course as the years go on. A very

*successful company naturally attracts more and more competition,
while troubled companies are usually forced to make major changes
to get back on course. The corporate history of this country is one
of both intense competition and survival: cyclical leaders and
cyclical laggards seem to eventually gravitate toward each other
because of natural free-market forces.*

While there will always be some exceptional (high-PE)
companies that continue to grow at a very high rate year
after year, chasing these companies is fraught with danger.
The low-PE strategy is based on the premise that most
companies will gravitate toward average growth because
of those natural forces of competition. Fortunately for
the low-PE investor, the vast majority of other investors—
individual and institutional—still get swept away by current momentums. Like the emotional investor who throws
in the towel at the bottom and returns to the market after
long advances, most investors perceive current earnings
trends of individual companies as never ending. This
tendency is another example of both the herd instinct
and the overreactions of fear and greed.

Low-PE, out-of-favor companies are also infinitely better takeover candidates than high-PE, popular companies.
Corporations, like wise investors, look for bargains, and
try to make their acquisitions in the down cycles of target
companies. The larger company considers all the fundamentals of the smaller company, including its current
price relative to both its earnings and underlying assets.
Since the acquiring company usually must pay a healthy
premium in order to accumulate enough shares of the
other company, real intrinsic value is particularly important.
The shares cannot be overpriced from the start, and its
earnings should be good compared to that price.

It doesn't take any research to locate low-PE stocks.
Most daily newspapers list PEs along with prices in their
stock columns. Every stockbroker's quote machine and
Standard & Poor's Stock Guide (a handy reference for any
investor) provide up-to-date information about a company's
earnings. Some publications even do the selecting and

grouping process for you: *Financial Weekly* categorizes all actively traded stocks according to PE groupings; and *Value Line* runs an updated list of low-PE/high-yield companies every week.

PE'S AND THE MARKET CYCLE

There certainly appears to be a correlation between current PE ratios and the future direction of stock prices. The average PE ratio (measured by the S&P 500 Index) in 1949, for example, reached an all-time low of 6:1 after plummeting from an all-time high of 21:1 just three years before. The year 1949, we now know, turned out to be the beginning of an almost uninterrupted twenty-year bull market.

More recent periods of low PEs have preceded even more dramatic bull markets. The average ratio hit a low of 7:1—by far the lowest since 1949—just before the market began a six-year surge in 1974, during which the average stock more than doubled in price. After a two-year market correction starting in 1980, the average PE ratio hit another low of 7:1 in the famous summer of '82. This time stocks doubled in just one year.

Conversely, several market *declines* in recent years have been preceded by dangerously *high* PE averages. The disastrous two-year tumbles that began in mid-1968 and mid-1972 were each forewarned by PE averages of 18:1.

● BIG BOARD BARGAINS ●

THE LOWEST PE STOCKS ON THE NYSE
AS OF 6/30/83 (EXCLUDING UTILITIES)

STOCK SYMBOL	COMPANY	INDUSTRY	STOCK PRICE IN DOLLARS	EARNINGS PER SHARE FOR PAST 4 QUARTERS IN DOLLARS	PRICE-EARNINGS RATIO
LUN	LEUCADIA NATIONAL CORP	*life insurance*	14.875	3.920	3.795
AZ	ATLAS CORP	*mining*	27.000	6.470	4.173
GLM	GLOBAL MARINE INC	*oil*	10.250	2.360	4.343
TEL	TELECOM CORP	*transportation*	3.875	0.830	4.669
CMB	CHASE MANHATTAN CORP	*banking*	53.375	11.320	4.715
CHL	CHEMICAL NEW YORK CORP	*banking*	47.500	10.030	4.736
BT	BANKERS TRUST NEW YORK CORP	*banking*	42.000	8.770	4.769
ZOS	ZAPATA CORP	*construction*	18.500	3.790	4.881
V	IRVING BANK CORP	*banking*	49.375	9.730	5.075
SJM	SMUCKER (J.M.) CO	*jams and jellies*	33.750	6.600	5.114
CES	COMMONWEALTH ENERGY SYST.	*energy*	20.375	3.950	5.158
FWB	FIRST WISCONSIN CORP	*banking*	38.750	7.500	5.167
BKB	BANK OF BOSTON CORP	*banking*	40.500	7.790	5.199
BK	BANK OF NEW YORK CO INC	*banking*	59.250	11.110	5.333
MHC	MANUFACTURERS HANOVER CORP	*banking*	44.000	8.230	5.346
NBD	NBD BANCORP INC	*banking*	38.125	7.010	5.439

STOCK SYMBOL	COMPANY	INDUSTRY	STOCK PRICE IN DOLLARS	EARNINGS PER SHARE FOR PAST 4 QUARTERS IN DOLLARS	PRICE-EARNINGS RATIO
MM	MARINE MIDLAND BANKS	banking	27.000	4.850	5.567
RD	ROYAL DUTCH PETE–NY GLOR 10	oil	46.250	8.100	5.710
FNS	FIRST NATL STATE BANCORP	oil	39.250	8.880	5.722
WMS	WILLIAMS ELECTRONICS INC	video games	15.000	2.610	5.747
TOD	TODD SHIPYARDS CORP	ship-building	35.250	6.100	5.779
MST	MERCANTILE STORES CO INC	dept. stores	72.000	12.400	5.806
BG	BROWN GROUP INC	apparel	35.000	5.910	5.922
KEY	KEY BANKS INC	banking	24.125	4.040	5.972
WFC	WELLS FARGO & CO	banking	37.250	6.220	5.989
TSO	TESORO PETROLEUM CORP	oil	15.875	2.640	6.013
GBS	GENERAL BANCSHARES	banking	27.125	4.510	6.014
SW	STONE & WEBSTER INC	engineering	43.750	7.190	6.085
BAY	BAY FINANCIAL CORP	banking	14.000	2.300	6.087
FNC	CITICORP	banking	39.500	6.470	6.105
FBT	FIRST CITY BANCORP (TEXAS)	banking	23.250	3.790	6.135
BKV	BANK OF VIRGINIA CO	banking	28.125	4.580	6.141
FBC	FIRST BOSTON INC	insurance	61.750	9.855	6.266
FNB	FIRST CHICAGO CORP	banking	23.000	3.660	6.284
XON	EXXON CORP	oil	33.750	5.350	6.308
HBC	HARRIS BANKCORP INC	banking	38.500	6.100	6.311

Symbol	Company	Industry			
JPM	MORGAN (J.P.) & CO	banking	71.625	11.290	6.344
CIL	CONTINENTAL ILLINOIS CORP	banking	21.625	3.390	6.379
SNT	SONAT INC	energy	33.375	5.210	6.406
RPT	REPUBLICBANK CORP	banking	36.750	5.710	6.436
IFC	INTERFIRST CORP	banking	21.375	3.290	6.497
MEL	MELLON NATIONAL CORP	banking	50.375	7.740	6.508
BRF	BORMAN'S INC	supermarket	19.375	1.590	6.525
FIS	FISCHBACH CORP	contractor	50.500	7.720	6.541
FAC	FIRST ATLANTA CORP	banking	27.500	4.190	6.563
ANR	AMERICAN NATURAL RESOURCES	energy	39.250	5.930	6.619
CHD	CHELSEA INDUSTRIES INC	shoes	18.000	2.700	6.667
WOC	WILSHIRE OIL OF TEXAS	energy	7.750	1.160	6.681
FIN	FINANCIAL CORP OF AMERICA	banking	39.125	5.850	6.688
RNB	REPUBLIC NEW YORK CORP	banking	39.500	5.880	6.718
USH	USLIFE CORP	insurance	24.000	3.570	6.723
ASO	AMSOUTH BANCORPORATION	banking	29.375	4.340	6.768
MTD	MERCANTILE TEXAS CORP	banking	28.375	4.170	6.805
CAF	CNA FINANCIAL CORP	insurance	19.750	2.900	6.810
SPC	SECURITY PACIFIC CORP	banking	49.250	7.147	6.891
UJB	UNITED JERSEY BANKS	banking	26.625	3.840	6.934
FLT	FLEET FINANCIAL GROUP INC	banking	45.625	6.570	6.944
ABS	ALBERTSON'S INC	supermarket	26.250	3.780	6.944

DISCOVERING VALUE

The Phoenix investor uses just three approaches in his all-important determination of value. Each is logical and quantitative. Each is based on the belief that real value will eventually be reflected in a stock's price. The first method is that of *asset valuation,* which is a determination of value through what a company owns, using such measurements as cash value per share, working capital per share, and stated book value per share. The second method is one we have just looked at: the *relative value* approach, in which the investor searches for stocks that are selling at lower PEs and higher yields than other stocks. And the third valuation method is an *appraisal* approach, where the investor "capitalizes" future income and appreciation potential and compares the estimated annual return on a stock to less risky alternative investments, such as money funds and treasury bonds. Sound technical? Some of it is, but, as I said from the outset, no sound investment strategy is all easy. Don't worry about where to find all this information. I'll cover that as we go along (there's even a chapter in Part IV on how to read a financial report).

A. The *asset valuation approach* is basically straightforward. *If a company's working capital (current assets minus current liabilities) per share is even close to its stock price, then the stock may be a bargain. And if its net* cash *value per share is close to its stock price, the stock would appear to be even more attractive.* If you find that a $15 stock, for example, has some $13 in working capital—$8 of which is cash—then an investor would be paying only $2 per share for all the other assets of the company: property, equipment, land, inventories, receivables, etc. If further investigation (often just an annual report) reveals that the company's fixed assets are carried on the books at only nominal prices, then you may have discovered even greater value. Surprisingly, it's not that unusual to find companies that sell below even their cash value, much less their working capital value. Just before the record-breaking 1982–83 bull market, in fact, most large-capitalization companies actually traded slightly below book value and well below replacement value.

Book value alone, however, is not an accurate price determinant. The asset valuation that a company carries may just as often be above real market value as below it. Furthermore, book value is simply a measurement of the theoretical value of a company's assets if that company were broken up and liquidated piece by piece, which rarely happens in reality. So the asset valuation approach, as useful as it is, should be used only in conjunction with other measurements of value.

B. We have just discussed David Dreman's theory of out-of-favor stocks. He has collected evidence that low-PE and high-yield stocks have consistently outperformed the rest of the market over the years. His view represents the *"relative-value"* theory: that all stocks tend to eventually have about the same values relative to what they earn and what they pay. Natural free-market forces will correct the stock price of an overvalued company and increase the price of an undervalued company.

Based on the relative-value approach, it would be wise to buy stocks which have below-average PEs in combination with above-average yields. A strict approach to this method would be to buy the ten lowest-PE (non-utility) stocks with yields over 8% on the NYSE (regardless of the company, industry, or any other factors), and purge your portfolio every year, replacing any stocks that are no longer in the top ten. Relative-value purists argue that this simple strategy actually works consistently over time, and can cite some pretty convincing price surveys as evidence.

But, like book values, PE ratios and yields should be looked at carefully. While a stated book value does not necessarily tell us what a single share of stock represents, PEs and EPSs (earnings per share) don't necessarily tell us the whole story about the company's earnings. Non-recurring gains and losses, for example, can distort real earnings (such as when Chrysler sold its tank-making business to raise cash). Besides, reporting methods themselves vary from company to company.

C. Our third valuation technique, in the great search for value, is the *appraisal method:* pricing a stock by comparing its estimated future income and appreciation to other (less risky) available investments. The future total return of any stock is obviously unknown; only estimates of dividend increases and growth prospects can be used. If a company has a long record of consistent dividend increases, however, it is reasonable to make an estimate of what you think the stock's yield might be at some point in the future. Earnings form less consistent patterns. Some appraisals are made by projecting a company's past earnings pattern into the future and assuming that its stock price will increase at the same rate. This return, combined with current and future dividend yield, can give the investor an estimate of total annual return. He must then figure in the risk factor of the equity investment versus a fixed-rate return.

THE CONTRARIAN PARADOX

Buying out-of-favor (low-PE) companies is a sensible strategy for almost anyone. Despite its suspiciously simple approach, it has been proven to work more consistently than many of the much more complicated investment strategies that you might hear about. Since many of the traditional methods of security analysis also are very sensible, both fundamental and technical information should be considered within the low-PE realm. Fundamental input actually is of substantial importance in shopping for distressed and bankrupt securities. The health of a company, after all, is perceived through any accurate fundamental information that you can derive from any source.

This chapter has presented a very simple but surprisingly effective way of taking advantage of stock market opportunities. Although there is certainly no such thing as fool-proof strategy, the general contrarian principle of limiting your field of choices to out-of-favor companies has clearly proven to beat the average results over time. It is based on the hypothesis that the market almost always overreacts to both good and bad reports about the investment environment.

If this sensible approach can improve results so easily, why isn't everyone an investment contrarian? There's an interesting paradox built into the theory itself: contrarianism, by its very nature, can never become popular. As soon as enough people get interested in an out-of-favor stock, it is no longer out-of-favor; if enough people act oppositely to the popular direction of the market, the direction changes and they become the crowd instead of being the contrarians. *The whole idea of contrarianism, in any field, is difficult for most people to grasp because it goes against our traditional way of thinking. Both the advice of experts and the influence of popular opinions are usually more persuasive than rationality itself. Both offer a sense of security.*

It's easy to be insecure as a novice Phoenix investor. Any kind of contrarian investing takes a healthy combination of faith and patience. It's true with Dreman's low-PE investing; it is especially true with the more venturesome Phoenix strategies that we are about to look at. The risks are greater, but so are the potential rewards.

5

The Phoenix Approach to the Distress Market

Distressed companies (ones operating in the red) don't jump at you from the stock listings, like low-PE stocks do. They don't have any earnings to make a ratio out of. And when they do break into the black, their PEs are typically very high because of those diminutive initial earnings. But this group is generally undervalued in the marketplace for the exact same reason as the low-PEs: the overreaction of investors to the companies' problems.

Just as several conclusive studies point toward low-PE stocks consistently outperforming high-PE stocks over the years, we also have conclusive evidence of distressed companies consistently outperforming healthy companies. Marine Midland Bank conducted a very revealing survey that tracked the performance of stocks of distressed companies versus those of profitable companies over a twenty-year period. The findings are startling: distressed stocks, on average, appreciated approximately twice as much as the Standard & Poor's Index itself in all time segments ranging from one to five years. The average distressed stock (between 1948 and 1967) bought on December 31st of the deficit year, for example, appreciated 23% over the next twelve months. During the same measurement periods the S&P Index averaged only 12.1% appreciation.

EVALUATING STOCKS OF DISTRESSED COMPANIES

Like their out-of-favor cousins, distressed stocks often sell at prices well below their real value because of investor overreaction. Both institutional and individual investors routinely sell out holdings of companies that report even quarterly losses: institutions because of fiduciary responsibility, and individuals because of fear and the inability to accurately assess the situation. *Most investors don't even consider the underlying intrinsic value of a company that's losing money; they sell at any price out of fear of a total loss. And yet in many cases the troubled company will be selling for far less than its underlying assets are really worth, and it may have a good chance of an earnings recovery in the not-too-distant future.*

The number of oversold companies that rebounded magnificently just in the last few years are too numerous to list in these pages. The top two performers on the New York Stock Exchange in 1982, for instance, were both troubled companies just one year earlier: Coleco Industries went from under $7 per share to over $50 in the same year because of the sudden popularity of its video games, and Chrysler Corporation went from $3 per share to $18 that year (and then to $35 in early 1983) thanks to an upturn in car sales and government loan guarantees. In Chrysler's case, the company's earnings went from a negative $26 per share in 1980 to a $1.12 gain in 1982 and an estimated gain of $6.50 in 1983.

But how do you know what to buy when bottom fishing in the battered end of the market? How do you identify a genuine recovery candidate among the hundreds of companies that just look cheap but really deserve their lowly market status? The key is to locate the companies that have the financial strength to not only survive but to reverse their current trends. To find these companies, the Phoenix Approach combines the theory of contrarianism with the tactics of fundamental analysis.

The following is a Phoenix Approach to the distress market: a dozen considerations for the value-seeker to weigh when kicking the tires of troubled companies. You may find it helpful to use the guide to understanding financial reports in Section IV for some of the material ahead. And remember: general financial data on many companies can be found in Standard & Poor's sheets, which your broker can get you, or *Value Line*, which you can find in the library, as well as quarterly and annual reports, which you get directly from the company.

Normal Earnings. Since companies that are losing money have no price-earnings ratios, we have to extrapolate this factor from past and future performance. *Look for companies whose stock is selling at a very low multiple of its normal earnings, companies that you think have the ability to regain those earnings.* For example, if Distressed, Inc., has been earning between $4 and $5 per share for several years in a row before posting a loss this year, it would be worth looking into further if its stock were selling for $9 or $10 (which would be just two times its normal earnings). This single criterion, however, tells us nothing at all about the company's ability to get its earnings back up to its former level.

Type of Business. Some businesses are harder to analyze than others. The distress investor should *stay with companies that can be judged in terms of normal industry competition and the direction of the general economy.* You can eliminate much of the unpredictable by staying away from esoteric businesses with fad products. This still leaves you with hundreds of choices among the highly cyclical, but essential industries.

Real Book Value. A true Phoenix investor never pays full price for any investment; he looks for discounts to hedge his risk. *Experienced distress investors will often pay no more than fifty cents for every dollar of estimated underlying asset value.* The place to start is by checking the stated book value of a company that you are interested in. Book value, remember, represents the amount that each share of stock would be worth in a liquidation. Based on a company's own balance sheet values, book value tells us how much money would be left if the company closed down, sold off all its assets, and paid off all its debts.

Since asset values that are carried on a balance sheet may not be up to date with current market values, however, the wise investor should read beyond what he sees in a financial report. Some industries' book values are fairly accurate because their assets are mainly liquid; banks and insurance companies fall into this category. Other industries traditionally carry assets on their books at outdated prices that are now worth much more because of inflation; paper companies, with their vast real estate holdings, fall into this category. Still other industries traditionally carry assets on their books at old values that are now worth far less than they once were; the steel companies, with their antiquated factories and equipment, usually have far overstated book values. *You should buy a distress stock only at a price which is well below what you estimate its real book value to be.* Ask yourself if the company's primary assets are apt to have increased or decreased in value over the years, whether they would be valuable to another company, and how liquid they would be on an open market.

Asset Liquidity. While we're still looking at balance sheets and asset valuations, an important consideration during corporate distress or possible bankruptcy is how fast assets can be sold. Securities, for example, can be turned into cash a lot faster than factories or real estate. *The wise distress investor attaches extra value to "current assets" and other relatively liquid holdings that a company might have.* The highest asset value should be attached to actual cash, of course. If our Distress, Inc., has a stated book value of $20 per share, and $5 of that is actually in cash reserves, then its financial position may be strong enough to absorb its current income losses.

Hidden Liabilities. Companies often have liabilities that are found only in the footnotes of their financial statements. A company may have a costly legal settlement pending or a pension liability hanging over its head that is not listed on its balance sheet. Troubled companies, of course, are much more apt to have unusual liabilities than are healthy companies. *Check the footnotes of the liability side of the company's balance sheet before deciding on a distressed stock.*

Debt-Equity Ratio (Leverage). A company is highly leveraged if it has a high proportion of bonds and preferred stocks in comparison to the value of its common stock. A high degree of leverage is good when the company is making money (because the leverage magnifies the earnings), but can spell doom for the same company during hard times. Since bond interest and preferred stock dividends are fixed costs, a decline in earnings can harshly affect the company's cash flow. Heavy debt, as we will see in the upcoming section on bankruptcy, is the most common cause of downfall for companies now in Chapter 11. *A relatively low percentage of debt (50% or less) to total capitalization is a big advantage to the survival of a troubled company.*

Dividends. Yes, companies that are losing money often still pay a dividend; the money comes from accumulated earnings from earlier years. Since the distress investor often must wait for a few years (sometimes a full economic cycle) before his company returns to its past productivity, it's a big advantage to be paid a respectable yield while you wait. *Look for companies that still pay a good dividend and have a history of dividend consistency.* High dividend companies, as we discovered in the last chapter on PE studies, have also proven to be better total-return investments over time (despite what most people think). But always be aware that a troubled company can reduce or suspend its common stock dividend at any time if it feels it must.

Competition. It is important to assess the nature of a distressed company's competition and what effect this competition has on its current troubles. In the early 1980s, for example, the U.S. automakers were stifled by competition from more efficient foreign manufacturers. The U.S. farm equipment makers, however, who were equally distressed during this same period, had almost no competition from abroad at all. Their problems were related almost entirely to general economic conditions and the terrible plight of the agriculture industry at that time. While farming cycles always come around, foreign competition doesn't go away easily (not without enormous philosophical and legislative changes). The auto industry, incidentally, recovered not by an increase in efficiency, but by a fortunate and dramatic decline in interest rates and the establishment of "voluntary" Japanese import restrictions. *Favor companies that have manageable foreign competition; favor companies even more that have an edge on their domestic competition.*

Management. A troubled company will often make key management changes in an attempt to reverse its fate. Sometimes the board of directors will even replace the company's president or CEO with someone more experienced in dealing with the particular circumstances that created the distress to begin with.

A corporation is nothing more than a combination of people and assets. Sometimes new leadership is just what a distressed company needs. GEICO Corporation, as I said earlier, is a classic example of a company saved from the brink of disaster by a key change in leadership.

Look for key management changes in distressed companies. Major improvements in top management positions can be as important as any of the financial factors discussed above.

Survival History. Many companies in the most cyclical industries—airlines, autos, railroads, steel, and others—are not strangers to recessionary distress. *How prepared a company is for hard times is an important consideration when looking for recovery candidates. Companies that have weathered periods of high interest rates, cyclical business slumps, intense product competition, or adverse government regulations in the past usually are more capable of bouncing back from their current problems than are companies that are suffering severe setbacks for the first time.*

New Products. Oftentimes, a single product will lead a distressed company back to financial good health. Coleco Industries, 1982's best NYSE performer (from $7 to $50), was a troubled swimming pool manufacturer just a few years earlier (in 1978, the company lost over $3 per share). Its toys and games division, however, rode the crest of the early 1980s video games craze and turned a profit of almost $6 per share for the company in 1982.

New models brought Winnebago back from red ink to black ink in recent years; even GEICO's turnaround was helped considerably by the success of new insurance products. *Try to find out what new products your recovery candidate might have in the works.* Read research reports or even call the company itself. How does it match up with the competition's new products in the same industry? How much bottom-line effect could the products have on the company to help turn it around?

Timing. Exactly when to step in and buy a distressed stock is a difficult decision to make. If a stock drops in price from $40 to $30 after reporting a loss, is this the time to jump in quickly before the price rebounds back up? Many investment managers feel that it's better to be too early than too late in market timing decisions. But in the arena of troubled companies, the opposite advice is safer. *I prefer to wait until a falling stock not only stabilizes, but actually starts back up.*

Don't ever expect to buy any stock at the very bottom or sell it at the very top; that's an unrealistic expectation. Within the strategy of distress investing, there is plenty of opportunity for cyclical gains without having to take unnecessary risks. So if you have been following a distressed stock and think that it has hit bottom, don't be afraid to give up a few points of appreciation in order to confirm your hunch.

All right, you've got some rules for selecting distressed stocks. Once you've narrowed down your field of candidates, choose the stocks that have fallen the most in price. Companies with reported losses have been proven to appreciate at twice the rate of the general market indices (based on Marine Midland's comprehensive study covering a twenty-year period).

● DIRECTORY OF CORPORATE DISTRESS ●

THE FOLLOWING NYSE COMPANIES WERE REPORTING NEGATIVE 12-MONTH EARNINGS THROUGH 6/30/83

STOCK SYMBOL	COMPANY	INDUSTRY	EARNINGS PER SHARE FOR PAST 4 QUARTERS IN DOLLARS	STOCK PRICE 6/30/83 IN DOLLARS
ATC	ATLANTIC METROPOLITAN CORP	real estate	-0.03	1.62
RON	RONSON CORP	metal	-0.03	5.00
TXF	TEXFI INDUSTRIES	textile	-0.05	9.75
AD	AMSTED INDUSTRIES	construction	-0.06	28.50
RBI	R B INDUSTRIES INC	furniture	-0.07	23.25
KML	KANE-MILLER CORP	food	-0.07	13.12
GEL	GELCO CORP	management	-0.07	17.37
AAE	AMERACE CORP	metal	-0.08	28.00
PS	PROLER INTERNATIONAL CORP	metal	-0.09	31.75
B	BARNES GROUP INC	mechanical	-0.10	20.75
ARE	ARLEN REALTY & DEVELOPMENT	real estate	-0.10	1.62
FLX	FLEXI-VAN CORP	transportation	-0.10	25.50
NAP	NAPCO INDUSTRIES INC	consumer products	-0.11	14.75
UPR	UNITED PARK CITY MINES	energy	-0.11	3.12
PUL	PUBLICKER INDUSTRIES INC	chemical	-0.11	4.62
TOW	TOWLE MANUFACTURING CO	silverware	-0.11	25.12
EA	ELECTRONIC ASSOCIATES INC	computer	-0.11	13.75

STOCK SYMBOL	COMPANY	INDUSTRY	EARNINGS PER SHARE FOR PAST 4 QUARTERS IN DOLLARS	STOCK PRICE 6/30/83 IN DOLLARS
ITH	INTERMEDICS INC	health	-0.12	21.25
BC	BRUNSWICK CORP	recreation	-0.14	39.00
BKI	BEKER INDUSTRIES	fertilizer	-0.16	8.37
WYL	WYLE LABORATORIES	electronic	-0.17	17.50
MX	MEASUREX CORP	electronic	-0.17	26.12
LEH	LEHIGH VALLEY INDS	textile	-0.18	2.37
THK	THACKERAY CORP	banking	-0.18	7.87
MAT	MATTEL INC	toys	-0.18	9.12
GFH	GIFFORD-HILL & CO	metal	-0.20	21.50
MSY	MODULAR COMPUTER SYSTEM	computer	-0.20	14.00
AAL	ALEXANDER & ALEXANDER SERV	insurance	-0.20	24.50
UCO	UNION CORP	various	-0.21	6.87
MH	MOBILE HOME INDUSTRIES	mobile home	-0.23	8.12
NI	NL INDUSTRIES	energy	-0.23	17.87
DMN	DAMON CORP	health	-0.23	37.50
FNM	FEDERAL NATL MORTGAGE ASSN	mortgage	-0.23	25.00
TBU	TACOMA BOATBUILDING INC	boats	-0.24	14.00
TMO	THERMO ELECTRON CORP	electronic	-0.25	30.62
PTO	PETROLANE INC	oil	-0.26	15.87
TAR	TRANSAMERICA RLTY INVESTORS	real estate	-0.26	13.50
GWF	GREAT WESTERN FINANCIAL	banking	-0.27	23.50

Symbol	Company	Industry		
NGX	NORTHGATE EXPLORATION LTD	mining	-0.27	5.50
OJ	ORANGE-CO INC	citrus	-0.27	6.25
EN	ENTERRA CORP	energy	-0.27	17.00
SFA	SCIENTIFIC-ATLANTA INC	electronic	-0.29	20.87
MAR	MARCADE GROUP INC	apparel	-0.30	4.50
PKD	PARKER DRILLING CO	drilling	-0.30	10.50
CNW	CHICAGO N WESTN TRANSN-CL A	railroad	-0.31	43.00
PRN	PUERTO RICAN CEMENT CO INC	cement	-0.35	7.87
DE	DEERE & CO	farm equip.	-0.35	34.87
CCH	CAMPBELL RESOURCES INC NEW	mining	-0.37	11.50
ST	SPS TECHNOLOGIES INC	fasteners	-0.37	28.25
TTC	TORO CO	motors	-0.38	10.62
TW	TRANS WORLD CORP	airline	-0.39	34.37
AEE	AILEEN INC	apparel	-0.39	6.62
AA	ALUMINUM CO OF AMERICA	aluminum	-0.41	37.00
PIO	PIONEER ELECTRONIC CORP-ADR	audio	-0.43	21.50
FGN	FLOW GENERAL INC	health	-0.43	14.62
DMC	DIVERSIFIED INDUSTRIES INC	metal	-0.46	5.62
WIE	WIEBOLDT STORES INC	dept. store	-0.48	9.12
KB	KAUFMAN & BROAD INC	insurance	-0.48	24.00
EQK	EQUIMARK CORP	banking	-0.49	5.75
MOH	MOHASCO CORP	furniture	-0.49	21.50
SE	SUN ELECTRIC CORP	automotive	-0.50	14.25
NHX	NATIONAL HOMES CORP	homes	-0.52	8.12
SSC	SUNSHINE MINING CO	mining	-0.52	15.87
BKO	BAKER INTERNATIONAL CORP	energy	-0.56	19.62

STOCK SYMBOL	COMPANY	INDUSTRY	EARNINGS PER SHARE FOR PAST 4 QUARTERS IN DOLLARS	STOCK PRICE 6/30/83 IN DOLLARS
NOM	NATOMAS CO	oil	−0.58	24.25
DM	DOME MINES LTD	gold	−0.59	17.50
INV	INSTITUTIONAL INVESTORS–DEL	real estate	−0.59	1.25
DCI	DONALDSON CO INC	automotive	−0.60	22.00
NSM	NATIONAL SEMICONDUCTOR CORP	electronic	−0.61	38.37
ARW	ARROW ELECTRONICS INC	electronic	−0.61	33.50
CEA	CESSNA AIRCRAFT CO	aircraft	−0.62	28.37
FHR	FISHER FOODS INC	supermarket	−0.65	11.62
CCF	COOK UNITED INC	dept. store	−0.66	6.75
SLF	SCOT LAD FOODS	food	−0.66	6.75
TCL	TRANSCON INC–CALIF	trucking	−0.71	8.50
POR	PORTEC INC	railroad	−0.73	16.00
PKR	PARKER PEN CO	writing utensil	−0.74	20.00
RAM	RAMADA INNS	hotel	−0.75	10.62
AGR	AMERICAN AGRONOMICS	citrus	−0.76	3.12
CMZ	CINCINNATI MILACRON INC	machine tools	−0.76	33.75
GFE	GF CORP	furniture	−0.78	8.25
CAW	CAESARS WORLD	hotel	−0.78	12.62
SCI	STORER COMMUNICATIONS INC	tv and radio	−0.79	30.62
SFE	SAFEGUARD SCIENTIFICS INC	automotive	−0.79	5.87
RCE	REECE CORP	apparel	−0.83	9.12
PCO	PITTSTON CO	energy	−0.85	16.87

Symbol	Company	Industry		
BNR	BANNER INDUSTRIES INC	*automotive*	−0.87	10.12
SMF	SINGER CO	*machinery*	−0.90	28.00
KMT	KENNAMETAL INC	*metal*	−0.91	26.87
CST	CHRISTIANA COMPANIES	*real estate*	−0.94	6.75
FPA	FIRST PENNSYLVANIA CORP	*banking*	−0.95	8.25
FLS	FLORIDA STEEL CORP	*steel*	−0.96	26.50
NVF	NVF CORP	*steel*	−0.98	2.87
AL	ALCAN ALUMINUM LTD	*aluminum*	−0.99	33.00
GCO	GENESCO INC	*apparel*	−1.00	8.37
GST	GENSTAR CORP	*real estate*	−1.00	27.75
KFM	KROEHLER MFG CO	*furniture*	−1.07	21.87
PPC	PATRICK PETROLEUM CO	*energy*	−1.07	5.75
UNC	UNC RESOURCES INC	*energy*	−1.08	7.12
TDI	TWIN DISC INC	*energy*	−1.09	20.50
CRA	CRAIG CORP	*electronic*	−1.09	8.75
MLR	MIDLAND-ROSS CORP	*metal*	−1.10	20.50
IR	INGERSOLL-RAND CO	*compressed air*	−1.13	52.75
HUF	HUFFY CORP	*bicycle*	−1.21	15.75
VI	VALLEY INDUSTRIES	*steel*	−1.27	6.62
DRV	DRAVO CORP	*engineering*	−1.29	15.00
TXN	TEXAS INSTRUMENTS INC	*electronic*	−1.33	119.12
ATH	ATHLONE INDS	*metal*	−1.36	21.37
KOP	KOPPERS CO	*construction*	−1.42	19.25
GRW	GROWTH REALTY COS	*real estate*	−1.43	4.50
UDE	UNIT DRILLING & EXPLORATION	*drilling*	−1.48	7.50
BNK	BANGOR PUNTA CORP	*aircraft*	−1.48	20.87

STOCK SYMBOL	COMPANY	INDUSTRY	EARNINGS PER SHARE FOR PAST 4 QUARTERS IN DOLLARS	STOCK PRICE 6/30/83 IN DOLLARS
SVB	SAVIN CORP	marketing	–1.51	6.50
CRO	CHROMALLOY AMERICAN CORP	metal	–1.51	14.50
WUR	WURLITZER CO	piano	–1.52	7.50
PLA	PLAYBOY ENTERPRISES	entertainment	–1.52	11.75
CKE	CASTLE & COOKE INC	farming	–1.57	14.62
IDL	IDEAL BASIC INDUSTRIES INC	cement	–1.62	19.12
LUC	LUKENS INC	steel	–1.63	15.00
IRF	INTL RECTIFIER CORP	health	–1.65	36.37
ADP	ALLIED PRODUCTS	automotive	–1.68	8.37
KEN	KENAI CORP	energy	–1.73	5.75
APL	APL CORP	health	–1.77	9.87
ABZ	ARKANSAS BEST CORP	trucking	–1.78	20.12
GLE	GLEASON WORKS	machinery	–1.82	12.75
LCE	LONE STAR INDUSTRIES	construction	–1.83	31.00
CCX	CCX INC	steel	–1.84	8.87
OXY	OCCIDENTAL PETROLEUM CORP	energy	–1.96	24.50
PD	PHELPS DODGE CORP	copper	–1.96	28.25
CR	CRANE CO	construction	–1.97	32.25
SUL	SULLAIR CORP	compressor	–2.02	7.62
HSI	HI-SHEAR INDUSTRIES	aerospace	–2.04	13.37
GCA	GCA CORP	electronic	–2.06	53.50
NP	NEWPARK RESOURCES	oil	–2.06	8.00

Symbol	Company	Industry		
CLF	CLEVELAND-CLIFFS IRON CO	iron	-2.11	23.62
NSD	NATIONAL-STANDARD CO	steel	-2.13	16.25
MAN	MANVILLE CORP	construction	-2.18	15.50
MME	MCNEIL CORP	support system	-2.18	18.75
DAL	DELTA AIR LINES INC	airline	-2.18	42.50
DLT	DELTONA CORP	real estate	-2.25	13.75
CLC	CLC OF AMERICA	transportation	-2.28	10.75
HES	HESSTON CORP	heavy machinery	-2.32	11.37
GHX	GALVESTON HOUSTON	oil	-2.34	12.00
TKR	TIMKEN CO	mechanical	-2.34	66.75
GVL	GRANITEVILLE CO	fabric	-2.40	16.87
FTR	FRUEHAUF CORP	automotive	-2.46	36.75
ALN	ALLEN GROUP	automotive	-2.50	18.37
GR	GOODRICH (B.F.) CO	rubber	-2.50	41.00
VRC	VARCO INTERNATIONAL	energy	-2.66	8.75
NMS	NATIONAL MINES SERVICE CO	mining	-2.69	8.62
AP	AMPCO-PITTSBURGH CORP	railroad	-2.81	14.50
VX	VULCAN INC	metal	-2.84	10.50
WCI	WARNER COMMUNICATIONS INC	entertainment	-2.96	28.37
UMM	UNITED MERCHANTS & MFRS INC	various	-3.02	13.62
MEA	MEAD CORP	paper	-3.03	30.62
COS	COPPERWELD CORP	steel	-3.05	15.62
HAY	HAYES-ALBION CORP	automotive	-3.12	10.87
N	INCO LTD	metal	-3.13	14.50
GX	GEO INTERNATIONAL CORP	oil	-3.14	10.87
CZ	CELANESE CORP	chemical	-3.16	63.62
ATA	ARTRA GROUP INC	chemical	-3.18	22.50

STOCK SYMBOL	COMPANY	INDUSTRY	EARNINGS PER SHARE FOR PAST 4 QUARTERS IN DOLLARS	STOCK PRICE 6/30/83 IN DOLLARS
AMT	ACME-CLEVELAND CORP	machine tools	-3.19	25.50
ICA	IMPERIAL CORP OF AMERICA	banking	-3.19	13.37
AMO	AMERICAN MOTORS CORP	automotive	-3.24	9.50
SWF	SOUTHWEST FOREST INDUSTRIES	wood products	-3.25	15.75
KLU	KAISER ALUMINUM & CHEM CORP	aluminum	-3.26	20.00
CYL	CYCLOPS CORP	steel	-3.29	30.00
SSP	SUPERSCOPE INC	audio	-3.37	5.12
ETN	EATON CORP	automotive	-3.43	41.50
GPO	GIANT PORTLAND & MASONRY CEM	cement	-3.48	7.87
CEN	CENTRONICS DATA COMPUTER	computer	-3.51	27.75
TKA	TONKA CORP	toy	-3.58	24.50
WOL	WAINOCO OIL CORP	energy	-3.76	8.00
BNS	BROWN & SHARPE MFG CO	waste	-3.78	16.25
NSW	NORTHWESTERN STEEL & WIRE CO	steel	-3.78	24.00
MMB	MACMILLAN BLOEDEL LTD	wood products	-3.79	25.75
CUM	CUMMINS ENGINE	automotive	-3.91	63.00
EVY	EVANS PRODUCTS CO	construction	-3.93	17.00
LMS	LAMSUN & SESSIONS CO	railroad	-3.97	6.37
HD	HUDSON BAY MINING & SMELTING	energy	-4.08	13.25
CGG	CHICAGO PNEUMATIC TOOL CO	machinery	-4.09	15.87
AG	ALLEGHENY INTERNATIONAL INC	construction	-4.26	34.50

Symbol	Company	Industry		
ABA	AMERICAN BAKERIES CO	*food*	-4.27	16.62
NX	QUAMEX CORP	*steel*	-4.46	8.62
ZH	CROWN ZELLERBACH	*wood products*	-4.51	30.00
RAY	RAYMARK CORP	*manufacturing*	-4.55	12.75
LLC	LLC CORP	*banking*	-4.67	5.50
PN	PAN AMERICAN WORLD AIRWAYS	*airline*	-4.68	8.12
DMG	DMG INC	*real estate*	-4.90	4.12
KSC	KAISER STEEL CORP	*steel*	-5.02	31.00
AHO	AMERICAN HOIST & DERRICK CO	*construction*	-5.39	14.50
EAL	EASTERN AIR LINES	*airline*	-5.47	11.37
CAT	CATERPILLAR TRACTOR CO	*construction*	-5.58	47.25
WOA	WORLD AIRWAYS INC	*airline*	-5.84	6.50
MUN	MUNSINGWEAR INC	*apparel*	-5.96	14.62
IAD	INLAND STEEL CO	*steel*	-6.11	32.50
RAI	REPUBLIC AIRLINES INC	*airline*	-6.13	7.87
AC	AMERICAN CAN CO	*container*	-6.75	43.75
AMX	AMAX INC	*natural resource*	-6.83	27.37
WTD	WEAN UNITED INC	*steel*	-6.94	6.75
NSH	NASHUA CORP	*copier*	-7.10	20.50
X	U S STEEL CORP	*steel*	-7.20	24.75
LTV	LTV CORP	*steel*	-7.30	15.62
PGO	PENGO INDUSTRIES INC	*energy*	-7.73	2.75
AS	ARMCO INC	*steel*	-7.79	17.87
RLM	REYNOLDS METALS CO	*aluminum*	-7.95	33.00
HLY	HOLLY SUGAR CORP	*sugar*	-8.21	45.50
MSE	MASSEY FERGUSON LTD	*heavy machinery*	-8.41	4.62

STOCK SYMBOL	COMPANY	INDUSTRY	EARNINGS PER SHARE FOR PAST 4 QUARTERS IN DOLLARS	STOCK PRICE 6/30/83 IN DOLLARS
WAL	WESTERN AIR LINES INC	airline	−8.90	6.12
HPH	HARNISCHFEGER CORP	heavy machinery	−9.77	8.87
TGR	TIGER INTERNATIONAL	air cargo	−10.01	11.12
HNM	HANNA MINING CO	mining	−10.57	21.75
HRT	HRT INDUSTRIES INC	dept. store	−11.06	5.62
KES	KEYSTONE CONS INDUSTRIES INC	steel	−11.79	14.25
CKL	CLARK EQUIPMENT CO	heavy machinery	−11.80	33.50
UB	UNITED BRANDS	food	−12.25	21.50
TOS	TOSCO CORP	oil	−12.46	11.75
MP	MCINTYRE MINES LTD	coal	−13.60	31.00
RS	REPUBLIC STEEL CORP	steel	−14.49	22.25
GRX	GENERAL REFRACTORIES CO	steel	−15.55	5.75
NRL	NORLIN CORP	music	−19.48	27.00
MCC	MESTA MACHINE CO	steel	−20.22	8.62
RVB	REVERE COPPER & BRASS INC	metal	−23.53	11.50
AH	ALLIS-CHALMERS CORP	heavy machinery	−23.63	17.62
BDW	BALDWIN UNITED CORP	financial service	−25.65	8.62
WHX	WHEELING-PITTSBURGH STEEL	steel	−27.03	24.00
NS	NATIONAL STEEL CORP	metal	−27.74	26.50
BR	INTL HARVESTER CO	heavy machinery	−36.07	10.12
BS	BETHLEHEM STEEL CORP	steel	−37.23	23.62

EVALUATING BONDS OF DISTRESSED COMPANIES

Bonds that are rated BBB or better (A, AA, and AAA) are considered "investment grade." These securities are thought to have relatively little chance of default because of their well-financed backers. They are bought as high-quality income instruments by both institutional investors and conservative individual investors. The yields on high-grade bonds are very competitive, based almost entirely on exact ratings and maturity dates. There are no undiscovered bargains, as there sometimes are in the stock market.

Bonds that are rated BB or below (B, CCC, CC, C) are fondly referred to as "junk bonds." These are the debt securities of troubled companies that the rating services think could default. Because of their low ratings, the yields on junk bonds are considerably higher—sometimes twice as high—than those on investment grade bonds.

The perception of risk in bonds is one of Wall Street's more time-honored peculiarities. Investors are obsessed with the risk of default (which is the only risk that the ratings measure). *Yet they seem to entirely ignore the real risk: changes in market conditions.* Whereas a typical conservative investor will feel sublimely secure about his AAA rating on one bond and quake in fear over the BB rating of another, he's likely to be oblivious to the chance that rising interest rates could halve the value of either bond. The actual number of defaults, as it turns out, is only about one in a thousand even among the lower-grade bonds. But ask anyone who owned even U.S. Treasury bonds during the 1978 to 1982 period of soaring interest rates how much their high ratings helped preserve their capital. Even the highest grade bonds lost up to half their principal value during that period.

Normally, the only reason to buy any bond to begin with is if you think that interest rates will, at least for the foreseeable future, stay at current levels or decline. That's what makes bond prices hold their value or increase in value. The only other reasons to buy bonds are these: to lock in a yield in a bond that you keep until it matures, to take advantage of the "oversold" (underpriced) situation of the bond of a distressed company, or to make a claim on the assets of a bankrupt company by buying its undervalued bonds (which I'll get to eventually). It is the bonds of distressed companies that I'll rattle on about here.

Skeptical about junk bonds? Consider these facts:

A. Junk bonds, over the years, have proven to yield a total return that is 50% greater than investment-grade bonds as a group, even after figuring in losses resulting from default.

B. The default rate is, amazingly, only slightly higher with the lower-grade bonds than the higher-grade bonds: far fewer than 1% of all low-grade bonds have defaulted during the entire twentieth century.

C. Even when default does occur, the investment potential for most bonds is anything but finished. Debt securities of bankrupt companies provide all sorts of investment opportunities.

Based on the normal risk-reward relationship of investments, facts A and B above seem incongruous. The combination of these facts reveals one of the most overlooked investment bargains available today: *junk bonds, as a group, are not nearly as risky as their high returns would imply.*

The yields on junk bonds are high because their prices are inordinately low. And the low prices are a result of the same investor overreaction to bad news that we often see in equities. While a 50% premium in yield (for example, an 18% yield-to-maturity versus 12%) should normally be the reward for a 50% increase in risk, price history clearly points out an exception with the bonds of distressed companies. Even in measurements that include the Great Depression, the incidence of default is surprisingly low: less than 2% of all lower-grade bonds defaulted between the turn of the century and the end of World War II. Since then, the record has improved substantially: fewer than one-eighth of 1% (about one out of every thousand issues) of junk bonds defaulted from World War II through 1983.

Bond defaults are like shipwrecks. They don't happen often, but when they do, it's all over the newspapers. The rest of the time, perfectly rational people become afraid to go to sea. Likewise the failures of such major corporations as Braniff International, Itel Corp., and Manville Corp. With all the financial casualties they've produced, who wouldn't be skittish? But considering the vast network of total debt securities—some 20,000 issues of publicly traded companies alone—the incidence of even delayed interest payments is actually very low.

The investment strategy for going after underpriced debt securities is very similar to that for distressed equities. The rules for stock selection all would apply to the bonds as well. As with the stocks, diversification is essential. For those investors who want even greater diversification and less decision-making responsibility than they can get on their own, there are several mutual funds that specialize in junk bonds. The objectives of these funds are a combination of a higher-than-average yield and capital appreciation.

JUNK BOND FUNDS*

FUND NAME ADDRESS AND PHONE	MINIMUM INITIAL INVESTMENT	MINIMUM SUBSEQUENT INVESTMENT	12 MONTH RETURN**
AMERICAN GENERAL HIGH YIELD INVESTMENTS, INC 2777 Allen Parkway Houston, TX 77001 713/522-1111	$ 500	$ 50	34%
AMERICAN INVESTORS INCOME FUND, INC. 88 Field Point Road P.O. Box 2500 Greenwich, CT 06836 800/243-5353	$ 400	$ 20	47%

FUND NAME ADDRESS AND PHONE	MINIMUM INITIAL INVESTMENT	MINIMUM SUBSEQUENT INVESTMENT	% RATE OF RETURN Y/E 6/30/83
COLONIAL HIGH YIELD SECURITIES, INC. 75 Federal Street Boston, MA 02110 800/225-2364	$ 250	$ 25	40%
FEDERATED HIGH INCOME SECURITIES, INC. 421 Seventh Avenue Pittsburgh, PA 15219 800/245-2423	$1,500	$100	34%
FIRST INVESTORS BOND APPRECIATION FUND, INC. 120 Wall Street New York, NY 10005 212/825-7900	$1,000	$100	30%
KEMPER HIGH YIELD FUND, INC. 120 South LaSalle Street Chicago, IL 60603 312/781-1121	$1,000	$100	40%
KEYSTONE B–4 FUND 99 High Street Boston, MA 02110 800/225-1587	$ 250	none	38%
LORD ABBETT BOND– DEBENTURE FUND, INC. 63 Wall Street New York, NY 10005 212/425-8720	$1,000	none	40%
MASSACHUSETTS FINANCIAL HIGH INCOME TRUST 200 Berkeley Street Boston, MA 02116 617/423-3500	none	none	52%
OPPENHEIMER HIGH YIELD FUND, INC. 3600 South Yosemite Street Denver, CO 80237 303/770-2345	$2,500	$ 25	35%
PIONEER BOND FUND, INC. 60 State Street Boston, MA 02109 800/225-6292	$1,000	$100	29%
UNITED HIGH INCOME FUND, INC. One Crown Center P.O. Box 1343 Kansas City, MO 64141 816/283-4000	$ 500	$ 50	36%

FUND NAME ADDRESS AND PHONE	MINIMUM INITIAL INVESTMENT	MINIMUM SUBSEQUENT INVESTMENT	% RATE OF RETURN Y/E 6/30/83
VANGUARD FIXED INCOME SECURITIES FUND–HIGH YIELD PORTFOLIO P.O. Box 876 Valley Forge, Pa 19482 800/523-7910	$3,000	$ 50	29%
VENTURE INCOME PLUS, INC. 309 Johnson Street Post Office Box 1688 Santa Fe, MN 87501 505/983-4335	$1,000	$ 25	36%

*Based on *Forbes* magazine annual mutual fund survey, Aug. '83
**Total return on fund for past twelve months ending 6/30/83.

JUNK BONDS LISTED ON THE NEW YORK BOND EXCHANGE
BY CURRENT YIELD

COMPANY NAME	ISSUE DESCRIPTION	RATING	6/30/83 PRICE	CURRENT YIELD
Telecom Corp	SDB 13.75% 10/01/88	CCC	$ 47⅛	29.2%
Telecom Corp	SDB 13.375% 10/01/99	D	50.000	26.8
International Harvester Co.	DEB 18% 12/15/2002	NR	96.500	18.7
Baldwin Utd. Corp	S DEB 10% 07/20/2009	BB-	59.125	16.9
Global Marine Inc.	SR S DEB 16.125% 03/01/02	B	95.500	16.9
Pam Am. World Airways Inc.	SR DEB 13.5% 05/01/2003	CCC	79.750	16.9
Global Marine Inc.	SR S DEB 16% 09/15/2001	B	95.125	16.8
Western Air Lines Inc.	SR NT 10.75% 06/15/98	B	64.000	16.8
Eastern Air Lines Inc.	2nd EQ TR 17.5% 07/01/97	CCC	104.625	16.7
Eastern Air Lines Inc.	EQ TR 16.125% 10/15/02	CCC	100.500	16.0
CTI Intl. Inc.	S NT 18.25% 07/15/1989	B	113.750	16.0

Company	Issue	Rating	Price	Yield
Hunt Intl. Res. Corp.	S DEB 9.875% 12/31/04	NR	62.125	15.9
International Harvester Credit	NT 13.5% 08/01/88	CCC	86.500	15.6
Leucadia Natl Corp.	S DEB 13.75% 08/01/99	NR	88.375	15.5
Allis Chalmers Credit	NT 16% 06/01/1991	B	103.250	15.5
World Airways Inc.	EQ TR 11.25% 04/15/94	CCC	73.000	15.4
Genesco Inc.	SR NT 15.25% 12/15/94	NR	100	15.3
Puritan Fashions Corp.	SR DEB 16% 05/01/1997	NR	105.000	15.2
Global Marine Inc.	SR S DEB 12.375% 08/01/98	B	81.250	15.2
Palm Beach Inc.	S DEB 16.125% 04/01/2002	B	106.250	15.2
Public Svc. Co. of NH	DEB 15.75% 10/01/88	B	104.250	15.1
Montgomery Ward Credit	NT 16% 03/15/1986	BB	106.625	15.0
CCI Corp.	S DEB 13.875% 07/15/00	CC	92.250	15.0

6

The Phoenix Portfolio

All that information in the first chapter of this section, about traditional investment theory, was very important: you have to know the other guy's thinking before you can understand bottom fishing. With this as a background, we looked at some of the specific rules and techniques of successful Phoenix investing in both the out-of-favor and distressed markets. By now, I hope you are eager to get started actually investing. You didn't pay $15.95 just to read theories and rules. In this chapter you will learn, step by step, exactly how to put together a Phoenix portfolio.

Perhaps you are a novice investor. Or, perhaps you have some experience in the market, but not a great deal. Or perhaps you are a full-fledged investment expert who reads a balance sheet like some people read a box score. Whichever category most closely describes you, the Phoenix Approach is a strategy by which you can profit. What follows are three checklists of easy-to-follow instructions on how to get started using the Phoenix Approach. The first is as elementary as they come, amounting to barely more than a random selection of stocks deemed eligible based on a simple qualifying formula. It is so simple, in fact, as to suggest implausibility. But implausible it is not.

Remember, historical data show that out-of-favor and distressed securities, as a group, have outperformed the averages consistently over time. With this strategy, and the requisite patience, you would have to turn the odds upside down not to prosper.

The second checklist is nominally more complicated, geared as it is to the person with a moderate amount of experience in the market. The third checklist is the real dandy; it contains an elaborate compilation of guidelines involving relatively sophisticated financial analysis.

The more work you do in choosing securities for your portfolio—using the Phoenix guidelines—the better your portfolio is likely to perform. However, as I said a while back, the Phoenix Approach is a strategy for everyone. Even the sublimely simple Strategy No. 1 will allow you to cash in on the only true bargains in today's market.

STRATEGY NO. 1 (NOVICE)

1. Get out a newspaper, preferably *The Wall Street Journal.* Turn to the stock listings. Find the listing for the NYSE (New York Stock Exchange). For the sake of simplicity we will stay with NYSE companies in these examples, although some of the best bargains are found on other exchanges or over-the-counter.

2. Find the column headed "PE" (price-earnings ratio). Mark each stock with a PE of 7 or less. (On pages 67 to 69 I listed all non-utility NYSE companies that were still valued below 7:1 in mid-1983.)

3. Find the column headed "Yld" (yield). This is a measurement of dividends per share as a percentage of price per share. (A stock that costs $20 and pays an annual dividend of $2.50 has a yield of 12.5%.) Mark a second time those low-PE stocks that also have a yield of 5% or greater. (Be sure that you are marking just common stocks, not preferred.) These are your 7–5 stocks. (Dividends tend to stay relatively stable. So, as the price of the stock goes up, the yield goes down. But 7–5 stocks are a good place to start.)

4. Look for the name of the stock. It will be abbreviated and some are more easily deciphered than others. IBM stands for IBM; Grum, for Grumman; MinPL, for Minnesota Power & Light. If you don't know which companies you've marked as 7–5s, you can find the answer in your Standard & Poor's Stock Guide which you can subscribe to or get from your broker.

5. Many of the 7–5s will be utilities. Cross them off your list. As a rule, their prices are affected mostly by interest rates and therefore they don't figure into our bottom-fishing growth strategy.

6. Since we are looking for depressed securities that might regain popularity as conditions change, we will favor stocks that are selling near the low end of their yearly price range. So look under the "52-week High/Low" column for each of your Phoenix candidates and put a star next to each one whose current price (column titled "Last") is much closer to its yearly low price than to its high price.

7. This method will leave you with several potential buys. Now, how much do you want to invest? $5,000? OK. Select five stocks in five different industries and buy $1,000 worth of each.

If you have $50,000 to invest you can afford to diversify even more. Buy ten stocks, all in round lots.

[**Note:** It's cheaper to buy in even lots of 100 shares. When you buy odd lots (less than 100 shares), your commissions go up. But if your means are modest—since you want to diversify your portfolio—you're better off buying the odd lots anyway if it's necessary. Since you'll be holding onto these shares for a long time, the difference in commissions will be minor in the long run.]

8. Although just staying with the same portfolio of low-PE stocks for several years will very likely beat the averages, a continual pruning strategy has been shown to improve results still more, even considering the transaction costs of making those changes. Every six months, sell any stock in the portfolio which no longer fits in under the 7–5 rule and replace it with a new, eligible one. (Hopefully, you will be doing most of your selling at a profit, with higher PEs and lower yields both the result of increased prices.)

9. Sit back and watch for another six months, then take step #8 again.

10. Should one of your stocks really take off, as a few will, you may be tempted to stick with it after your six months have elapsed even though it will have long since soared out of 7–5 range. Holding is usually a mistake. (Stick with your *strategy*.) If you feel the upward trend has a long way to go, and you just can't sell it, then keep it, but not in your bottom-fishing portfolio. Shunt it off into a separate portfolio—one for more speculative stocks—and replace it with another 7–5 bottom fish of your own choosing.

[**Note:** There is nothing magic about 7 and 5. In a very depressed market—when the Dow Jones Industrial Average is 800 or below—the bottom-fish guide number is more like 5–8 (lower PEs and higher yields). In a mature bull market, the bottom-fishing PE could be 10 or below, and the yield 4% or above. I ran a 7–5 screen in mid-1983, after a dramatic one-year market rise, and found 38 NYSE non-utility candidates. A year earlier, there would have been hundreds more to choose from.]

STRATEGY NO. 2 (INTERMEDIATE)

1. Locate, in *The Wall Street Journal* stock listings, all NYSE stocks with a PE of 7 or less and a yield of 5% or greater. Exclude utilities.

2. As with Strategy No. 1, favor companies that are low in their price range, and then diversify by industry.

3. On a separate sheet, list all of the companies that operated at a loss for the past year. These can be identified by the absence of a PE figure in the paper. (My screen in mid-1983 identified some 234 NYSE companies in the red. Your field by now should still contain at least 100 companies.) These distressed companies will represent a whole separate category within your Phoenix portfolio, and should account for 20% to 30% of the total portfolio. Since these companies are naturally riskier, a certain amount of effort is required to select a variety of different industries.

[**Note:** A paradox exists in our theory of low-PE, high-PE, and distressed securities. Distressed stocks, which, as a group, we like, can quickly become high-PE stocks, which, as a group, we don't like. This happens when a company's earnings rise from the red to the barely black. Since we are obviously not interested in companies whose profits will remain minute, careful selection of distressed companies is necessary to find those long-term, high-potential turnaround candidates.]

4. Start your selection by finding out a little more about the distressed companies through your handy little S&P Guide. For this portfolio, exclude all companies that are widely perceived to be on the very brink of bankruptcy. Then narrow your field by eliminating industry repetitions.

5. Now ask yourself two questions about the money-losing companies that remain in your field:

> **A.** Does this company have products or services that people continue to demand at a price that's competitive with other companies in the industry?

B. Are there creditors, employees, government bodies, and suppliers in whose overwhelming interest it is to keep this company in business?

If the answer to either of those questions is "no," cross it off your list.

6. The final selection process in Strategy No. 2 can be applied to both your out-of-favor and distress candidates. Look for *quality* in these companies before putting them in your portfolio. Three considerations:

A. *Management.* A company's most important asset is often its management team. A top-level executive, with experience in making profits and with good contacts in the financial community, can be invaluable to a corporation. *I prefer stocks in which management holds a large equity stake in the company;* personal ownership goes a long way during rough times. *But be careful of companies that are ruled by a single dominant executive.* Such companies tend to become very dependent on that person and can suffer greatly from his or her loss.

B. *Capital Structure.* The total value of a company's securities is commonly known as its "capitalization." The specific proportioning of all those securities—common and preferred stock as well as various bond issues—is known as its "capital structure." These securities are the financial resources of the company; they are the very sources of the company's money. Although leverage (proportion of debt to equity) varies from industry to industry, you should *avoid companies that are hopelessly burdened with short-term debt.* Common stockholders are hurt by heavy debt (especially when it's non-callable) and a large number of preferred issues.

    C. *Stock Distribution. Wide distribution of a company's stock among many investors is usually preferable to its shares being controlled by relatively few larger investors.* (The number and percentage of institutional holdings in many companies can be found on the back of an S&P sheet.) Even though institutional investors add a certain amount of prestige to a company, its stock will generally be more liquid and stable with greater distribution.

These are just a few of the favorable characteristics that you should look for in a company before buying its stock. Other factors are very important too: dividend potentials, earnings trends, cash flow and working capital, labor relations, consistency of sales, shape of equipment and facilities, diversification of products, research and development, industry position, and the all-important "intangibles" such as the company's name and reputation. (When the best part of a company's management team is under indictment, for example, the total-debt-versus-tangible-assets ratio suddenly assumes less importance.)

    7. Make your final selections, buying as many shares as you can in five to ten different issues, spending about three-quarters of your money on low-PE companies and the rest on turnaround candidates.

    8. Prune your portfolio as in Strategy No. 1.

STRATEGY NO. 3 (ADVANCED)

    1. Again, find all NYSE stocks with a PE of 7 or less and a yield of 5% or greater. Get rid of the utilities.

    2. Create a separate list of distress companies—those with a year of negative earnings.

    3. Divide both lists by industry, and use the methods in Strategy No. 2 to choose a manageable number of candidates in each category that you want to analyze further.

4. Scrutinize these finalists according to the appraisal methods I'm about to give you. (This is the more sophisticated stuff; I hope you like arithmetic.) I should precede this information with three warnings: **(A)** These tests are the very tools of Wall Street's fundamentalists. As we have seen, when used on an open field of selections, they may produce no better results than random guesses over time. But when used within the context of the Phoenix strategy—on the narrowed field of selected unpopular companies—your results should improve considerably. **(B)** Employing the appraisal techniques described ahead requires a little work. It should be attempted only by the dedicated investor, properly equipped with the financial reports of his prospective companies. **(C)** Many of these tests won't work for distressed companies because of their negative earnings; most will be more helpful in your final selection of low-PE stocks, which represent the lion's share of your portfolio anyway.

You can give any company a complete financial physical by looking at its financial reports and applying the information to several commonly used health-measurements called "ratios." There are four categories of financial ratios: those that measure a company's assets, liquidity, leverage, and profitability.

    A. *Asset Ratios:* measure how efficiently a company uses its assets.

        1. Inventory vs. revenues: a measurement of the company's inventory investment. A low inventory in relationship to revenues is usually a good sign.

        2. Assets vs. revenues: reveals productivity of assets by measuring how much revenue they produce. High sales per assets is a good sign.

3. *Receivables vs. revenues:* measures how effectively a company can collect what it is owed. A rising ratio could be a sign of trouble.

B. *Liquidity Ratios:* measure the all-important cash resources of a company. This is particularly useful information to know about troubled companies since they are more apt to need liquidity to meet obligations on short notice.

1. *Current assets vs. current liabilities:* measures the company's available cash reserves. Usually referred to just as "current ratio," this is probably the most commonly used financial ratio of all. A healthy company is said to require at least a 2:1 current ratio for safety, but a wider range of comfort is often necessary depending on the industry and circumstances. The net excess of current assets over current liabilities is known as "working capital."

2. *Liquid current assets vs. current liabilities:* an even tougher measurement of a company's liquidity. This ratio—often called the "acid test"—excludes inventory values from other current assets. A general guideline is 1:1 for safety under this test.

3. *Working capital vs. revenues:* measures the company's net current assets on hand compared to the company's total sales. There is no accepted guideline to this ratio since there are so many variables.

C. *Leverage Ratios:* measure the amount and safety of a company's debt structure.

1. *Earnings vs. fixed expenses:* measures the company's ability to meet built-in obligations such as interest payments and leases. A ratio of at least 3:1 is minimum for safety.

2. *Short-term debt vs. total debt:* indicates degree of immediate (next twelve months) liquidity and ability to meet unexpected obligations. Too much short-term debt, and the inability to roll it over upon maturity, is the main cause of corporate bankruptcy.

3. *Total debt vs. tangible assets:* measures a company's ability to borrow more money. The less debt (both long-term and current debt) already outstanding compared to the company's tangible assets (excludes intangible assets, such as patents and goodwill), the more stable the company generally appears and the more it can probably still borrow against those assets.

D. *Profitability Ratios:* tell a stockholder how efficiently and productively his equity is working for him.

1. *Return on Equity (ROE):* a standard measurement of how much profit a company's capital is producing, figured by dividing earnings by net worth. High-growth companies sometimes average a 20% ROE annually.

2. *Operating Ratio:* measures the fixed costs of doing business, figured by dividing operating expenses by revenues. The lower the ratio, the safer the company is. The opposite of this ratio, the percentage of revenues that net earnings represent, is known as the company's "profit margin." Overall industrial margins average only about 5% annually.

5. Follow Strategies No. 1 and 2 for pruning. Stick with your strategy, and be patient. You're not in it for the quick kill. The Phoenix Approach, remember, is for a lifetime of investing.

[**Note:** When selling *losers* from the distress list after only one year, be sure to do it *before* the full year is up to take advantage of the short-term capital loss. When selling *gainers* after a year, make sure you've gone *past* a full year for the long-term gain.]

SOME REMINDERS

Before going on to a whole new sector of the market, let's briefly summarize some of the Phoenix advice given so far in the book on how to select out-of-favor and distressed companies:

1. Buy low, sell high.

2. Buy on bad news, not on good news—unless the news is very, very unexpected and you somehow get a very, very, very early start.

3. What looks like a dog may not be a dog; real value eventually establishes itself.

4. Buy mostly stocks with low price-earnings ratios, but remember that the key is future, not present, earnings.

5. Buy at a discount—a price per share lower than book values per share—but remember that real asset value is not always as stated. Inflation and appreciation can make it higher than it appears, obsolescence and market glut lower than it appears.

6. Buy stocks with high yields. Investment value includes appreciation plus yield, and high-yielding stocks historically perform better.

7. Choose companies with competition and in established industries. It will be easier to judge their worth.

8. Faced with a choice, choose companies whose stock prices have plummeted the most. The comeback could be all the more lucrative.

9. Do not try to catch a stock at the bottom of the market. Wait for it to come back at least a little before you buy. If the big comeback never occurs, you've minimized your risk.

Favor companies with:

10. A history of dividend consistency.

11. A record of previous comebacks.

12. A promising new product on the shelf or on the horizon.

13. A wide distribution of stock ownership (as opposed to five institutions owning 75% of the shares).

14. High asset liquidity.

15. Changes for the better in management.

16. A sound debt-to-equity ratio.

Beware of companies with:

17. Hidden liabilities. (Read those footnotes!)

18. Heavy loads of short-term debt.

RECOVERY SELECTIONS

Making specific investment recommendations is a dangerous task for the financial writer. With a lag-time of six to eight months between a manuscript deadline and publication date, specific recommendations can be far outdated long before the first book is even available. But since my strategy is long-term by nature, and should endure shorter-term fluctuations, I'll stick my neck out just this one time. The following is a list of a few of my own favorite turnaround candidates among low-PE and negative-earnings stocks as of June 30, 1983. I will review both lists by year-end.

I. OUT-OF-FAVOR FAVORITES

COMPANY	INDUSTRY	EPS FOR PAST 4 QTS. A/O 6/30/83	STOCK PRICE A/O 6/30/83	PE
1. NBD Bancorp	banking	$7.01	$38.12	5.43
2. Key Banks	banking	$4.04	$24.12	5.97
3. Exxon	oil	$5.35	$33.75	6.30
4. Bay Financial	real estate	$2.30	$14.00	6.08
5. Smuckers	food	$6.60	$33.75	5.11
6. Stone & Webster	engineering	$7.19	$43.75	6.08
7. Financial Corp./Amer.	banking	$5.85	$39.12	6.68
8. Sonat	gas	$5.21	$33.37	6.40
9. Harris Bancorp	banking	$6.10	$38.50	6.31
10. First Chicago	banking	$3.66	$23.00	6.28

II. DISTRESS FAVORITES

COMPANY	INDUSTRY	EPS FOR PAST 4 QTS. A/O 6/30/83	STOCK PRICE A/O 6/30/83
1. Brunswick	marine	-$0.14	$39.00
2. Measurex	control syst.	-$0.17	$26.12
3. Natl. Semiconductor	integ. circ.	-$0.61	$38.37
4. Intl. Rectifier	semicond.	-$1.65	$36.37
5. APL	tissue	-$1.77	$ 9.87
6. Gleason Works	tooling	-$1.82	$12.75
7. Hesston	farm equip.	-$2.32	$11.37
8. Celanese	chemicals	-$3.16	$63.67
9. Kaiser Steel	steel	-$5.02	$31.00
10. Nashua	office prod.	-$7.01	$20.50

SUPER-CONTRARIANISM

In Section I—Searching for Value—we learned about Wall Street's traditional methods of securities analysis: the fundamental and technical approaches. We then reviewed the origins of contrarian thought. The principle is straightforward: don't buy what is popular. Buy unpopular stocks that have the potential to become popular in the future. Once they are, sell them.

Knowing how to find those undiscovered bargains is a little more difficult. I've tried to show you how and where to fish for them, and how to recognize real value when you come across it, by outlining specific steps to take and things to look for. As you now know, much of the Phoenix Approach makes use of fundamental analysis within the realm of contrarian theory.

What you have already read is a complete investment book by itself. The strategy is sound, and it works. Anyone can use it; it is safer than any other strategy if used as prescribed. Buying carefully selected, low-PE companies and high-quality companies with cyclical troubles is a strategy for almost any investor in almost any investment climate.

The extreme, but logical, extension of the contrarian investment world has to be the dark world of bankruptcy investing. Here we find the most troubled companies of all. They are the most feared of all possible investments (and the most sure way to make an investor cringe). But in the rubble of these broken companies, the true bottom fisher sometimes finds his biggest catches. The arena just can't be ignored.

The smart money has always explored the bankruptcy market. Over the past year or so thousands of new investors have entered this market too; interest in this area seems to be growing rapidly. But little information is available on the subject of bankruptcy investing. Most research and brokerage firms shy away from Chapter 11 companies, and I have found no other book on the subject. I first decided to explore this intriguing investment arena because of the growing interest in the field, even among my own clients.

Unlike investing in unpopular and cyclically troubled companies, bankruptcy investing—the subject of Section III—is clearly not for everyone. The risks are much greater and the selection process much more demanding. So proceed with caution. What you are about to read offers an overview of the bankruptcy field as well as a strategy (a stance) that the Phoenix investor can use to prosper in Wall Street's most challenging environment.

III

Up From Ashes

7

Financial Crisis

So the widget market has gone south and Continental Widget is in deep trouble.

Distress signals begin emitting from the corporate boardroom; earnings are so low and cash is so squeezed that the company's fixed debts, including interest payments, can barely be met. The main problem is an old bond issue; it's about to mature and Continental will never be able to refund it by bringing another issue to the market. The distressed company, while solvent for the time being, must make a significant financial adjustment to stay out of bankruptcy court. In this kind of fix, it has but two options short of bankruptcy: a special arrangement for debt restructure acceptable to creditors and bondholders, or a rescue by another company that is interested in buying some or all of the troubled company's assets. International Kelp, eyeing Continental's Widgetworld theme park subsidiary, is one possible white knight. But in this case, Continental's board tries to stave off bankruptcy proceedings by making last-minute arrangements with creditors.

That's one distress scenario.

Meanwhile, over at Mr. Freezer Paper, the discount household paper supplies chain, things are much worse.

Faced with a big drop in consumer demand, MFP has reached *insolvency*—it cannot meet its current debts and has no other recourses because its liabilities far exceed its assets. Analysts call that negative net worth. What it means is trouble—and court-supervised bankruptcy proceedings. Negotiations between MFP and creditors are fruitless. Chapter 11 time is here.

Through it all, both Continental and MFP—each a former glamor stock—continue to have their securities bought and sold on Wall Street. Trading on MFP is suspended for a day after it files, but then resumes.

What does the Phoenix investor do? It depends on the company and the degree of risk he's willing to take. So he'd better know what he's getting into:

1. What's going on in the distressed companies.
2. What bankruptcy is all about.
3. What kind of securities are on the market.
4. Who stands to get what from which.

AVERTING INSOLVENCY

Most corporate distress over the past few years has been the result of a combination of recessionary sales and extreme changes in the economic climate or financial markets, poor management and corporate strategy, or stifling government regulations that choke off profitability. (Bad management, you could argue, is really the ultimate problem in all business failures since good management foresees and prepares for any of the other problems.) The specific solution to the problems of a company that is close to insolvency is determined by the cause of the distress.

Poor earnings and inadequate cash flow sometimes necessitate voluntary changes in the structure of a company's securities, such as the exchange of regular bonds (whose interest payments must be met on schedule) for *income bonds* (whose payments are met only when the company has the money). Sometimes bondholders will even be willing to extend a maturity date in order to avoid bankruptcy if the company just doesn't have the money to pay off a bond issue about to mature and cannot raise new money by way of floating another bond issue. Other creditors may be asked to restrain their payment demands so that a new means of financing or a line of credit can be established to keep the company in business. Securities holders and creditors do not comply out of sympathy or generosity. Their alternative is simply less attractive: letting the company go under and waiting in line, often for years, for a compromise court settlement on what is owed them. Helping to keep a company afloat until it gets back on track is almost always a better choice for everyone involved.

In cases where liabilities are about to exceed assets, rendering a company technically insolvent, a quick merger or acquisition is often sought. Sometimes the sale of just specific assets, or a division of the company, will raise the needed cash. A total liquidation of assets is almost always avoided if possible. Even in the case of insolvency, a reorganization under bankruptcy law is usually preferable to liquidation.

Corporations, government agencies, and security holders will often go to great lengths to save a company from insolvency—namely, changes in the company's capital structure and terms of its securities. These changes, possible only with majority consent among debt holders, are called *adjustments*. Some adjustments are rarely used, such as the one available to troubled railroads under the Mahaffie Act of 1948. In times of financial peril, a railroad may either alter the terms of the securities or exchange some of the securities for new ones, if the company gets the approval of both its regulatory agency (the ICC) and its securities holders. Another seldom-used provision for adjustments can be found in the laws of Delaware, where tens of thousands of companies are incorporated. A Delaware corporation can make virtually any financial adjustment that meets the approval of a Delaware court of equity and a majority of the securities holders involved.

The most common adjustments made by troubled corporations concern bond issues. Most *bond indentures* (the original contract stating the terms of the issue) provide for adjustments of certain conditions upon majority approval. Indenture-based changes automatically apply to the entire bond issue (all bondholders) once approved. Other proposals for bond adjustments are not provided for by an indenture and, therefore, must be presented to each bondholder individually. Changes of this type are usually the more significant ones, such as those affecting maturity dates, exchange of existing bonds for income bonds or the lowering of interest rates. Since the decisions of whether or not to comply to such provisions are made on an individual basis by each bondholder, the corporation usually adds some kind of enticement (such as a cash bonus) to go along with the proposed change.

Sometimes large security holders of a troubled company will form what is called a *protective committee* to negotiate with the managers of the company. In order to increase its bargaining power, the protective committee will solicit the proxies or powers of attorney of the other security holders. Investors are well advised to get an expert opinion of the particular situation before necessarily going along with the wishes of such a committee. Although a common interest prevails among all investors, the expense of negotiation can be very high, and the *deposit receipts* that often replace certificates during negotiations are usually not as liquid as the certificates themselves.

The most extreme action, other than bankruptcy proceedings, taken with troubled companies is something called *equity receivership*. Although seldom used today, receivership was the method of resolution for most corporate insolvencies until the 1930s. Either the corporation itself, or its creditors, can ask for a receiver to be appointed by a state court. The duty of the receiver is to protect the insolvent company's assets from being picked apart by anxious creditors until such time that an equitable solution to all its debts can be found. As in modern-day bankruptcy proceedings, this solution could take the course of either liquidation or reorganization.

Unlike bankruptcy proceedings, however, equity reorganizations (where an ongoing successor corporation is formed) require the consent of each individual security holder. Anyone who does not agree with the receivership plan can simply file a federal bankruptcy petition. Bankruptcy court, however, does have the power to force compliance to a fair reorganization plan.

ALL ABOUT BANKRUPTCY

The English word "bankrupt" is derived from Italian words meaning "broken bench" (*banca* and *rotta*). In common-law England, the custom was to break the bench of merchants who could not meet their obligations.

Today, in the United States, the procedure of bankruptcy is a sophisticated legal process of fair treatment to both creditors and debtors, used as a last resort in cases of corporate insolvencies. All bankruptcy cases are heard in federal court.

The Constitution (Article 1, Section 8) gave Congress the right to enact federal laws governing both personal and corporate bankruptcy procedure. Not until 1898, however, did Congress enact a comprehensive bankruptcy act. The 1898 Nelson Act, although amended some fifty times in the twentieth century, stood for eighty years. The Chandler Act of 1938 was the only significant revision of the Nelson Act during those years. By the 1970s, a major reform of bankruptcy law was long overdue.

That came with the Bankruptcy Reform Act of 1978. The new Bankruptcy Code became effective on October 1, 1979, after nine years in the making.

One big difference today is in the role of the bankruptcy judge. Under the old law, he acted as both judge and administrator. Now these roles are separated. The new Act also introduces a whole new federal bankruptcy court system, effective April 1, 1984, consisting of ninety-five judicial districts.

The Bankruptcy Code is made up of various odd-numbered chapters:

—Chapter 1 defines several of the rules and procedures, and describes who is a debtor.
—Chapter 3 tells us how a bankruptcy case is initiated for both voluntary and involuntary cases, and defines the role of trustees in the proceedings.
—Chapter 5 covers the duties and obligations of both creditors and debtors.
—Chapter 7 is important to investors. This section of the Code applies to cases where *liquidation* of corporate assets (straight bankruptcy) is sought by the party that petitioned the proceedings.
—Chapter 9 deals with debt adjustments of municipalities.
—Chapter 11 is of the greatest importance to us as investors. This chapter of the new code is a synthesis of old Chapters 8 (railroad reorganizations), 10 (other corporate reorganizations), 11 (arrangements), and 12 (real estate arrangements). The new Chapter 11 deals with any corporate *reorganization*: where the company continues to operate under the protection of the court, while it attempts to work out a plan for paying its creditors.

A bankruptcy petition may be filed voluntarily by the debtor company, or against the debtor by any of its creditors. All petitions are now based solely on the debtor's inability to meet its obligations. (Negative net worth insolvency is no longer a cause for petition.)

In the case of Chapter 11 reorganization, the court protects the company against creditor suits and sometimes appoints a *trustee* to run the company's operations and oversee its assets during the reorganization. Even if the company is allowed to retain its own management, the court may appoint an examiner to keep an eye on the company by checking its records.

Several securities holders committees also crop up during Chapter 11 reorganization proceedings. Each class of security usually has its own representatives.

The first step in Chapter 11 proceedings is the all-important *reorganization plan*. If the company's own management is still in control (known as "Debtor in Possession"), then it has 120 days to submit its own plan to the court. After that time period, or such time as a trustee is appointed to take over the company's operations, any investor or creditor also may file his own reorganization plan.

The plan itself is a complex proposal on how to recapitalize the company's securities and how to proportion the distribution of those new securities in any equitable way to its creditors and the holders of its old securities. A strict plan of fair distribution must be adhered to during reorganization. The *rule of absolute priority* compels the court to make sure that senior and secured creditors are compensated in full before junior or unsecured creditors get anything. Another court rule of reorganization is known as the *best interests of creditors test*, which says that creditors must get at least as much out of reorganization distributions as they would get out of a Chapter 7 liquidation procedure.

A majority of each class of securities holders must accept a reorganization plan before it can be approved by the court. The plan must not only provide equitable compensation for creditors and security holders but must also provide for the company's future solvency.

The goal of Chapter 11, after all, is to have the company emerge as a better-organized, slimmed-down operation more fit for survival in the unforgiving world of business. If little hope is held for survival, proceedings can be switched from Chapter 11 reorganization to Chapter 7 liquidation. This situation is usually dismal news for all concerned, but especially for the common-stock holders. By the time bondholders and creditors get finished picking over the wounded company's last possessions, the shareholder will usually find nothing left.

THE HIERARCHY OF SECURITIES

There are at least a dozen ways that you can invest in a company. But what you actually own, or what you are owed, is very different from one class of security to the next.

The absolute priority doctrine provides that creditors should be compensated for their claims in a certain hierarchical order and that more senior claims must be paid in full before less senior claims can receive anything. In the event of a default, for example, secured bondholders have the first claim on mortgaged assets. If the sale of these assets does not sufficiently cover their claims, they become creditors equal to the next class of securities holders: senior unsecured bondholders. (Investors holding senior debentures have a general claim on unmortgaged assets, and a "junior" claim on the mortgaged assets. After the property is sold, and secured bondholders are repaid, any excess funds are directed to unsecured bondholders. Junior, or subordinated, bondholders have a junior claim on all assets. Preferred shareholders and common shareholders have a residual claim on the balance of assets.)

The following is a list of the order in which investors will be repaid in the event of liquidation:

(1) secured debt holders
(2) senior unsecured debt holders
(3) junior (subordinated) unsecured debt holders
(4) preferred stockholders
(5) common stockholders

In order of increasing priority, the descriptions ahead will give you a good idea of what you're buying with the various classes of these securities.

A. *Common Stocks.* All corporations are owned by, and operated for the benefit of, stockholders. The issuance of equity (common stock) shares is normally the largest source of raising new funds for companies of any size.

Common stocks are the very meaning of the term "the market"; people are referring to the equity markets when they use this term. The buying and selling of ownership in publicly traded corporations has been an American obsession for a hundred years that rivals football when the market is hot. (And bloodletting when the market is not.)

Along with all the rights of ownership (such as voting power, participation in dividends, and the possibility of capital appreciation), there are some pitfalls that come with owning common shares. Prices of common stocks are often volatile and unpredictable, and stockholders are only residual owners when it comes to the liquidation or reorganization of a company. *Remember: Common stockholders are last in line, behind all other securities holders and creditors who have contractual claims on a company's assets.*

B. *Preferred Stocks.* Like common stockholders, preferred stockholders are equity owners of a corporation. What is "preferred" about this class of security is a dual priority claim ahead of common shares: stated dividends of preferred shares must be paid before common shareholders are paid, and preferred shareholders have a priority claim on assets in the case of bankruptcy. Preferred stock, however, is not a debt security; preferred stockholders are not creditors of the corporation as bondholders are.

There are several different types of preferred stocks. Some carry voting rights and some don't. Some are convertible to common shares, giving the investor the possibility of greater appreciation (in return for a lower yield). Some preferred stock has the stipulation that unpaid dividends must be made up (called "cumulative preferred") before any dividend can be paid to common stockholders. Many corporations have a variety of preferred issues outstanding at the same time.

In bankruptcy proceedings, the preferred stock investor stands in line between the common stockholder and the lowest ranking bondholders.

C. *Debentures.* Bonds are debt obligations of a corporation. A company can borrow money from the investment public agreeing to pay a certain interest rate and to return the money on a particular date. Being creditors of the corporation, bondholders have no ownership rights such as voting privileges.

Some bonds are secured by property or collateral, and others are unsecured. Debentures are unsecured corporate bonds; they are backed only by the good faith and reputation of the corporation. If a company has secured bonds outstanding as well as debentures, the debentures are generally not as safe in times of financial trouble. Because of this, unsecured bonds usually pay more interest and sometimes have a lower rating than secured bonds of the same company.

Debentures can be designated as junior (subordinated) or senior by the corporation. The priority of the senior issue comes into play only in the case of bankruptcy proceedings: senior unsecured bonds have priority claims on interest and assets over subordinated unsecured bonds. But all debentures stand in line behind secured debt.

D. *Secured Bonds.* These debt securities have a lien on some of the company's property, such as real estate or equipment. In the case of reorganization (where new securities are issued) or liquidation (where all assets are sold off), secured bondholders get full value back before unsecured bonders, preferred stockholders, or common stockholders get anything. If the company happens to have enough money to start making interest payments to bondholders during Chapter 11 proceedings, secured bondholders have first claim on that interest.

The most common type of security for bond issues is the *mortgage bond.* This is a bond backed by a lien on specific property. You may have seen a prospectus or ad for a new bond called a "first mortgage," "prior lien," "first leasehold," or "first refunding" bond. These are all mortgage-backed borrowings with various degrees of security.

Some bonds are backed by securities that the company pledges as collateral; these are called *collateral trust bonds.* The securities, which are held by a trustee, can be the stocks or bonds of the company borrowing the money, one of its subsidiaries, or the securities of other companies that the borrowing company owns as an investment.

A common type of secured bond for transportation companies is a chattel security known as an *equipment trust certificate.* A public offering bond issue is the usual way of financing a new jet for an airline company or a new locomotive for a railroad company. The equipment can be either leased to the company by a trustee (known as the Philadelphia plan or equipment lease plan) or sold to the company by a trustee as the trustee receives funds from a series of equipment trust notes (known as the New York plan or conditional sale plan).

CAVEAT EMPTOR

Remember United Merchants and Manufacturers? How about Miller Wohl, National Mortgage Fund, Yuba Consolidated Industries, Pantry Pride, Orion Capital, or Quality Egg? With the help of Uncle Sam and the 1978 Bankruptcy Act, they have held on through years of rebuilding and reemerged as profitable enterprises. And they have lots of company. Of the last fifty NYSE firms to file for bankruptcy, only three have been liquidated. The others all are in various stages of reorganization, with the expectation of continued employment, products, and profits. Today's bankruptcy laws invite the ultimate American success story: from riches to rags and back to riches.

Not that there aren't pitfalls. You may lose some money by buying G.E. at the top of a bull market, but you won't lose your shirt. Investors who dive into bankrupt companies unprepared can lose their entire wardrobes.

The companies above are real; each rose triumphantly from its own ashes. The following is an example of a company—fictitious for the sake of clarity—that didn't come back.

Continental Widget seemed to be the Phoenix investor's dream. When it filed for Chapter 11, bankruptcy didn't even seem necessary. True, management failed to rearrange debt with creditors—chiefly suppliers who were also suffering in a depressed steel market—but there always appeared to be a way out by selling Widgetworld. Those five theme parks in the Southeast had an asset value of about $50 million. International Kelp, which already had vague ties to theme parks, seemed an eager buyer. Also, Federated Boutique Stores, operators of Widgets 'N' Things retail stores in the Midwest, expressed an interest in the Widgetworld division.

Even $30 million from the sale of Widgetworld would have staved off bankruptcy. Only because Continental held off on negotiations so long, as it tried to rearrange its debt, did it have to file. When talks with creditors broke down, the old bond issue had matured and the company had no cash with which to repay bondholders.

So when the company filed, many investors knew that—timing aside—the resources were there. The stock was trading at $2.00 a share, and $1,000 bonds were there for the picking at $500.

A perfect opportunity? No. The first warning was the fact that Continental had to file in the first place. If a company has assets with which to avoid bankruptcy and can't cash them out, that's a sign of big trouble. Not only had management failed to prepare against a predictable depression in the widget market, it also failed to accurately read the position of its creditors. Once Continental filed, the would-be buyers of Widgetworld—already trying to pick up the assets at bargain prices—no longer made offers that would provide enough cash to do any good.

What's more, the theme park subsidiary was really the only attractive element of the firm. Though industrialized nations had long since found high-tech substitutes for widgets, the company had never diversified into other products.

"There are a lot of emerging nations out there," Continental's chairman was quoted by *The Wall Street Journal* as saying in 1979. "They'd love to have our widgets."

And they would have loved it. But the Third World has cash problems, too. The outflow of their currency was devoted to other products. And Continental's sales never recovered. Continental was a company which, largely due to management intransigence, had very little future. Two dollars per share was not a bargain. Six months later, Chapter 11 became Chapter 7. The company was in liquidation; the stock was worth zero. The holders of the $1,000 bonds, even though they were secured, got $37 for them. Why? The widget machinery, though it had a very high book value, was worth nothing in the market-place. Like the inventory that remained. Trustees did sell the entire Widgetworld business. International Kelp, by then bidding alone, bought it lock, stock, and widget for $9 million—roughly the value of the real estate upon which the four parks rested.

Caveat emptor. Let the buyer beware.

On the other hand, if it weren't for the extra risks involved, bottom fishing wouldn't be bottom fishing. The prices of troubled companies wouldn't plunge quite so precipitously in the market place, and bankruptcy wouldn't be a contrarian strategy to begin with. But the rewards *can* be great. Consider *Mr. Freezer Paper.*

Who would have thought, in the mid-1960s, when stretch wrap was coming into its own, that a company like Mr. Freezer Paper could burst on the scene in 1971 with such drama.

Spun off a small, successful Oregon hardware store chain when the owner realized freezer paper was a high-turnover, high-profit item, the first Mr. Freezer Paper in Eugene, Oregon, led to a string of forty-nine stores in the Pacific Northwest. "Serving all of your household paper needs of a decade" was the company slogan when it filed under Chapter 11 in 1982. A company that had ridden the crest of the "back to basics/all natural" wave suddenly also was the victim of old-fashioned business pressures:

1. Competition from another chain—Freezer Paper City—which was using the financial resources and merchandising know-how of its monolithic discount-retailing parent company to undersell Mr. Freezer Paper market for market.

2. Spiraling operating costs at its lumber mills in Washington, Oregon, and Ontario.

3. Heavy start-up costs for its Mr. Freezer Snax line of frozen yogurt treats introduced in 1977 and distributed nationally in supermarkets. (The yogurt was wrapped in freezer paper and squeezed out bit by bit for consumption.)

From the time the company went public in 1973, it was a high flier. It was a go-go company, if ever there was one, selling for an incredible ninety times earnings in 1975. In 1982, the recession had taken only a nominal toll, despite the fact that earnings growth—averaging 80% per year from 1971 to 1981—was down to only 40%. The chain was still growing, and Mr. Freezer Snax was off to a remarkable start in the stores.

On the day the company filed for Chapter 11, the common stock sold for $57 per share—20 times the previous year's earnings. One week later, it was selling for $7. It was one of the most precipitous drops in trading history; the analysts had been caught by complete surprise. Complicating matters, the SEC was rumored to be investigating the company for alleged failure to disclose key financial details—chiefly on an above-market, 23%, $20 million loan from a Portland bank in connection with the Freezer Snax start-up.

On the face of it, everything about this situation told the Phoenix investor to stay away. Too risky, it seemed.

Wrong.

Though on paper the company was insolvent, the real problem was only cash flow. Here's why.

1. The bank loan that precipitated the crisis was bound to be renegotiated. The $20 million credit line was struck at the zenith of the early '80s interest-rate escalation. Though the bank was reluctant to give up the profits of what became a dream loan (rates were down to 12% when Mr. Freezer Paper filed under Chapter 11), it was easier to renegotiate a nightmare loan when it realized the company hadn't been bluffing about its financial crisis.

2. The Mr. Freezer Snax line was, indeed, a phenomenal success. It wasn't yet contributing to profits, but it was the right product for the right time, and sales were booming. Once start-up costs were amortized, it would be a big money-maker.

3. Book-value assets, many of them in the form of timberland, were grossly understated. Sale of the Canadian property alone—having appreciated by 200 percent during the 1970s—would get the company out of its cash bind. It had, in fact, been on the market for months when the company filed.

4. Because of the SEC investigation, management was not talking to the press to explain how its position was not as desperate as it looked. But all the data were available in footnotes to the quarterly report and other SEC filings.

In the end, the reorganization lasted only a year, the loan was renegotiated at prime-plus-one and the Canadian property (purchased with equity capital during the go-go years) was sold for $10 million. And Mr. Freezer Snax became the biggest new food product introduction since instant iced-tea.

Today, Mr. Freezer Paper stock sells for $35 on the FSE (Fictional Stock Exchange). The Phoenix investor earned a 267% return on investment.

The moral: Do your homework.

8

Bankruptcy Investment Strategy

WHEN TO INVEST

A key to the high-stakes game of bankruptcy investing is determining your objectives before you even get started. How much risk you are willing to take, how long you are willing to have your money tied up, and how much time you want to spend analyzing companies, can all be deciding factors as to what you buy and when you buy.

I divide bankruptcy investing into three time frames: *the speculative stage, the buy-and-hold stage,* and *the arbitrage stage.* The speculator goes in early, soon after the company files for bankruptcy and before much information is available about its future course. This early stage always has the greatest risk, and sometimes the greatest reward. The speculator is perhaps the truest contrarian in that he steps in right after a dramatic price decline, on the theory that most investors have overreacted to the situation. The speculator is a short-term investor, looking for a quick bounce back after a big panic sell-off.

In the second stage of bankruptcy investing, the "buy-and-hold stage," the investor moves only after preliminary information is known about the direction the company plans to take in the proceedings. If he sees the security as underpriced, he will buy it with the belief that eventually the market will realize the security's value. This strategy is, by its very name, a long-term approach. Chapter 11 proceedings often take years to evolve. (Penn Central investors waited eight years before the company emerged from bankruptcy, but they were eventually rewarded handsomely.) This investor is willing to stay with his position through short-term price swings, waiting until the actual value of the security is realized. His success is dependent on two things: that he has valued the security accurately, and that the public will eventually agree with that valuation. Analysis of all available information is extremely important to the long-term investor as well as to the speculator and arbitrager.

In a bankruptcy situation, the buy-and-hold stage usually begins soon after some future direction can be determined for the company (such as whether or not the company will attempt to reorganize, and, if so, what plan it will use), and continues until the company is ready to emerge from Chapter 11.

The third stage of bankruptcy investing begins once the company's plan of liquidation or reorganization has been approved, and values can finally be more accurately figured. The arbitrager capitalizes on market inefficiencies by investing in known quantities which are undervalued. He attempts to identify temporary price disparities between quantifiable elements. He is waiting for the market to make a mistake, selling assets for less than they are worth, or buying assets for more than they are worth. The key to an arbitrager's success is his ability to determine both current and future values of securities with a reasonably high degree of accuracy.

An arbitrager will sometimes invest in a security in one market when he is reasonably certain that he can sell it at a profit in another market. If a stock were selling for more on the Pacific Stock Exchange than the NYSE, as they sometimes do, the arbitrager would buy on the NYSE and sell on the PSE at the same time. It is this type of activity that is supposed to maintain uniform pricing among the various markets on which a security trades. In another instance, the arbitrager may spot a temporary price disparity between a convertible bond and its underlying stock. If, for example, a convertible bond is selling for less than what it is worth if the conversion privilege is exercised, the arbitrager might buy the debt, convert it, and sell the stock.

In most Chapter 11 situations, the arbitrager will enter the market after the company has determined to liquidate or reorganize, and plans have been made public. At this stage, the investor can most precisely determine the value of these securities and identify price disparities between his valuation and current market prices. The arbitrage strategy is the safest of the three investment stages, provided that its analysis is performed quickly and accurately.

WHAT TO INVEST IN

The problem is difficult because every situation is unique. You can greatly improve your chances of success, however, by doing two things: predetermining whether a bankrupt company will liquidate or reorganize, and getting a feel for the value of the company's assets.

There is little consistency of performance among bankruptcy issues within a certain security class. While an equipment trust certificate may turn out to be the best investment in one case, common stock may be the best buy in another. In the case of W.T. Grant, for example, senior debtors have done very well while junior debtors are still waiting for 20¢ on the dollar. But common stockholders have had the best gain in the case of United Merchants and Manufacturing, with junior debtors coming in second and senior debtors last. As with Toys 'R' Us, and countless other corporate disasters, common stockholders bailed out in droves, making the stock simply oversold. United Merchants, once $32 a share, dropped to $2.50 in 1978 when the company filed for Chapter 11. Today it sells for around $15.

Sometimes the best plays can be found in the less obvious situations, such as the securities of a healthy subsidiary. Gamble-Skogmo, a credit subsidiary of bankrupt Wickes Co., for example, has various debt issues outstanding, including a 9⅜% note due in 1986, secured by customers' installment credit accounts. While this collateral is fairly solid, the notes still dropped from $550 to $420 the day after Wickes filed for bankruptcy on April 24, 1982. The bonds had still risen to only $485 as of early 1983. Each bankruptcy case is as individual as a fingerprint. You've got to go out and kick the tires of every troubled company that you are interested in.

While there is no steadfast rule for predicting whether a Chapter 11 company will liquidate or reorganize, there are several things an investor should consider in attempting to determine the direction a bankrupt company will take.

One rule of thumb in trying to determine whether a company will emerge from Chapter 11 in reorganized form is to ask yourself if you, as a trade creditor, would want the company as a client in the future.

"If a trade creditor has a choice of getting 70% of his money from a liquidated firm, or 35% from an ongoing concern, he will almost always take the latter choice," writes Richard Greene in *Forbes* (March 15, 1982). Take, for instance, the case of a clothes manufacturer that sells a significant percentage of its products through a company that goes bankrupt. Should the company liquidate, the creditor might recover 70% of its investment. But this is all it will ever get. It will, however, lose a lot more than just 30% of its investment; it will lose a customer with which it did a large portion of its business. It may be more attractive for the creditor to take 35% now, and maintain a relationship with a customer who will allow the creditor to eventually more than recover its investment as well as retaining a major source of business.

Another thing to consider is who else can benefit through liquidation of the firm. Is the company worth more to others dead or alive? In most bankruptcy situations there is a significant amount of outstanding debt. If a company's loans are federally guaranteed, for example, the banks would have no incentive to keep the company afloat. Bank creditors do not have the same ongoing relationship with debtors as do trade creditors. They are more than happy to recover their investment from a combination of the sale of the company's assets and federal funds. This can mean the end of the bankrupt company.

This should not serve as a warning to stay away from liquidating companies. It merely suggests that it is important to get a grasp on which way proceedings will go. *In the case of liquidations, secured debt issues are almost always more favorable than either unsecured or equity issues.* Thus, the early identification of liquidations should serve to steer the investor away from the other issues and toward the secured debt.

It's nice to have guidelines in attempting to assess the future course of a bankrupt company, but bear in mind that more and more concrete information comes out in every case as the proceedings go on. *Any analysis or information that the investor can gather before the liquidation/reorganization decision is made can help him take an earlier position, often at a more attractive price.*

For several reasons, of which safety is the foremost, investors in Chapter 11 securities tend to view debt as the favored investment medium, particularly in the early stages. David Salomon, who heads the First Investors Bond Appreciation Fund (a mutual fund that invests in bankruptcy securities), claims that "becoming a creditor of a company going into, or in, bankruptcy by buying its bonds is a reasonable bet. The biggest gains in the bond market have been made in defaulted securities. Defaults have been stellar performers." (Stanley Kulp, *Barron's*, February 8, 1982.) In the event of liquidation, creditors (including bondholders) are paid off before shareholders see a penny.

Even in successful reorganizations, the common shares of a company in bankruptcy are almost always diluted during the restructuring process, as bondholders are paid off with a package of new securities (typically a combination of new bonds, new stock, and cash). Shareholders, who own 100% of a company going into bankruptcy, may end up with only a fraction of the ownership upon emergence. In the case of Penn Central, bondholders ended up with almost 90% of the equity of the new firm, while common stockholders were left with a 1-for-25 reverse split (one share of new stock for every twenty-five shares of old stock). Although the stocks of some bankrupt companies have turned out to be magnificent performers (e.g., Toys 'R' Us), the informed equity investor must realize the dilution risks in the case of reorganization, as well as the possibility of a total loss in the case of liquidation.

Regardless of which type of debt one invests in, the strategy should involve analysis of the company's assets. Investing in either liquidations or reorganizations is a complex business which is based on interpreting the company's balance sheet, rather than its earning power. The object of the game is finding values where other people fail to see them. If the company is planning to liquidate, it is obvious that the only value is in its assets. If it is spared from corporate demise, it is still reasonable to assume that many assets, including whole subsidiaries, will be sold to provide the necessary cash to pay off creditors and service future debt. The investor must determine what these assets are worth in order to know what the underlying debt is worth.

SECURED DEBT INVESTING

In cases of liquidation, secured debt is almost always more favorable than unsecured issues or equity, since secured debtholders usually take a strong ownership position. The secured bond investor is backed by the pledge of a specific asset, which he often becomes the owner of. If the sale of this asset does not satisfy his claims, he then gets in line with the same priority as senior unsecured creditors.

Braniff Airlines currently has $8.9 million dollars of equipment trust certificates outstanding (in the form of 11⅛% due in 1987). These are secured by a 747 aircraft with a book value of roughly $12 million. If the company were to liquidate today, its *junior unsecured* creditors would probably get only a few cents on the dollar. But the equipment trust certificate holders, on the other hand, stand to receive full value, as long as the plane can be sold for at least $8.9 million. (This allows for a 25% discount from book value which seems highly probable even in today's depressed airline market.)

It is generally a lot easier to place a value on secured bonds than on any other type of investment since the assets themselves are easy to price if they have a ready market (such as a piece of transportation equipment). In the case of an equipment trust certificate, for instance, the valuation process is relatively straightforward, and, therefore, the security's price will reflect actual value fairly accurately. There are, however, situations in which the asset pledged to secured debt holders is extremely difficult to evaluate, such as highly specialized industrial machines or equipment, where there is not a ready market. For companies with very specialized technology-oriented assets, liquidation is sometimes impossible, making reorganization the only choice.

Even if a company does reorganize, the worst the secured debt holder can do is realize the value he would have gotten in liquidation, thanks to the absolute priority rule. This rule protects secured debt holders in these three ways:

1. The secured debt holder retains his lien on the company's property whether the asset is kept by the company or transferred to another company. Therefore, whether Braniff reorganizes and continues operations, or is taken over by another corporation, equipment trust certificate holders are still secured by the 747 aircraft pledged to them.

2. If the property is sold or the lien transferred, the secured debt holder must receive deferred cash payments equal to at least the value of the claim on the date that it is decided to sell the property. So, if Braniff has to sell its fleet, equipment trust certificate holders are guaranteed at least as much as the planes are worth at the time the plan is confirmed.

3. The secured debt holders must receive value at least equal to liquidation estimates in order for a reorganization plan to be approved. Therefore, if Braniff offered a package (of various cash, debt, and equity components) to secured creditors in a reorganization plan, that package must at least equal what they would have received had the company liquidated.

Investors who desire more risk, in search for greater returns, cite the limited appreciation potential of secured issues as unattractive. Generally, the most a secured debt holder can expect to receive is the value of his claims. *The highest return a secured debt holder can even hope for is the difference between his investment and par value of the bonds. (And usually the prices of secured bonds start off much higher than the company's other securities.)* Unsecured debt holders, and stockholders, on the other hand, have the potential of much greater reward if a reorganization proves successful.

Investing in secured debt, if accurate assessment is made, can be almost a pure arbitrage play because of the relative ease of evaluating secured assets. If any information concerning asset value is available, it should be used. Secured debt investing in Chapter 11 companies does not have to be that speculative, because there is always some information to help the investor to minimize risk.

Most individual investors have limited resources when it comes to determining the value of the assets of troubled companies. As with other kinds of investments, most reliable information comes from professional researchers. There are, however, three important questions when considering secured debt:

1. What is the debt secured by?
2. Is the underlying asset marketable? Have technologies changed enough to outdate the asset?
3. What is the economic condition of the industry in which the asset would be disposed?

Information can be obtained from several sources. Once a company enters bankruptcy, some facts become available to the public through the financial news media. This information allows both the large and small investor to determine asset values more precisely. *The Wall Street Journal* and *Barron's* often provide estimates as to how much a bankrupt company's assets are worth. While these figures may not be precise, they are usually helpful in making educated guesses as to the real value of the company's securities. There has, for instance, been a great deal of daily coverage of the plight of Braniff Airlines. The longer you wait until entering the market, the more light will be shed on your prospects, although fewer bargains will be available as time goes on. *An essential source of information for the serious bankruptcy investor is the company's proposed Plan of Reorganization, which is available from the Securities and Exchange Commission.*

Just because you determine that an underlying asset will not cover secured debt holders' claims does not necessarily preclude further analysis of the investment. Look at the price of the security in relation to the property. If a bond is selling for fifty cents on the dollar, it doesn't have to ever pay off in full to still be a very successful investment.

Another important factor to consider in analyzing bond values is time. How long will it take a company to pay off its secured bondholders? The time value of money is significant: if it takes ten years to double your money, this is only about 7% per year. Why take the risk?

Three more questions to ask yourself when considering secured debt:

1. How much does the underlying asset seem to be worth?
2. If this is not enough to pay off the claims, how much is the secured bondholders' share of the company assets worth? (More on this analysis in the section on unsecured debt.)
3. How long is it expected to take to recover claims? What is the calculated yield-to-maturity on your prospective investment, based on current price and number of years before expected payoff?

The three bankruptcy investment stages, speculation, buy-and-hold, and arbitrage, apply more to unsecured issues than secured debt. There is not really a speculative stage for investing in secured debt, since some information is available right from the beginning. Investing in secured debt issues of Chapter 11 companies usually has to be a buy-and-hold strategy. Within this stage, as the court proceedings continue, more information will become available. *If you don't have a feel for the value of a secured debt, you should wait until you do.* With this cautious approach you might end up buying at 50¢ on the dollar, rather than 30¢, but at least you avoid the risk of buying at 30¢ and ending up with nothing. The market usually supports the secured debt investor once values can be determined. Arbitragers move in once they get a grasp on the time element associated with the company's bankruptcy process.

UNSECURED DEBT INVESTING

If secured debt is the safest medium for investing in bankrupt securities, unsecured debt must be considered the most intriguing. There are several types of unsecured bonds, but for the sake of clarity in this discussion, I'll talk about unsecured debt as just senior and junior. Senior debt is a higher class security than either junior debt or equity. After secured debt holders, bank creditors, and trade creditors, senior debt holders are the next in line. In the event of liquidation, secured creditors can become senior unsecured creditors if they have not been made whole by the sale of collateralized assets. Junior debt holders (often referred to as subordinated) stand behind all other creditors. Investment analysts who stress secured debt—especially if there is a potential for liquidation—agree that investors should consider senior unsecured debt in reorganizations because of the likelihood that they will receive securities which might, in turn, provide appreciation. Whereas secured debt holders often are paid in cash, unsecured creditors usually receive a variety of debt and equity securities that can prove quite attractive in the long run.

Junior debentures should generally be bought only later in the reorganization process. If a reorganization attempt turns into a liquidation, most junior creditors will not fare well. As mentioned earlier, W.T. Grant, one of the largest liquidations in bankruptcy history, saw its senior and junior debentures fall to 20¢ on the dollar several days after filing for bankruptcy, on May 10, 1975. While senior debentures then began a steady rise toward par value, junior creditors watched their investment drop to just 2¢ within a month.

In the process of reorganization, senior debtors usually end up with more cash and equity, and higher grade debt (if new bonds are issued) than junior debt holders. Like secured creditors, senior unsecured creditors are protected by the rule of absolute priority: they cannot do any worse than they would do in liquidation.

But don't rule out junior bonds. Just remember that there is much more risk involved, and therefore more analysis is needed. The priority concept tells us that junior creditors must know exactly what is available for each class in front of them. Junior debentures make more sense as more information becomes available and reorganization approaches.

There are two unique features of unsecured debt that make it an especially interesting investment. The first is its movement through all three investment stages: no other security adheres as closely to this classic pattern. (I'll show you what I mean soon by following Itel Corporation's senior unsecured bonds through the reorganization process.) The second unique feature has to do with the evaluation of unsecured debt. Unlike secured debt holders, who generally end up with a large amount of cash and little equity (even in the case of reorganization), unsecured creditors usually become the majority owners of the new corporation, and end up determining the future course of the company. It is, therefore, particularly important for the unsecured bondholder to judge the value of the reorganization package and the viability of any ongoing business of the corporation.

It is not unusual for unsecured bondholders to end up with a variety of unusual securities, ranging from "liquidating preferred stock" to "zero coupon bonds." In the case of Food Fair, which emerged as Pantry Pride not long ago, debt holders received a package of four different preferred stocks in addition to common shares, a promissory note, and cash.

Let's take a look at an unsecured bond as it travels through the three stages of the bankruptcy investment cycle. A complete cycle can take a sick company from a panicked oversold position immediately following the bankruptcy announcement, all the way back to financial good health after a successful reorganization.

The first stage begins immediately after a company files for bankruptcy. While a sudden drop in investor confidence might reduce market values of its securities to a very tempting level, there is a great deal of risk involved in this stage. The greatest risk is the lack of information concerning both the direction of the company and the current health of the company. W.T. Grant and Saxon Industries are perfect examples of problems encountered in Stage One investing in unsecured debt. In the case of Saxon Industries, which went bankrupt on April 15, 1982, information uncovered during Stage One led to a major loss for speculators in its junior debt. Immediately after its filing, Saxon's 5¼% junior convertible debentures, due in 1990, dropped to $220, a 37% discount from their $350 level only a month earlier. In June the company disclosed that it had overstated its inventories by at least $24 million. The junior convertibles dropped immediately to the $140 level where they since have hovered.

On the other side of the spectrum, however, Braniff's 9⅛% debentures due in 1997, after experiencing a $100 price drop the day after their filing for Chapter 11 on May 13, 1982, gained $150 per bond over the next five months.

The second stage begins a month or two after a company enters bankruptcy. By this time, the initial price swings have been calmed and more information is available. Accountants have had a chance to analyze the financial position of the firm, and more educated guesses as to the future course of the company can be made. Itel Corporation's senior unsecured bonds rose from $250 to $450 during Stage Two.

The main risks involved with Stage Two are these: the uncertainty of information element and the time element. Until final reorganization plans are announced and confirmed, a company's future is in doubt. Braniff Airlines, a company currently in Stage Two, has made several attempts to remain in operation through an intricate plan involving another airline. But at this writing it is anyone's guess as to whether the company will reorganize or liquidate. Those who have bet on reorganization, investing in unsecured debt and equity during Stage One or Stage Two so far have lost money. In the cases of W.T. Grant and Saxon, too, major losses could have been avoided by waiting until later in Stage Two.

Then there is the matter of time. It isn't uncommon for the buy-and-hold investor to have to wait a few years, and in some cases even longer. Miller-Wohl took one year to reorganize; Penn-Dixie Corp. took two years; and Toys 'R' Us took four years to emerge. Penn Central investors waited eight years before reorganization was complete. *(Railroads have a tendency to take longer than usual to reorganize, which is why many analysts suggest staying away from them. You should certainly not consider them if you need liquidity, or are looking for short-term appreciation.)* The patient Stage Two investor must endure the ups and downs that a company attempting to reorganize experiences. This investor is willing to pay a little more for his unsecured debt than the speculator paid if the extra time gives him a more accurate picture of what he is getting.

Stage Three, the most conservative time to invest, begins immediately after reorganization plans have been made public. At that time, values can be more accurately determined, and the arbitrager is enticed into the market. Curiously, it is not unusual for a security's price to remain undervalued for a short period of time following the confirmation of a reorganization plan. This is explained by the difficulty of evaluating reorganization packages filled with unusual securities, as well as the market's continual skepticism of a Chapter 11 company. Arbitragers thrive on this peculiarity.

BANKRUPTCY STOCKS

If secured debt is the favorite investment medium of bankruptcy issues, and unsecured debt the most intriguing, then equities must be the most daring vehicle for investing in Chapter 11 firms.

The arguments against stocks of bankrupt companies

include the possibility of total loss in the event of liquidation, the possibility of significant dilution of ownership in the event of reorganization, and the difficulty in accurately evaluating common stock in either case. Three pretty good arguments.

If a company is forced to liquidate, stockholders are last in line to be paid off. Because of the priority bankruptcy rules, it is not unusual for common stockholders to end up with worthless certificates, after all prior claims have been made whole in a liquidation.

The lack of information necessary to perform an analysis of common stock values until very late in the reorganization process adds to the risk of an equity play. Until organization plans are confirmed, the real value of equity securities is not only a guess, but a wild guess.

On the other hand, it can pay to be a wild guesser. Because of the risks, stocks of bankrupt companies usually sell for just a fraction of their former prices. At the first mention of the word bankruptcy, most stockholders panic, selling their holdings at any cost, which lowers the stock price even more. Often, this reaction creates an oversold situation that can bounce back. Since bankruptcy stocks are usually very cheap to begin with, there can sometimes be tremendous rewards. As we know, investors in Toys 'R' Us (then Interstate Stores) saw their stock rise from 12¢ a share to over $60 a share. Miller Wohl, Orion Capital, and others have also provided stellar returns to daring equity investors.

Investors in "junk" stocks also cite the limited downside risk of these already low-priced securities as an attractive advantage. Dealing in bankruptcy stocks often is equated to purchasing options: high risk at a low price but with the possibility of a huge return. Should stockholders benefit by a major turnaround, as in the case of Toys 'R' Us, the return is magnified by the larger number of shares they're able to buy at such a low price.

There are two Phoenix strategies for investing in the

Stock Price Range by Year 1968-1981 for Four Phoenix Investments

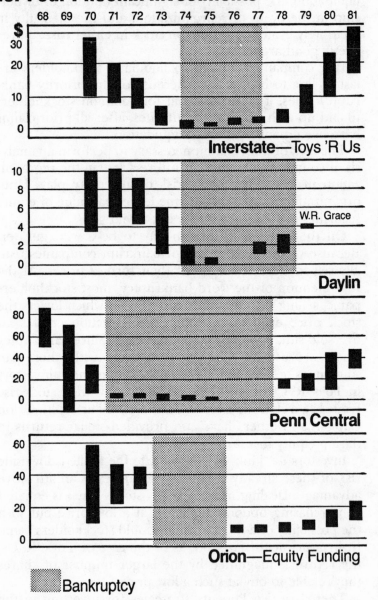

68 69 70 71 72 73 74 75 76 77 78 79 80 81

Interstate—Toys 'R Us

W.R. Grace

Daylin

Penn Central

Orion—Equity Funding

Bankruptcy

common stock of Chapter 11 companies. The first, a speculative play, capitalizes on short-term price savings. The second, a buy-and-hold play used later in the game, takes advantage of future profitability of the new firm. Unlike debt, equities do not support an arbitrage stage, because values rely too heavily on market whims that are not quantifiable enough for the arbitrager.

Stage One investing in bankruptcy stocks involves the speculative, contrarian play of catching a price rebound after the initial shock wave of selling. Penn-Dixie, for example, was trading on the New York Stock Exchange for $2⅜ a share the day before entering Chapter 11, on March 18, 1982. Over the next three days, the securities dropped down to the $1⅜ level. After being delisted, the stock rebounded to a stunning $3½ price within four weeks while trading over-the-counter. The speculators who played this stock received a 135% return in one month.

Use this strategy only if there has been at least a 50% drop in price from recent prebankruptcy levels. If a stock has already been declining in price prior to the bankruptcy, because of publicity and rumors, there may not be nearly as dramatic a price swing (dip and rebound) after the filing date.

The more conservative Stage Two strategy of bankruptcy stock investing begins right before, or immediately after, a company has come out of reorganization. A clean balance sheet, an accumulation of tax losses that can be carried forward to offset future earnings, and a talented new management team often make these companies very attractive for the buy-and-hold investor.

Security values often are not recognized by the market until after emergence from the depths of Chapter 11. Once a company has cleaned up its balance sheet, and sold off unhealthy subsidiaries, the investor has a much better idea of what he is buying. Quite often, a firm leaves Chapter 11 with an entirely different identity.

SUMMARY OF
CHAPTER 11 INVESTMENT STRATEGIES

	STAGE I (SPECULATIVE)	STAGE II (BUY-AND-HOLD)	STAGE III (ARBITRAGE)
Secured Debt	No speculative play.	Secured debt is primarily a buy-and-hold strategy. Investor goes in after estimating the value of assets that secure his bond and figuring the yield-to-maturity based on how long he has to hold it.	Arbitrager goes in late, after decision to liquidate or reorganize has been made, using quantified analysis of values.
Unsecured Debt	Speculator buys severely distressed unsecured debt shortly after company files, and well before much information is available. Buys with no real value estimate, looking for short-term price recovery. Sells to Stage II investor.	After waiting a few months to see what the company's going to do, the buy-and-hold investor has much better idea of real value of security, but time element still unknown. Has much less risk than speculator but may have to pay more.	Arbitrager comes in after the reorganization plan is made public, when he can quantify expected real return and finds security undervalued. Usually the most analytical investor taking the least risk.

Equity	Speculator buys right after stock drops on bankruptcy news, and holds only for short-term rebound.	Buy-and-hold investor goes in after reorganization plan is accepted or even after company emerges from Chapter 11, and holds long-term until market reflects company's turnaround.	No arbitrage play.

WHERE ARE THEY NOW?
STATUS OF MAJOR BANKRUPTCIES 1970–82

COMPANY	INDUSTRY	BANKRUPTCY DATE FILED	STOCK PRICE	DATE EMERGED	RECENT PRICE	EXCHANGE TRADED	CURRENT STATUS
Penn Central Co.	*railroad*	6/21/70	6½	10/24/78	29½	NYSE	Reorganized as Penn Central Corp.
Reading Co.	*railroad*	11/23/71	2⅜	12/31/80	11	Phila.	Reorganized
Dynamics Corp. of Am.	*appliances*	8/ 2/72	2¼	12/27/74	8⅜	NYSE	Reorganized
Ancorp Nat'l Services	*tobacco distr.*	3/20/73	5	5/13/75	—	—	Acquired by Sodexho, Inc.
Equity Funding	*fin. services*	4/ 5/73	14⅜	3/31/76	16	NYSE	Reorganized as Orion Capital
U.S. Financial	*fin. services*	7/23/73	24½	—	—	—	No recent information
Unishops, Inc.	*retailer*	10/13/73	2	4/25/75	3	NYSE	Name changed to Marcade Group
Arlan's Dept. Stores	*discount stores*	3/10/74	2½	—	—	—	Liquidated
Interstate Stores	*discount stores*	5/22/74	1⅞	4/ 6/78	41⅜	NYSE	Reorganized as Toys 'R' Us
Hartfield-Zodys	*discount stores*	11/10/74	¾	12/22/81	8¾	NYSE	Reorganized as HRT Industries
Fidelity Mtg. Inv.	*REIT*	1/30/75	1½	—	—	—	Merged into Lifetime Communities Inc.

Cavanagh Communities	*REIT*	2/ 5/75	5/8	12/13/76	5/8	OTC	Reorganized
Daylin Corp.	*diversified svcs.*	2/12/75	1	10/20/76	—	—	Acquired by W.R. Grace
Chicago-Rock Is. RR	*railroad*	3/17/75	5¼	—	—	—	In liquidation
W.T. Grant	*retailer*	5/10/75	2⅛	—	—	—	Liquidated
Penn Fruit	*supermarkets*	9/ 3/75	1½	—	—	—	Assets sold to MCP Corp.
GAC Corp.	*REIT*	1/23/76	¼	10/ 1/80	11½	OTC	Reorganized as Avatar Holdings
National Mortgage Fund	*REIT*	6/30/76	¼	3/ 1/77	15⁄16	OTC	Reorganized
Continental Mtg. Inv.	*REIT*	10/21/76	¼	—	—	—	In reorganization
Continental Inv. Corp.	*REIT*	11/ 5/76	4⅞	—	—	—	Acquired by Liberty Nat'l Insurance
United Merchants & Mfg.	*textile*	7/12/77	3¼	6/30/78	5⅞	NYSE	Reorganized
Apeco Corp.	*office copiers*	10/19/77	1⅛	1/16/80	9⁄32	OTC	Reorganized
Colwell Mortgage Trust	*REIT*	2/10/78	1¾	4/29/79	4	OTC	Reorganized as CMT Invest. Co.
Commonwealth Oil	*oil refining*	3/ 2/78	2¼	7/24/81	½	Pacific	Reorganized
Food Fair, Inc.	*supermarkets*	10/ 2/78	3¼	7/ 6/81	4⅝	Pacific	Reorganized as Pantry Pride
Citizens Mtg. Inv. Trust	*REIT*	10/ 5/78	¼	—	—	—	In reorganization
Allied Supermarkets	*supermarkets*	11/ 6/78	2	3/30/80	2¼	Phila.	Reorganized

COMPANY	INDUSTRY	BANKRUPTCY DATE FILED	BANKRUPTCY STOCK PRICE	BANKRUPTCY DATE EMERGED	RECENT PRICE	EXCHANGE TRADED	CURRENT STATUS
Chase Manhattan Mtg.	*REIT*	2/22/79	5/8	6/ 5/80	7/16	Pacific	Reorganized as Triton Group Ltd.
City Stores	*department stores*	7/27/79	2½	6/23/81	2⅜	Phila.	Reorganized
Penn-Dixie Ind.	*steel products*	4/ 7/80	2	3/18/82	11/16	OTC	Reorganized as Continental Steel Corp.
White Motor	*heavy-duty trucks*	9/ 4/80	3⅛	—	¼	Pacific	In reorganization
Combustible Equip. Ass.	*energy systems*	10/20/80	2⅜	—	⅜	OTC	In reorganization
ITEL Corp.	*diversified services*	1/ 9/81	1¼	—	¾	Pacific	In reorganization
Seatrain Lines	*container lines*	2/11/81	1½	—	⅜	Pacific	In reorganization
Arctic Enterprises	*snowmobiles*	2/17/81	2	12/ 4/81	2⅞	OTC	Reorganized
Sambo's Rests.	*fast-food chain*	11/27/81	1⅛	—	1⅞	Pacific	In reorganization
McLouth Steel	*steel mfg.*	12/ 8/81	2⅝	—	13/16	OTC	In reorganization
Bobbie Brooks	*women's apparel*	1/15/82	1½	—	2 1/16	OTC	Reorganization plan filed
J.W. Mays	*department stores*	1/25/82	2⅝	—	½	Pacific	In reorganization
Lionel Corp.	*toy supermarkets*	2/19/82	3⅝	—	3½	Pacific	In reorganization
AM International	*business equip.*	4/14/82	1⅛	—	1⅛	Pacific	In reorganization
Saxon Industries	*copiers; paper prod.*	4/15/82	1¾	—	⅝	Pacific	In reorganization

Wickes Cos.	bldg. retailer	4/24/82	2¼	—	6	Pacific	In reorganization
Braniff International	airline	5/13/82	⅞	—	1⅜	Pacific	In reorganization
UNR	steel producer	7/29/82	7⅞	—	2	OTC	In reorganization
KDT Industries	department stores	8/ 5/82	15/16	—	15/16	Pacific	In reorganization
Manville Corp.	bldg. paper prds.	8/26/82	5⅛	—	7	NYSE	In reorganization
Revere Copper	fabr. aluminum	10/27/82	10	—	5⅝	NYSE	In reorganization

From *Financial World* 11/15/82.

9

Itel: A Case Study

Until 1979, Itel Corporation's business was selling and leasing various types of capital equipment, including computers and railroad equipment. It also provided related administrative, operating, and financial services. In its heyday, the company was known for its outgoing management style, with luxury perks such as Mercedes-Benz company cars and water coolers filled with Perrier. But, in early 1979, the company was forced to discontinue its involvement in computer equipment and services because of competitive pressures, a highly leveraged capital structure, and unprofitability.

Itel suffered through 1979 and 1980 while posting losses of more than $500 million. As of December 31, 1980, common stockholders had a deficit of $339.8 million (liabilities outweighed assets by that much) and creditors had $1.2 billion outstanding. On January 19, 1981, the company entered Chapter 11, in an attempt to reorganize its capital structure.

Prior to Itel acknowledging the severity of its financial problems in the beginning of 1981, its 10½% senior (unsecured) debentures due in 1998 were selling for $400, or 40¢ on the dollar. As news of the firm's imminent bankruptcy spread, the price dropped to $250. Stage One had begun. *(If a bankruptcy filing is preceded by rumor and speculation, prices usually fall and Stage One begins early since the market's discouragement would be already reflected in the price of the bonds.)* Itel's bond prices did not experience continued drops after bankruptcy was declared because of the dramatic decline prior to the filing, as well as the early investor opinion that the company would indeed reorganize.

In the months following Itel's bankruptcy, speculators started selling to investors as this unsecured bond began to regain its value. This was Stage Two. The picture was unfolding. In the first year, two creditors' committees attempted to develop a concrete plan to reorganize Itel's operating and capital structures. The 10½% of 1998 bond investors followed this process, pushing its price up from $250 to $450, for an 80% gain in one year.

When an outline of reorganization was announced on February 4, 1982, the biggest question in investors' minds was the time element. Because of the uncertainty of how long the workout process would take, many arbitragers held out, waiting until they could get a better feel for the timing. And yet there was great potential for arbitrage, with a wide discrepancy between current value and future value. A classic Stage Three.

Let's take a look at what Itel's reorganization plan for holders of its 10½%–1998 unsecured debt looked like in early 1983, two years after the company filed for Chapter 11 and eight months before it emerged from reorganization. The plan provided unsecured creditors (who had claims totaling $850 million) with $228 million in cash ($414 per $1,000 bond), plus a combination of new debt and equity securities.

A. *The debt portion* of the package included a $190 million new issue 14% secured note due in 1996 (secured by a lien on Itel Corporation's new common stock), and a $110 million new issue 10% debenture due in 2002. The value of the new secured debt (the 14% note) was estimated at between $149 and $199 per $1,000 of the old bonds. The new unsecured debt (the 10% debenture) was valued at between $49 and $56, making the total debt package worth between $198 and $255 per $1,000 of the old bonds.

B. *The equity portion* consists of $97.5 million (par value) of a new series of liquidating preferred stock. (The liquidating provision allows Itel to periodically reclaim this stock at a given price.) Each bondholder will get 1.3 shares of this issue per $1,000 bond, which was estimated to be worth about $15 a share (or $20 for 1.3 shares). The old bondholders were offered 70% of the new common stock of the reorganized Itel, which comes out to fourteen shares for every old $1,000 bond. With the stock valued at approximately $2.50 a share, that translates to about $35 per bond. Thus, the value of the equity portion of the package was estimated to be about $55 for each old bond.

C. Furthermore, the plan provided that "a holder of a senior unsecured claim in an amount of $10,000 or less may elect to receive payment of 50% of the allowed amount of his claim in cash" (Itel Corporation, *Disclosure Statement of Amended Plan of Reorganization*, December 8, 1982), but forfeits the 10% notes, preferred shares, secured bonds, and common stock.

Estimates of the total value of the package offered to holders of Itel's 10½% of 1998 bonds were in the $650–$700 range in early 1983. Itel's own estimate was $663. Despite the calculated value of the package, market values of these unsecured bonds rose at a turtle's pace, reaching only $560 by January 1983. Arbitragers began to infiltrate the market as a time horizon became more determinable, and prices hit the $685 level as of February 28, 1983.

When the company finally emerged from Chapter 11 in September 1983, bondholders were pleasantly surprised with an initial distribution worth about $770 and the likelihood of an additional 5% or so to come later. Investors who had bought the bonds for $220 just two years earlier were very pleased. The table below illustrates the September, 1983 distribution:

ITEL CORPORATION'S INITIAL
DISTRIBUTION TO BONDHOLDERS
(Per $1000 of 10½% Senior Unsecured Bonds Due 1998)

	COMPONENT VALUE*	TOTAL VALUE
Cash	$471	$471
New Debt (Bonds)		
14% secured note	$143	
10% unsecured note	$ 59	
Debt package		$202
New Equity (Stock)		
preferred stock		
(1.3 shares at $21 per share)	$ 28	
common stock		
(14 shares at $5 per share)	$ 70	
Equity package		$ 98
Value of total package		$771

*Based on actual market prices of each new security shortly after the distribution.

HOW TO EVALUATE UNSECURED DEBT

Valuation techniques of unsecured debt securities differ depending on both the investment stage the company is in, and the direction it will take. In the event of liquidation, or potential liquidation, investors must look mainly at the company's balance sheet. But once it has been determined that the company will reorganize, investors must attempt to measure the future success of the company as well as continue to analyze the company's assets. I'll go through the three investment stages and present valuation techniques for each.

ITEL Corporation Investment Cycle
10½% Notes Due 1998

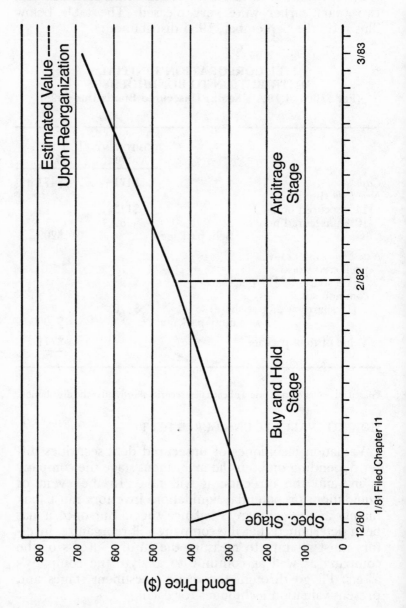

(1) In *Stage One,* we do not know whether a troubled company will liquidate or reorganize. While we can make some educated guesses about which course looks more likely, we still do not know for sure. *Therefore we must use a worst-case scenario, evaluating the security based on liquidation.*

The unsecured investor first must determine where he stands in line; usually, there are secured bondholders as well as bank creditors ahead. The speculator must identify all assets pledged to secured creditors, and determine if the sale of those assets will cover the specific debt. If they don't, then the remaining portion of secured debt will be included in the senior unsecured debt class. If the assets do cover all secured debt, then the investor still must consider all unsecured debt that is senior to him. Once this is done, it is possible to determine how much his particular class will be repaid in the event of liquidation.

This is the most difficult stage in which to evaluate a Chapter 11 company because adequate information is usually not available. Some information can be gleaned, however, through annual reports, quarterly reports, and 10-K reports available through the company itself, the SEC, or your stockbroker. It is very important to do this analysis early. *(Don't be fooled into buying subordinated bonds of a liquidating firm just because the maturity date is coming up soon; maturity dates mean nothing in these situations.)*

(2) *Stage Two* investors have the benefit of more information on the future direction of the troubled company, and on the financial position of the firm at the time. In the case of liquidation, priority rules again should be applied; know where you stand. If reorganization is forecasted, the investor must look at other factors, such as the form that capital structure will take after reorganization, the makeup of the new company's core business, the value of the assets sold and retained by the company, and the future business potential of the ongoing concern.

In the case of Itel, Stage Two investors had the advantage of knowing precisely what the firm planned to sell off. It was clear that it would divest itself of its computer equipment and services activities, which would generate a tremendous inflow of cash. Itel officials also made it clear that they were confident of getting back on their feet after a few tough years.

The second stage may continue after the initial plan of reorganization has been presented; in this case, investors have a great deal of information with which to evaluate securities.

(3) By *Stage Three,* arbitragers generally have an adequate amount of information with which to evaluate potential bankruptcy investments. There are two basic problems that their evaluation process tries to solve: what exactly the investor will get in the reorganization package, and how much that package will be worth. *All numbers needed to perform the evaluation of these securities can be found in the disclosure statement of the company's plan of reorganization, which must be filed with the SEC.* We will break down both problems in the context of the Itel case.

A. How much of the total reorganization package being offered goes to holders of my specific bond issue?

In order to determine exactly what is included in a reorganization package, the arbitrager must first figure how much cash, how many bonds, and how many shares of preferred and common stock will be allotted to each specific bond issued within the creditor class (priority class) that the package is being offered to. This is accomplished by determining what percentage of the total creditor class his particular issue represents. (After this is calculated, the investor can analyze just how much in cash, bonds, and stock will be allotted to each $1,000 bond that he holds, or is planning on buying.)

In the case of Itel Corporation, holders of the 10½% unsecured bonds due in 1998 belonged to a creditor class which consisted of the following: $584 million of private unsecured debt, $110 million in other public, senior, unsecured issues, and $67 million in other assorted claims. The 10½% of 1998 bondholders' $84 million claim represents 9.94% of the total creditor class. These calculations are presented below:

ITEL CORPORATION
SUMMARY OF CREDITOR CLASS 5-A*

ISSUES	CLAIMS (MILLIONS)	% OF CLASS
Private Issues	$ 584	69.13%
10½% of 1998	*84*	*9.94*
10½% of 1993	47.6	5.64
9¾% of 1988	28.3	3.35
9¾% of 1990	34.1	4.03
	778	92.09
Other	67	7.91
Total Claims of Creditor Class 5-A	$ 845	100.00%

*Source: Itel Corporation Plan of Reorganization.

These percentages tell us precisely how much of the reorganization package (offered to the entire class) belongs to the holders of each specific bond issue.

B. What exactly will holders of my particular bond issue get?

What Itel offered this creditor class in its reorganization plan is the following: $312 million in cash, $171.9 million (face amount) in new 14% secured notes, $110 million in new unsecured 10% notes, 975,000 shares of new preferred stock, and 10.5 million shares of new Itel Corporation common stock. The share of this package that is due to former holders of the old 10½%–1998 bond is calculated by multiplying each portion of the package by 9.94%. This is exhibited below:

TOTAL PACKAGE OFFERED TO CREDITOR CLASS 5-A	TOTAL AMOUNT DUE TO 10½%–1998 BONDHOLDERS (9.94% OF CLASS 5-A)
$312,000,000 cash	$31,022,160
171,900,000 (face amount) new 14% secured notes	17,092,017
110,000,000 (face amount) new 10% unsecured notes	10,937,300
975,000 new shares preferred stock	96,944.25 shares
10,500,000 new shares common stock	1,044,015.00 shares

Of the $312,000,000 in cash pledged to creditor class 5-A, $31,022,160 (or 9.94%) is due to former holders of the old 10½%–1998 bonds. Of the $171,900,000 in new 14% secured notes pledged to the creditor class, $17,092,017 is due to former holders of the old 10½%–1998 bonds, and so on.

C. How much of all this do I get for the number of bonds that I hold?

Since there were $75 million worth of the 10½%–1998 bonds outstanding, dividing each part of the 10½%–1998 package further by the number of bonds outstanding gives the individual investor the precise amount that he will receive for each of his $1,000 bonds. Like so:

PACKAGE OFFERED TO HOLDERS OF 10½%–1998 BOND ISSUE AS A GROUP	EQUALS THIS AMT. PER $1,000 BOND (75,000 BONDS MAKE UP WHOLE ISSUE)
$31,022,160 (cash)	$413.62 face amount
$17,092,017 (face amount) new 14% secured notes	$277.89 face amount
$10,937,300 (face amount) new 10% unsecured notes	$145.83 face amount
96,944 shares preferred stock	1.292 shares/bond
1,044,015 shares common stock	13.92 shares/bond

The tables above are very useful to the investor who is considering an unsecured bond of a Chapter 11 company after the official plan of reorganization has been made public. They allow the investor to see precisely what he will receive for each bond that he buys.

D. What's it all worth?

The next problem to tackle is that of figuring out what all this is actually worth. There's no trick to that in the case of the cash portion of the package, but in analyzing the debt portion of the workout package, the investor should make assumptions based on the best-case and worst-case scenarios. In some reorganizations, for example, newly issued debt has a clause allowing for interest to be deferred, which could be a value factor by itself. *Keep your best-case assumptions conservative; although this advice may steer you away from some successful plays, it may save you from the disasters as well.*

How much return should you expect to get from bonds in a reorganization package? The total yield—both interest and price appreciation—on these securities must clearly exceed what you can get on safer, investment-grade bonds (BBB through AAA ratings), or they are not worth the risk. The Itel bonds offered an estimated yield of 20% at a time when BBB rated bonds were yielding about 16%. Any unusual characteristics of the new bonds, such as allowance for deferred interest, must be taken into consideration too. (Itel's 10% notes allow their interest to be deferred until maturity if necessary.)

Analysts calculated Itel's 14% bonds to be worth in the range of 83¢ to 87¢ (per dollar's worth) upon emergence from Chapter 11. Their valuation of the new 10% bonds was 34¢ to 38½¢ on the dollar.

In analyzing the equity portion of the package, the investor must estimate the value that each security will support once the company is back on its feet. Quite often, several different varieties of equity securities will be included in the reorganization package. As with bonds, income deferral clauses can influence the nature and value of preferred issues. (Liquidating preferred stock must be analyzed as a fixed income security, because it is discontinued once investors have received a certain return.)

Yes, it's a guessing game. If you don't have enough confidence, some experts do the guessing for you—namely, fundamental analysts at the big brokerage houses. Ask your broker for help.

When evaluating common stock, future earnings potential is considered the most important factor. Often, the plan of reorganization includes independent analysis and evaluation of each component of the package. In the Itel plan, Lehman Brothers provided the outside evaluation, and its estimates were very close to the figures that we've used here.

Looking closer at the Itel situation, both the new preferred stock and the new common stock require evaluation. The preferred issue (which is allowed to withhold payments) was valued at between $15 and $26 per share, and the common at between $2.50 and $5 per share. The following table is the kind of homework a Phoenix investor might have done in early 1983, trying to estimate the real value of Itel's 10½% of 1998 bonds:

**ESTIMATED TOTAL VALUE OF ITEL'S REORGANIZATION
PACKAGE OFFERED TO HOLDERS OF ITS OLD
10½%–1998 UNSECURED BONDS
(PER $1,000 BOND)**

	PRICE RANGE PER UNIT	WORST CASE	BEST CASE
Cash	$414	$414	$414
14% Note	83%–88% of par	$149	$199
10% Note	34%–38% of par	$ 49	$ 56
Preferred stock	$15–$26 per share (1.3 shrs)	$ 20	$ 34
Common stock	$2.50–$5.00 per share (14 shrs)	$ 35	$ 70
Totals Est. Value		$667	$773

On September 19th, 1983, Itel emerged from Chapter 11 reorganization just two years and eight months after declaring bankruptcy. The company came out one-third its former size, and limited to the leasing of boxcars and containers. No more computers. And no more Mercedes and Perrier.

10

Predicting Bankruptcies

Portfolio managers keep a constant eye on their stocks in hopes of detecting trouble ahead of time often using sophisticated prediction models to estimate the chances of a troubled company going bankrupt.

The Phoenix investor can use the same methods to get familiar with these companies well before they actually file for Chapter 11. Some of the very companies that the institutional investor is thinking about selling should be the ones that the wise bottom fisher is preparing to buy. The process of predicting a bankruptcy opportunity and determining the company's investment potential requires a close look at the latest financial reports.

The most fundamental reason for the majority of corporate bankruptcies is overleveraging; there are not many bankruptcies that don't involve a significant amount of debt. There are several industries that are always highly leveraged: the capital-intensive airlines, railroads, retailers, and energy companies. Other factors can signal bankruptcy risk too, such as susceptibility to severe economic swings and restrictive government regulation.

Consider the airlines. When a company decides to purchase a plane, it has two financing options. Since .most airlines don't have several million dollars in cash lying around, they have to either finance their new equipment through a bank or through the issuance of a public bond issue. For a variety of reasons, including the high failure risk inherent in the industry, airline bonds usually are secured by equipment. (The pledge of repayment is tied to the value of the airplane. If the company defaults on payment and enters bankruptcy, the creditors may find themselves the proud owners of a jumbo jet.)

Airlines often are affected greatly by regulatory pres-sures. Recently, with deregulation of the airline industry and the added pressures of competition, price wars have resulted in discounts that barely leave room for breaking even. *Any industry in which changing regulations can greatly affect the financial health of its companies usually has more bankruptcy risk.*

The airline industry also is very sensitive to the general health of the economy. When the economy is strong, people have money and they travel. But when it is in a downswing, and the nation is suffering through a reces-sion such as in 1980–82, individuals and companies alike cut back on travel, making cash flow extremely tight for the airlines. The probability of the industry encountering problems in servicing its huge debts is greatly increased. Then there are external events, such as the dramatic fuel price increases that clobbered the industry in the late 1970s and early 1980s.

No wonder that, at this writing, there are still several airlines identified as potential failure candidates, includ-ing Pan Am, World Airways, Tiger International, Eastern and Continental. Similarly, the steel, energy and railroad industries have more than their share of endangered companies.

When performing fundamental industry analysis to iden-tify possible corporate bankruptcies, the investor should start with these questions:

1. How much leverage is standard within the industry? Is this company more in debt than its competitors?
2. To what extent is the industry's success affected by government regulation?
3. To what extent is the industry's success dependent on another industry or on the economy in general?

After picking certain industries to concentrate on, you must next identify specific companies within these industries that are potential bankruptcies. You can do this with formulas called *analytical models,* all of which focus on corporate balance sheets.

FORECASTING MODELS

Over the past two years, one of Wall Street's favorite pastimes has been guessing which company will go bankrupt next. The stakes are high in this game, as bankers, brokers, insurance companies, lawyers, creditors and experienced bottom fishers are well aware.

The importance of this information, the significantly increased number of corporate failures in recent years, and the ever-increasing sophistication of financial analysis have brought us some surprisingly dependable forecasting methods from the academic world. Mathematical formulas, which plug in the financial data of troubled companies, use ratio analysis to predict the likelihood of bankruptcy.

One of the most accurate models was developed by Edward Altman, a professor at NYU Business School, and is called the *Z-Score Model.* Altman uses five financial ratios to measure the likelihood of a company's failing within a two-year period. Another model, known as the *Gambler's Ruin Model,* was refined and developed by Jarrod Wilcox while he was teaching at MIT's Sloan School. Also highly accurate, Wilcox's approach is based on changes in a company's liquidation value and makes predictions as far out as five years. Both models boast a proven rate of accuracy of about 80%.

After testing some twenty-two ratios, Altman chose just five to use for his formula, assigning different weightings to each for importance. By simply adding up the five figures, we have a good indication of a company's efficiency (based mostly on its return on assets). Failing companies usually reveal inadequate working capital, extreme debt (greater than the total market value of their stock), and diminutive retained earnings (relative to assets).

Any investor can make use of the Z-Score Model. The data is readily available in any company's financial statement. Here's the formula. Simply add these figures up for any company:

(1) *Working Capital/Total Assets* (then multiply this figure by the weighted value of 1.2). This ratio indicates what the net liquid assets of a company are relative to its total capitalization. (Working capital is current assets minus current liabilities.)

(2) *Retained Earnings/Total Assets* (multiply by 1.4). This ratio measures long-term cumulative profitability.

(3) *Earnings Before Interest and Taxes/Total Assets* (multiply by 3.3). The most heavily weighted ratio, this one indicates the real productivity of the company's assets.

(4) *Market Value of Equity/Total Debt* (multiply by 0.6). This least heavily weighted ratio indicates how much a company's assets can shrink before they are exceeded by its liabilities.

(5) *Sales/Total Assets* (multiply by 1.0). The final ratio measures how much revenue the company's assets can bring in.

Just add up the numbers and see what you get. Scores below 1.8 emit danger signals; scores above 3.0 indicate financial safety.

Let's see how Tiger International would have stood this model's test last year, at the height of its financial difficulties. Tiger International is a holding company for several aviation subsidiaries, the largest of which is Flying Tiger, the world's largest scheduled air cargo carrier. Tiger was hit extremely hard by the recession of 1980–1982, high interest payments due to its overleveraged debt position, and poor management. Over the past year, the company has been considered a bankruptcy candidate, and as recently as September 30, 1982, it scored only .76 on the Z-Score test, significantly below the 1.8 danger point. Tiger may be able to successfully turn around without the help of the courts, but the Z-Score Model told us at that time that Tiger was one of many companies to keep an eye on for a bankruptcy play. *Identifying bankruptcy candidates ahead of time gives the bottom fisher the big advantage of starting to evaluate the assets of these companies before they take the expected final plunge.*

Z-SCORE MODEL CALCULATIONS FOR TIGER INTERNATIONAL, INC. AS OF LATE 1982

Z-SCORE MODEL:

$$z = 1.2x_1 + 1.4x_2 + 3.3x_3 + 0.6x_4 + 1.0x_5$$

where:
- x_1 = Working Capital/Total Assets
- x_2 = Retained Earnings/Total Assets
- x_3 = Earnings Before Interest and Taxes/Total Assets
- x_4 = Market Value of Equity/Total Debt
- x_5 = Sales/Total Assets

TIGER INTERNATIONAL DATA (IN MILLIONS $):

Working Capital	50
Retained Earnings	0
Earnings Before Interest & Taxes	24
Total Assets	2175.9
Total Debt	1835.9
Sales	1446.0
Market Value of Equity	104.0

$$Z = 1.2(.023) + 1.4(0.0) + 3.3(.011) + 0.6(.057) + 1.0(.665)$$
$$Z = 0.76$$

In fiscal year 1982, Tiger ended up losing over $8 per share. By mid-1983, the company was in the red by over $12 a share on a yearly basis, but investors still found value in its stock, as it hovered in the $7–$8 range.

• BALANCE SHEET BARGAINS •

The pundits of Wall Street may be wrong much of the time, but there *is* some good research being generated by top Wall Street firms. The following report was put together by two savvy analysts, Michael Metz and Norman Weinger at Oppenheimer Co. Their report is geared to investors interested in acquiring entire companies, but the information is also a useful resource for the Phoenix investor. It shows that there are companies out there (see Metz and Weinger's list) whose stock is selling for less than the net value of their assets. In this specific example, Metz and Weinger arrive at a figure they call "net borrow power." This represents the kind of borrowing one should be able to do in order to buy the individual companies listed. To determine a company's net borrowing power in a conservative way, Metz and Weinger use a formula which combines cash, 20% of the gross value of the plant, and various percentages of receivables by subtracting 100% of current liabilities, 90% of long-term debts, and 100% of settlements with minority partners and preferred holders. As such it approximates each company's "real," or liquidation, value.

In their March 1983 list, Metz and Weinger identified 47 companies whose net borrow values far exceed their current market values. The two analysts do not suggest that these companies should or will be liquidated. They are simply identifying undervalued securities which they call balance sheet bargains. Here is their full report:

BUY A COMPANY
NOTHING DOWN, EASY PAYMENTS
by Norman Weinger and E. Michael Metz

Despite the precedent-shattering advance in stock prices since August 1982, the movement toward restructuring through leveraged buyouts, mergers and spin-offs shows little sign of abating. Numerous publicly owned companies are still appraised at large discounts from their going business value, and the restructuring phenomenon is expected to remain a feature of the investment environment.

In this screening we approach a stock from the perspective of a businessman seeking to acquire an entire company without putting any cash up front. Our parameters are designed to single out those companies that theoretically could be purchased entirely through funds raised from leveraging existing assets of the purchased company. In order to qualify, a company must have borrowing power, as we define it, in excess of its market valuation. In essence, a company must be selling at what we believe is less than the collateral value of its net assets.

The investor is cautioned that no investment decision is warranted on the basis of these figures alone. The data should be used as a starting point in a quest for unusually attractive values. This study is part of a continuing program, begun in 1974, to highlight particularly intriguing areas of undervaluation in the stock market.

The new era in the securities field that features asset restructuring, leveraged buyouts, reversions to private ownership and more frequent takeovers, capitalization shrinkages and mergers has stemmed from the undervaluation typical of many publicly owned companies. We use the term undervaluation specifically to mean that the market appraisal is below what a businessman might be willing to pay for an entire business. We have used our computer to screen out those companies that, on the basis of balance sheet entries, would be particularly attractive to an acquiror since their assets could theoretically provide sufficient collateral values to permit borrowing the entire purchase price. *In essence a buyer could conceivably use the borrowing power of the acquired company to completely finance the purchase of it.*

Column I is the reporting date for all the subsequent balance sheet entries. Column II is the market capitalization —the value in millions of dollars placed on the company, based on the present market price of the common shares. We have eliminated companies with a market valuation of less than $10 million.

The remaining columns are all per-share numbers. Column III is the cash included in current assets; of course, cash is valued at 100% in terms of its value as collateral. Column IV is receivables net of allowance for doubtful accounts, discounted by 25%. Our assumption is that a factor, for example, would lend 75% of face value. Column V is inventory, discounted by 60%, the assumption being that a lender would advance funds equal to 40% of its book value. Column VI is gross plant. Since that figure is the undepreciated cost of the original plant account, we have arbitrarily discounted its value by 80% to arrive at its value as collateral. Column VII is what we characterize as total borrowing power per share reached by adding the collateral value of Columns III through VI.

Columns VIII, IX and X represent liabilities already existing against the corporation which presumably would have to be paid off before new encumbrances could be placed on the assets. Column VIII is the amount of debt included in current liabilities. Column IX is long-term debt. Column X is the total of existing borrowing (Column VIII added to Column IX).

Next, total present borrowing (Column X) is deducted from total borrowing power, as computed (Column VII), to arrive at the net borrowing power per share (Column XI). To fit the parameters of this screen, this figure must exceed the current market price (Column XII). *The excess*

(Column XIII) is theoretically the amount of borrowing power still available to the purchaser of the subject company after having paid the market price for all outstanding shares. In essence, the buyer has leveraged out completely, using the acquired company's assets as collateral, and still has excess funds. Column XIV is the reported book value.

Various caveats should be noted. First, all balance sheet figures must be examined more closely. In the case of receivables (Column IV), we believe that a 25% discount for collateral purposes is generally reasonable. However, in the case of some businesses, particularly those dealing with numerous small, poorly financed customers (such as sole proprietor retailers), a larger discount might be reasonable. Conversely, where the government or a blue chip corporation is the major customer, a smaller discount would be in order.

Second, inventories (Column V) have to be analyzed closely. In the case of fungible items used, for example, in the metal fabricating or food processing industries, the 60% discount may be too large. In other instances, where finished consumer fashion items loom prominently in inventory, a much larger discount would be appropriate.

Third, regarding gross plant (Column VI), some obsolete or poorly located facilities would not command a collateral value much above salvage value. In many instances, however, the 80% discount would prove overly conservative.

Fourth, the liability side also merits scrutiny. In certain cases, some of the debt may take the form of mortgages on specific plants or pieces of real estate. The company may be in a position to incur additional debt without having to refinance existing obligations. Of critical importance is a consideration of whether trade relationships would be hurt by the injection of additional leverage. For example, suppliers might, as a consequence, insist on earlier or even simultaneous payment. Thus, the subject company might have greater working capital requirements than under its present, less leveraged financial structure.

Fifth, in many cases, borrowing power may prove materially larger than appears on the surface. A substantial LIFO reserve could considerably enhance the collateral value of inventories. The plant account might be dramatically understated and include unencumbered assets that would support large new secured borrowing. On the other hand, some off-balance sheet liabilities, such as pension obligations or pending litigation, could conceivably constitute prior liens and reduce borrowing power. In some instances, however, it is possible that pension plans are overfunded if more realistic actuarial assumptions can be adopted.

Ultimately, of course, the critical consideration is whether a leveraged purchase of a company makes business sense. That determination, in turn, is largely a matter of whether projected cash flow would be sufficient to service the new debt and to generate adequate funds for maintaining the profitability of the company.

Several smokestack companies appear on the list, such as Cyclops Corp., Interlake, National Steel and Republic Steel. In the case of many steel companies, however, off-balance sheet liabilities such as pension obligations are sizable. An offsetting asset is LIFO reserves that are in some cases significant relative to the market valuation of the companies. The major problem with many concerns, however, remains one of poor cash flows. Elsewhere, Jupiter Industries announced some time ago that it had considered and subsequently abandoned a plan to go private. McDermott has undergone a restructuring designed to counter the tax liability accruing from overseas operations. Michigan Sugar has dramatically strengthened an already sound balance sheet. Operating results are largely dependent upon sugar pricing. Perini Corp., which last year was the subject of a 13D filing and subsequently

OPPENHEIMER & CO., INC.
BUY A COMPANY—NOTHING DOWN, EASY PAYMENTS IX

Parameters: 1) Net Borrowing Power > Market Price
2) Market Capitalization > $10 Million
As of: 3/8/83

			I	II	III	IV	V	VI	VII	VIII	IX	X	XI	XII	XIII	XIV
				MARKET				20%	PER SHARE INFORMATION TOTAL	DEBT IN			NET			RPRTED
COMPANY NAME	TICK	X	REPORT DATE	CAP. $ MILL	CASH	75% RECEIV	40% INVENT	GROSS PLANT	BORROW POWER	CURR. LIAB.	L.T. DEBT	TOTAL BORROW	BORROW POWER	CURR. PRICE	EXCESS	BOOK VALUE
ALLIS-CHALMERS CORP	AH	N	12/81	154.1	9.56	17.36	11.11	10.75	48.78	3.91	22.92	26.84	21.94	12.25	9.69	46.92
ALTAMIL CORP	ALW	A	11/82	15.3	7.94	5.04	3.26	3.66	19.89	.46	4.49	4.96	14.93	14.25	.68	20.70
AMDISCO CORP	ADSO	O	9/82	18.4	30.61	1.24	.00	.03	31.87	.00	.00	.00	31.87	26.31	5.56	30.44
AMERICAN BAKERIES CO	ABA	N	9/82	29.8	1.05	12.27	1.58	13.18	28.08	2.03	8.37	10.40	17.68	12.25	5.43	16.04
AVONDALE MILLS	AVD	A	11/82	62.4	8.08	14.96	3.87	18.29	45.20	.22	5.84	6.06	39.14	31.00	8.14	46.13
BANISTER CONT LTD	BAN	A	9/82	37.8	.82	9.12	.00	2.31	12.25	.92	1.56	2.48	9.77	7.50	2.27	8.17
BANK BUILDING & EQUIP CORP AM	BB	A	10/82	15.2	.30	16.07	1.02	1.67	19.06	3.18	.62	3.81	15.25	9.50	5.75	7.06
BOBBIE BROOKS INC	BBKSQ	O	4/82	12.4	.32	1.04	1.71	.64	3.71	.03	.13	.16	3.55	2.69	.86	1.61
BORMAN'S INC	BRF	N	10/82	25.6	2.32	3.36	7.78	6.81	20.27	.53	9.79	10.32	9.95	9.00	.95	11.04
BUELL INDUSTRIES INC	BUE	A	10/82	18.3	8.28	4.06	1.66	4.67	18.68	.67	2.41	3.09	15.59	13.69	1.90	19.73
CDI CORP	CDI	A	10/82	21.6	.78	12.75	.00	1.56	15.10	.48	1.74	2.22	12.87	11.13	1.75	13.79
COMBUSTION ENGINEERING INC	CSP	N	9/82	1259.3	15.83	12.55	9.54	7.84	45.75	.82	3.99	4.81	40.94	38.13	2.82	24.82
COMMERCIAL METALS CO	CMC	N	11/82	88.2	4.58	10.86	6.41	4.52	26.37	.61	4.35	4.96	21.42	21.25	.17	26.34
CONCORD FABRICS INC	CIS	A	11/82	11.4	.48	5.67	3.62	.81	10.58	1.02	3.04	4.07	6.51	6.38	.14	10.69
CONTINENTAL STEEL CORP-DEL	CSCS	O	9/82	20.2	1.65	.91	.54	1.69	4.79	.06	.89	.95	3.84	1.91	1.93	1.31
COURTAULDS LTD	COU	A	3/82	367.2	.96	1.36	.96	1.28	4.57	.16	1.68	1.84	2.73	1.34	1.39	2.22
CRAIG CORP	CRA	N	9/82	15.7	3.67	6.81	8.98	1.06	15.52	1.43	.64	2.06	13.46	8.75	4.71	21.33
CYCLOPS CORP	CYL	N	9/82	90.9	.26	25.94	16.34	24.12	66.67	4.64	22.67	27.31	39.36	26.38	12.98	53.90
DRAVO CORP	DRV	N	9/82	177.5	1.61	12.61	2.58	7.56	24.36	2.16	7.32	9.49	14.88	13.63	1.25	18.58
DUNLOP HOLDING LTD	DLP	A	12/81	107.8	.61	3.11	1.87	1.88	7.47	2.27	3.36	5.63	1.84	.75	1.09	2.57

Company	Sym	X	Date													
DYNALECTRON CORP	DYN	A	9/82	109.0	7.38	7.56	.34	1.20	16.47	.10	3.34	3.44	13.03	12.75	.28	8.94
FAB INDUSTRIES INC	FIT	A	8/82	44.1	9.91	6.29	3.07	2.85	22.13	.11	.72	.83	21.30	19.00	2.30	21.53
FISCHBACH CORP	FIS	N	9/82	167.1	16.76	60.28	.00	7.18	84.22	.66	17.27	17.93	66.29	49.25	17.04	45.17
FISHER FOODS INC	FHR	N	9/82	49.3	8.37	1.24	3.23	5.87	18.71	.29	7.04	7.34	11.37	9.88	1.50	15.37
FOSTER WHEELER CORP	FWC	N	9/82	462.7	4.99	7.96	1.78	1.20	15.93	.34	.86	1.20	14.73	13.50	1.23	10.11
GENERAL REFRACTORIES CO	GRX	N	9/82	22.8	1.88	13.85	6.91	15.79	38.42	18.76	8.93	27.69	10.73	6.00	4.73	17.35
GF BUSINESS EQUIPMENT	GFB	N	9/82	16.3	.13	7.37	3.23	5.56	16.29	.40	6.77	7.18	9.11	6.50	2.61	15.98
HOLLY SUGAR CORP	HLY	N	9/82	45.0	2.62	8.99	4.45	21.72	37.77	.09	.86	.95	36.82	32.50	4.32	56.21
INTERLAKE INC	IK	N	9/82	174.7	9.76	19.79	13.16	24.93	67.64	3.16	26.45	29.61	38.03	37.13	.91	73.72
ISS INTL SERVICE SYSTEM	ISI	A	9/82	13.3	1.13	7.08	.00	.44	8.65	.10	1.27	1.38	7.27	5.25	2.02	5.42
JUPITER INDUSTRIES	JUP	A	9/82	15.2	15.90	19.60	2.64	18.68	56.81	7.94	23.74	31.68	25.13	14.81	10.32	22.16
KEYSTONE CONS INDUSTRIES INC	KES	N	9/82	24.4	10.25	15.72	13.65	26.02	65.65	3.94	30.36	34.30	31.35	13.00	18.35	51.06
MCDERMOTT INC	MDE	N	9/82	717.9	5.99	22.65	3.52	10.95	43.11	.45	11.16	11.61	31.51	19.50	12.01	32.67
MICHIGAN SUGAR	MGU	A	9/82	35.5	17.14	2.04	1.63	4.73	25.56	.25	1.07	1.32	24.23	23.50	.73	26.89
MOVIE STAR INC–CL A	MVS-A	A	11/82	10.6	3.55	8.18	6.93	2.30	20.96	3.24	4.95	8.20	12.77	12.69	.08	23.00
MYERS (L.E.) CO GROUP	MYR	N	9/82	25.1	2.39	16.21	.00	6.40	25.00	4.06	4.57	8.63	16.37	13.50	2.87	13.69
NATIONAL STEEL CORP	NS	N	9/82	432.0	4.16	20.26	10.57	40.16	75.15	6.46	40.26	46.71	28.44	23.13	5.31	68.83
PERINI CORP	PCR	A	9/82	101.8	8.80	33.97	.00	7.93	50.70	4.76	5.58	10.34	40.37	32.00	8.37	26.53
PITTSBURGH–DES MOINES CORP	PDM	A	9/82	43.3	14.08	27.35	1.53	6.82	49.78	.85	6.69	7.54	42.24	17.38	24.87	28.01
RAYMARK CORP	RAY	N	9/82	34.0	1.58	14.47	12.44	10.76	39.26	5.67	17.77	23.45	15.81	12.63	3.19	33.41
RAYMOND INTL INC–DELAWARE	RII	N	9/82	92.9	7.37	24.44	1.21	6.92	39.93	2.59	9.68	12.27	27.66	14.88	12.79	24.68
REPUBLIC STEEL CORP	RS	N	9/82	380.3	.07	14.40	13.10	45.39	72.96	6.30	42.66	48.96	24.01	23.50	.51	90.58
RESEARCH–COTTRELL	RC	N	10/82	81.2	4.26	18.65	2.21	4.29	29.41	1.04	7.05	8.09	21.32	16.63	4.70	23.16
SALEM CORP	SBS	A	9/82	17.4	5.13	12.67	1.01	1.60	20.41	.13	.32	.44	19.97	11.00	.51	14.08
TODD SHIPYARDS CORP	TOD	N	9/82	165.0	20.38	14.61	.45	8.05	43.49	.12	8.68	8.80	34.69	33.25	1.44	25.95
TURNER CONSTRUCTION CO	TUR	A	9/82	73.9	10.13	152.18	.00	2.70	165.01	9.56	4.95	14.51	150.50	39.50	111.00	21.49
WALLACE (SAM P.) INC	SWC	A	10/82	17.2	7.64	11.11	.52	.85	20.13	.04	.22	.25	19.87	5.50	14.37	7.44

X CODE: N = N.Y. EXCH.; A = AMER. EXCH.; O = O.T.C.; R = REGIONAL; P = PRIVATE.

repurchased holdings of that dissident group, recently announced that it was considering a move to spin off its valuable real estate holdings.

A total of 47 companies qualify under our parameters. At the time of our previous screening on February 7, of this year, 53 stocks qualified. The number was 75 on December 3, 1982 and 119 last August, at the onset of the market rise.

• THE CHAPTER 11 MARKETPLACE •

Familiarity with the marketplace is important for any investor but is especially for the Phoenix investor looking at companies in Chapter 11 because he must operate in several different arenas at the same time. Each of the major exchanges, as well as the over-the-counter market, plays a role in the bankruptcy game.

The New York Stock Exchange, the oldest (1792) and largest securities market in America, had followed, until recently, an unwritten policy of delisting all companies that enter Chapter 11. Over the last few years, however, this conservative exchange has relisted bankruptcy companies considered "reasonably healthy," after recognizing the success that other exchanges were having in trading these issues. KDT Industries, Manville Corporation, and Revere Copper are still trading on the Big Board as they reorganize under Chapter 11. The NYSE is no newcomer as a supplier of bankruptcy plays however. Since 1970, fifty NYSE-listed companies have declared bankruptcy.

The American Stock Exchange is the second largest stock exchange in the country. Since the Amex lists more emerging growth companies than its NYSE competitor, it has provided more than its share of bankruptcy plays. (The latest of these, at this writing, is Texas General Resources, an energy firm, which entered Chapter 11 on March 15, 1983.) Unlike the NYSE, the Amex has continued to suspend trading on all companies that file for bankruptcy. Although the Amex may change this policy because of the growing interest in Chapter 11 investing, bankrupt Amex companies now usually go to the Pacific Exchange or OTC market.

The Pacific Stock Exchange, founded in 1957, was formed by a merger of the San Francisco and the Los Angeles Stock Exchanges. The PSE dually lists approximately 1,000 securities traded on the NYSE and ASE, and lists another 100 companies whose stock is traded primarily on the Pacific.

The PSE began to build a reputation as the "bankruptcy exchange" in 1978 when it decided to list Commonwealth Oil and Pantry Pride, the two latest Chapter 11 companies at the time. Citing the abundance of information available on these two companies, the administrators of the exchange were confident that they could provide a liquid, active market for speculative bankrupt securities. (Firms in Chapter 11 are indeed subject to strict disclosure requirements, as creditors and owners need to know everything possible.) The experiment proved successful, and the PSE became a haven for Chapter 11 securities.

Ten companies in Chapter 11 currently trade stocks and some bonds on this exchange. All were listed on either the New York Stock Exchange or the American Stock Exchange in conjunction with the PSE prior to the larger exchanges delisting them upon entrance into Chapter 11. The market for these securities has been liquid and active: Four of the ten most active Pacific stocks for 1982 were current, or former, Chapter 11 securities. The exchange has declined the opportunity to list several other Chapter 11 companies because it felt the companies could not reorganize and would end up in liquidation. The PSE wants to trade only companies that it considers survivable.

CHAPTER 11 SECURITIES CURRENTLY TRADING ON THE PACIFIC EXCHANGE (AS OF AUGUST 30, 1983)

COMPANIES	STOCK PRICE
AM International	$5.62
Braniff	$2.75
KDT Industries	$0.50
Lionel	$4.62
Sambo's Restaurants	$2.25
Saxon Industries	$1.88
Seatrain Lines	$0.75
Wickes Co.	$6.88

A MUTUAL FUND THAT INVESTS IN CHAPTER 11 SECURITIES

Mutual Shares Corporation
170 Broadway
New York, New York 10038
(212) 267-4200

Sales Charge: None   Minimum Investment: $1,000

ANNUAL PERCENTAGE TOTAL RETURNS BY YEAR

	73	74	75	76	77	78	79	80	81	82	83 (1st half)
Mutual Shares	−8.5	8.6	35.0	55.2	15.4	18.3	42.8	18.5	8.7	13.3	28.1
S & P 500	−14.8	−26.4	37.2	23.6	−7.4	6.4	18.2	32.3	−5.0	21.3	20.3

10 Year Average Annual Return:

Mutual Shares Corp.	23.5%
S&P 500	10.1%

Since most individual investors don't have the time or financial background necessary to research Chapter 11 companies, and because a diversified portfolio of bankruptcy stocks can be an expensive proposition, the mutual fund is worth considering as a vehicle for the Phoenix investor.

• BANKRUPTCY INVESTING REMINDERS •

The following is a recap of rules, tips, warnings and other bits of information covered in the preceding section on the subject of bankruptcy investing:

1. In the case of liquidations, common stockholders are last in line, behind all other security holders and creditors who have contractual claims on a company's assets.

2. You can greatly improve your chances of success in bankruptcy investing by doing two things: predetermining whether a bankrupt company will liquidate or reorganize, and getting a feel for the value of the company's assets.

3. Sometimes the best plays can be found in the less obvious situations, such as the securities of a healthy subsidiary.

4. One rule of thumb in trying to determine whether a company will emerge from Chapter 11 in reorganized form is to ask yourself if you, as a trade creditor, would want the company as a client in the future.

5. Ask yourself if anyone else can benefit through liquidation of the firm. Is the company worth more to others dead or alive?

6. Any analysis or information that the investor can gather before the liquidation/reorganization decision is made can help him take an earlier position, often at a more attractive price.

7. Even in successful reorganizations, the common shares of a company in bankruptcy are almost always diluted during the restructuring process, as bondholders are paid off with a package of new securities which typically include new stock as well as bonds and cash.

8. The highest return a secured debt holder can even hope for is the difference between his investment and par value of the bonds.

9. A simple exercise in considering secured debt is this:

    A. What is the debt backed by?

    B. Are the underlying assets marketable? Have technologies changed enough to outdate the assets?

    C. What is the economic condition of the industry in which the asset would be disposed?

10. The longer you wait before buying a bankruptcy security, the more information will become available on your company. The risk you take by waiting is that of your price moving up.

11. Look at the price of a debt security in relation to the assets backing it. If a bond is selling for 30¢ on the dollar, it doesn't ever have to pay off in full to still be a very successful investment.

12. Another important factor to consider in analyzing a bond value is *time*. How long will it take the company to pay off its secured bondholders? The time value of money is significant: if it takes ten years to double your money, this is only about 7% per year.

13. If you don't have a feel for the value of a secured debt, you should wait until you do.

14. Junior debentures should generally be bought only later in the reorganization process. If a reorganization attempt turns into a liquidation, most junior creditors will not fare well.

15. Railroads have a tendency to take longer than usual to reorganize, which is why many analysts suggest staying away from them. You should certainly not consider them if you need liquidity, or are looking for short-term appreciation.

16. If a security has already been declining in price

prior to its bankruptcy announcement, because of publicity and rumors, there may not be nearly as dramatic a price swing (dip and rebound) after the filing date.

17. In Stage One, you do not know whether a troubled company will liquidate or reorganize. While you can make some educated guesses about which course looks more likely, you still do not know for sure. Therefore you must use a worst-case scenario, evaluating the security based on liquidation.

18. Don't be fooled into buying subordinated bonds of a liquidating firm just because the maturity date is coming up soon; maturity dates mean nothing in these situations.

19. Most of the numbers needed to perform an evaluation of the securities of bankrupt companies can be found in the *disclosure statement* of the company's Plan of Reorganization (filed with the SEC).

20. Keep your best-case assumptions conservative; although this advice may steer you away from some successful plays, it may save you from the disasters as well.

21. Any industry in which changing government regulations can greatly affect its financial health usually has more risk of bankruptcy among its companies.

DIRECTORY OF CORPORATE DISASTERS
1980–1983
PUBLIC COMPANIES FILING CHAPTER 11 PETITIONS
January 1, 1980 through February 28, 1983

| FILING DATE | COMPANY | ASSETS & LIABILITIES | | PUBLIC INTEREST | | | | |
| | | ASSETS (MILLIONS) | LIABILITIES (MILLIONS) | EQUITY | | DEBT | | |
				SHARES (MILLIONS)	HOLDERS	AMOUNT (MILLIONS)	HOLDERS
1980	G. Weeks Securities (1)	$ 16.0	$ 7.0	—	—	$6–8	100
1980	General Resources Corp.	1.9	2.3	—	7,500	—	—
1980	L.S. Good & Co. (2)	33.0	30.0	2.5	1,827	—	—
1980	Auto Train Corp. (2)	28.8	30.0	1.6	4,595	—	—
1980	Inforex, Inc. (1)	73.3	57.6	3.2	2,934	20.0	564
1980	Penn-Dixie Industries	176.0	121.0	5.2	11,000	9.0	775
1980	Mansfield Tire & Rubber	42.0	37.0	1.6	3,400	—	—
1980	Park Nursing Center	577	7.0	—	—	5.2	650
1980	Tenna Corp. (2)	26.1	16.7	9.4	3,381	—	—
1980	Coleman American Cos., Inc.	9.2	7.0	1.7	1,200	—	—
1980	White Motor Corp.	897.5	730.5	9.4	21,993	30.0	1,366
1980	Resource Exploration, Inc. (1)	27.6	22.9	4.7	3,700	39.0	4,000
1980	Western Farmers Assoc. (1)	80.0	88.0	.1	45,000	14.0	15,000
1980	Pleasant Grove Med. Ctr. (1)	15.0	13.0	—	1,200	10.0	1,200
1980	Topps & Trowsers (1)	21.1	15.5	2.1	3,520	—	—
1980	Christian Life Center (1)	7.2	6.1	—	—	5.7	1,248
1980	SBE, Inc. (1)	1.6	1.5	1.2	977	—	—

Year	Company						
1980	Southland Lutheran Home(1)	3.7	6.5	6.1	900	—	—
1981	Horizon Hospital, Inc.	9.2	15.5	—	—	—	1,700
1981	Airlift Int'l., Inc.	52.5	58.9	25.5	61,234	15.0	837
1981	NOVA REIT	30.5	21.0	1.2	3,260	4.9	1,500
1981	Combustion Equipt. Assn.	178.0	104.0	10.4	9,685	20.0	—
1981	Seatrain Lines, Inc.	570.5	785.5	15.0	6,200	46.6	1,800
1981	Fidelity Amer. Fin. Corp.	2.5	2.3	.2	300	7.6	750
1981	Arctic Enterprises, Inc. (1)	87.7	78.0	1.2	4,900	—	—
1981	FWD Corp. (1)	17.0	14.0	.7	485	—	—
1981	Goldblatt Bros., Inc.	58.0	50.0	3.0	3,100	—	—
1981	Unishelter, Inc. (1)	13.8	13.7	.3	1,200	—	1,500
1981	Grove Finance Co.	7.1	20.6	—	—	18.0	—
1981	Computer Communications	18.0	11.0	.7	2,750	—	—
1981	Omega Fin. Inv. Corp. (2)	4.6	3.0	—	1	—	—
1981	Am. Nautilus Fitness Ctr. (3)	.02	.22	—	3,000	—	—
1981	Itel Corporation	1457.0	1717.0	3.5	6,700	several series	
				11.8	12,500		
1981	Hawaii Nevada Inv. Corp. (2)	—	—	—	2	—	109
1981	Heritage Inv. Group of Ark. (3)	2.1	.8	—	1	—	—
1982	Rusco Industries, Inc.	39.0	39.0	4.4	11,500	6.2	1,175
1982	Colonial Commercial Corp.	51.9	52.3	3.1	1,653	23.1	12,000
1982	The Lionel Corp.	207.4	165.2	7.1	10,100	15.0	52
1982	Saxon Industries, Inc.	503.0	461.1	7.2	9,800	31.0	4,093
1982	KDT Industries, Inc.	239.0	203.0	7.3	7,100	—	—
1982	Manville Corp.	2200.0	1100.0	28.6	52,000	—	—
1982	Leisure Time Products, Inc.	5.9	2.7	3.1	2,113	—	—
1982	McLouth Steel Corp. (1)	435.5	322.8	5.5	6,000	—	—
1982	Spaulding Bakeries	9.4	8.7	.4	320	—	—

| | | ASSETS & LIABILITIES | | PUBLIC INTEREST | | | |
| | | | | EQUITY | | DEBT | |
FILING DATE	COMPANY	ASSETS (MILLIONS)	LIABILITIES (MILLIONS)	SHARES (MILLIONS)	HOLDERS	AMOUNT (MILLIONS)	HOLDERS
1982	Kenilworth Systems Corp.	1.4	1.0	9.2	2,500	—	—
1982	Medserco, Inc.	2.8	3.1	4.4	1,199	—	—
1982	Carnegie International	4.3	1.2	3.9	6,600	—	—
1982	Proprietors' Corp. (1)	4.9	15.8	—	—	—	—
1982	McCoy Industries	—	—	—	—	—	—
1982	Hyperion, Inc.	—	—	—	—	—	—
1982	Bennett Petroleum	4.5	5.2	—	—	—	—
1982	United Financial Oper. Inc.	—	—	—	—	—	—
1982	Oklahoma Gasohol, Inc.	4.9	2.0	5.5	1,117	—	—
1982	Petro West Inc.	—	—	—	—	—	—
1982	C.S. Group Inc.	12.0	8.6	2.3	989	—	—
1982	All American Burger, Inc.	1.2	.170	2.6	823	—	—
1982	International Diamond Corp.	15.0	12.0	—	—	—	—
1982	Haven Properties, Inc.	3.0	3.0	.001	2	2.0	300
1982	Stewart Energy Systems	2.0	5.5	—	—	4.5	350
1982	Bear Lake West	7.8	7.8	—	—	—	1,800
1982	Fashion Two-Twenty, Inc.	3.0	1.8	1.4	1,900	—	—
1982	Bobbie Brooks, Inc.	90.0	62.0	4.5	7,000	—	—
1982	Wilnor Drilling Inc.	12.5	13.4	—	—	7.5	415
1982	Colonial Discount Corp.	23.1	9.9	3.1	1,653	9.6	1,200
1982	Mid-American Lines Inc.	9.3	8.2	.7	824	—	—
1982	AM International	476.7	519.7	10.2	11,450	465.0	8,000
1982	Tax Info Ctr./P & K Fry	1.2	1.6	—	—	—	—
1982	UNR Industries	232.6	165.0	3.7	2,900	—	—

1982	Shelter Resources	20.8	24.0	4.0	5,110	11.0	—
1982	Lewis Energy Corporation	31.3	30.2	12.0	3,006	—	—
1982	Empire Oil & Gas Co.	41.3	39.0	20.9	5,779	—	—
1982	Braniff International	1008.0	1102.0	—	33,000	—	—
1982	Dreco Energy Service Ltd.	220.8	161.2	9.2	1,783	15.2	—
1982	Atlas Mortgage Loan Co.	38.0	46.0	—	2	—	2,600
1982	Sambo's Restaurants, Inc.	400.8	376.9	12.8	13,705	—	—
1982	Wickes Companies	1705.3	1376.5	14.2	26,079	—	—
1982	Nucorp Energy Inc.	777.1	603.6	28.2	10,295	119.1	—
1982	Super Stores, Inc.	.802	1.1	.36	617	—	—
1982	Captran Resorts Int'l, Inc.	.122	—	—	—	—	—
1982	Holistic Services Corp.	.167	1.1	—	300	—	—
1982	Unistat Corp.	—	.562	—	—	—	—
1982	Swiss Chalet Inc.	3.4	.71	.71	756	—	—
1982	Invesco Internat'l Corp.	7.0	6.5	2.1	500	—	—
1982	Farmer in the Dell Inc. (2)	.56	.14	.41	—	—	—
1982	RPS Products Inc.	6.0	7.0	1.2	1,081	—	—
1982	Morton Shoe Co., Inc.	23.0	16.9	1.5	1,342	—	—
1982	Data Dimension, Inc.	2.8	1.7	1.2	900	—	—
1982	Vermont REIT	—	—	—	—	—	—
1982	Bicycle Technology Corp.	.276	.425	1.2	119	—	—
1982	Elan Air Corp.	.100	.729	—	—	—	—
1982	Gamex Industries, Inc.	2.6	2.5	4.1	3,000	—	—
1982	Gilman Services	32.5	30.2	2.6	704	—	—
1982	Iotron Corp.	2.1	5.8	4.6	123	—	—
1982	Bodin Apparel, Inc.	1.7	5.6	2.1	690	—	—
1982	Barclay Ind., Inc.	5.1	8.0	1.4	735	—	—
1982	Stevecoknit, Inc.	24.9	25.0	2.1	836	—	—
1982	AFI Corp.	.71	1.1	1.5	746	—	—

FILING DATE	COMPANY	ASSETS & LIABILITIES		PUBLIC INTEREST			
				EQUITY		DEBT	
		ASSETS (MILLIONS)	LIABILITIES (MILLIONS)	SHARES (MILLIONS)	HOLDERS	AMOUNT (MILLIONS)	HOLDERS
1982	Internt'l Picture Show Co.	.5	2.0	2.0	1,000	—	—
1982	Cooper-Jarrett, Inc.	21.0	28.0	.75	1,300	—	—
1982	Quote Me., Inc.	3.7	7.7	.2	230	—	—
1982	Allvend Ind., Inc.	2.2	3.5	1.1	350	—	—
1982	Standard Dredging Corp.	1.7	2.9	1.1	2,200	—	—
1982	Fidelity Electric Co., Inc.	—	—	—	—	—	—
1982	J.W. Mays, Inc.	38.9	20.1	2.2	5,400	—	—
1982	P.K. Management Corp.	2.6	—	3.6	2,328	—	—
1982	Heywood-Wakefield Co.	18.0	18.4	.18	833	—	—
1982	Interlakes Finance	—	—	—	—	—	—
1982	Mego International Inc.	46.0	49.0	2.3	1,300	12.7	500
1982	Nano Data Computer	8.1	5.9	4.2	107	—	—
1982	Pubco Corp	19.0	17.0	3.6	5,793	1.2	—
1982	Fantasy Island, Inc.	.2	.06	.06	704	—	—
1982	Major Pool Equipment Corp.	4.6	5.3	.7	652	—	—
1983	South Atlantic Fin. Corp.	28.7	20.4	2.7	3,947	18.7	730
1983	Revere Copper & Brass Inc.	402.0	237.0	5.7	3,912	43.4	1,643
1983	HRT Industries Inc.	233.5	183.7	3.5	2,192	—	—
1983	Q-1 Corporation	.6	2.8	3.8	641	—	—
1983	Marva Industries Inc.	2.1	3.7	.7	281	—	—
1983	Video To Go Inc.	.7	5.3	1.1	300	—	—
1983	Threshold Technology, Inc.	1.9	1.5	3.0	1,200	—	—
1983	American Polymers, Inc.	3.5	4.5	.43	234	—	—

Year	Company						
1983	Comco Centurian Oil & Mineral	.19	.76	4.1			—
1983	Foundation Financial Corp.	.5	.62	3.7	2,518		—
1983	Data Access Systems, Inc.	39.0	47.0	3.3	3,200		—
1983	Magnetic Core Corp.	.3	.8	1.2	930		—
1983	Orth-O Vision	.3	.26	.2	305		—
1983	DeLorean Motor Co.	—	—	—	—		—
1983	Robert C. Labine/Pro. Assoc.						
1983	Briggs Transportation	19.5	24.7	1.8	2,406		—
1983	Leisure Dynamics	37.0	37.0	2.5	1,200		—
1983	Energy Sources, Inc.						
1983	Richmond Leasing Co.						
1983	Search Drilling Co.	39.5	64.6	—	—	—	340
1983	Flight Transportation Co.	56.4	32.6	4.3	3,038	.5	664
1983	Amarex Inc.	373.3	325.4	8.8	1,550	30.0	5,000
1983	North American Coin & Cur.	37.9	24.7	—	9	21.0	5,000
1983	Invesco International Corp.	7.0	6.5	2.1	500	—	—
1983	Newport General Corp.	6.0	5.6	1.6	1,100	—	—

(1) Plan of reorganization confirmed.
(2) Converted to Chapter 7.
(3) Petition dismissed.

IV

The Informed Decision

11

How to Read a
Financial Report

Examining financial information has never been a favorite pastime for nonfinancial readers. One of the most important sources of information for the individual investor, however, should be examined here. It's called an *annual report,* and it's not that difficult to decipher.

Annual reports use this standard format: the good news is in the front, surrounded by glossy pictures, and the bad news is in the back, hidden in the financial figures and footnotes that most investors fail to read. Amateurs read an annual report from front to back; professionals read from back to front.

What can you learn about a company from its annual financial report? A lot. The two main elements are the *income statement* ("profit and loss" statement), which tells us how much money the company made or lost in the past year, and the *balance sheet,* which is a snapshot of all the company's assets and liabilities on the last day of its year. (The company's fiscal year may be different from the calendar year.)

Although annual reports are by no means the only source of information that you'll need to investigate a company (they're outdated by the time they even come out), they are an excellent place to start. Even though these expensive brochures are written by the companies themselves, with public relations always in mind, strict SEC reporting requirements make all financial reports a reliable source of information.

Walking through a typical corporation's report should be particularly helpful to readers of this book since much of the investment strategy presented here is based on an understanding of the basic financial makeup of the corporations being examined. So the following pages will be a guided walking tour through the back pages (the ones without the pictures) of a corporation's yearly report to its stockholders. My goal will be to make these multifigure columns not only understandable, but interesting and revealing to the nonbusiness reader. They're really not that bad.

Below are some of the terms that we'll come across on our tour. You have probably heard them all, but perhaps are not exactly sure what they mean. Besides being good vocabulary for cocktail conversation when it turns to the subject of investments, these are words that I would call the eleven most important things to know about your company:

1. debt structure
2. working capital
3. book value
4. capitalization
5. margin (operating margin of profit and net profit ratio)
6. earnings per share: primary and fully diluted, and price-earnings (PE) ratio
7. leverage
8. retained earnings
9. dividends, dividend payment ratio
10. cash flow
11. return on equity (ROE)

Now we'll see what we can find out about each of these in an annual report. To make this a little more meaningful, refer to the sample financial statements at the end of this chapter as you read along.

• THE BALANCE SHEET •

As an investment adviser, I am often asked what a company's balance sheet looks like. Let's find out what this part of a company's financial statement tells us. A balance sheet is a statement of the company's financial condition on one specific day (the last day of its fiscal year). It tells us what the company owns (assets), what it owes (liabilities), and the difference between the two (which is known as stockholders' equity). What balances on a balance sheet is this: Total liabilities plus stockholders' equity always equals total assets.

The assets of a company include not only property and investments currently owned by the company, but also money owed the company. Liabilities include all its debts. If our company were to close its doors, sell off all its assets, and pay off all its debts, the amount of money left over represents the stockholders' equity.

ASSETS

Let's take a closer look at a typical company's assets. There are two types represented on its balance sheet: *current assets* and *fixed assets*. Current assets are the company's most liquid holdings, such as cash, bank accounts, securities, accounts receivable and inventories. The *securities* that most companies hold for their own accounts are simply money-market instruments that can be easily converted to cash. The *accounts receivable* entry on a balance sheet generally represents money owed to the company over the next three months, minus an allowance for bad debts. *Inventory* entries include both raw materials and unsold products held by the company. The total current assets are also known as *working assets* because they are the most fluid part of the company's business cycle: inventories are sold and become accounts receivable that are collected and placed in marketable securities, which eventually turn into cash.

Fixed assets (sometimes known as "property, plant and equipment") consist of the permanent assets of the company that are used in making its products. They include buildings, land, equipment, and machinery, among other things. The value of fixed assets is usually stated on the balance sheet as the original (acquisition) cost minus any depreciation of the asset since its purchase.

Depreciation is the constant deterioration of value on fixed assets that results from use, time, and obsolescence. The amount of depreciation figured for the purpose of a balance sheet (and for tax purposes) depends on the useful life expectancy of the particular asset. An item known as *prepayments* may be found on a balance sheet. This entry represents an advance payment that the company has made for goods or services not yet received. The reason for the balance sheet entry is that if the prepayment had not been made, this same amount of money would still be listed under current assets (cash).

Deferred charges represent expenses incurred in the current year for projects (i.e., research and development) that will provide longer term benefits to the company. The final entry found on our sample balance sheet's list of assets is known as *intangibles*. This item may include any asset that is not quantitatively measurable, such as a patent, trademark, or even goodwill. The company's valuation of this entry often requires some creative thinking.

LIABILITIES

Liabilities and *stockholders' equity* are what balance against assets on a balance sheet. Like the assets column, the liabilities column is divided into two parts: current and long-term. *Current liabilities* are simply the company's short-term debts, what it owes over the next twelve months. As you might have guessed, these debts are paid with money from the other side of the balance sheet (out of current assets).

Like current assets, current liabilities can be subdivided into various categories. *Accounts payable* are comparable to accounts receivable; this is money owed to the company's regular creditors, due within the next few months. Debts owed to banks or other lenders for short-term loans are listed here as *notes payable.* Unpaid operating expenses, such as payroll and interest payments, are listed as *accrued expenses payable. Federal income tax payable* is usually listed separately under current liabilities.

Bonds are simply another form of debt that a company might have. When a company issues a bond because it needs more money, it promises to repay its bondholders on a specific date and pay a certain rate of interest until then. Since bond debts are generally payable in more than twelve months, they are listed separately on the balance sheet as *long-term liabilities.*

STOCKHOLDERS' EQUITY

Just as you and I have, a company has a net worth that is the result of its total liabilities being subtracted from its total assets. Since this amount represents the net value that is actually owned by the company's stockholders, it is known as *stockholders' equity.* This entry appears on the liability side of the balance sheet because it represents the investors' claim (a liability) on the corporation.

A company's equity is made up of three elements of value: *capital stock, capital surplus,* and *accumulated retained earnings.* Capital stock consists of all shares of ownership, common or preferred, which make up the company. (The various classes of stocks and bonds are explained in the next chapter.) Capital surplus is the excess amount between the "par value" of the common stock and the actual price at which the company issued its original stock. For example, if a company issued a million shares of stock at $10 per share that has a stated par value of $5 per share (par is a totally arbitrary value for common stocks), then that company would have common stock valued at $5 million and capital surplus worth another $5 million. (The stock's actual value on the market has no reflection on either of these two balance sheet entries. Market value is the reflection of a multitude of factors, and the result of what investors are willing to pay for the company's shares at that particular time.)

Accumulated retained earnings is the total amount of money that the company has ever earned (net earnings after expenses and taxes) that has not been paid out to stockholders in the form of dividends. Thus the value of the stockholders' ownership of the company is found in each of the above items, which combined are called stockholders' equity.

INTERPRETING THE BALANCE SHEET

We have examined the three parts of every company's balance sheet: assets, liabilities and stockholders' equity. This information can tell us a lot about the financial condition of a company. In the next few pages we will take a look at a few ways that we can use this information to become more familiar with the prospects of our company. The next time you are asked what a certain company's balance sheet looks like, here are a few items that might come in handy:

1. *Working capital* is the amount of available cash that a company has (current assets minus current liabilities), and is an important determinant of the company's ability to take advantage of opportunities quickly. Although cash requirements vary from industry to industry, analysts generally like to see a *current ratio* of 2:1 (twice as much current assets as current liabilities).

2. You may have heard the term *quick assets*. Not nearly as exciting as they sound, these are simply the company's most liquid assets (its current assets not including inventories). "Net quick assets" is a measurement of the company's ability to meet its obligations on short notice and is determined by subtracting current liabilities from quick assets.

3. *Book value* is one of the most important corporate measurements indicated by a balance sheet. Book value, or asset value, tells us how much assets are backing each security (stock and bond) of the company. The value at which a company carries its assets on its books, incidentally, may be vastly different from its current market value. Real estate bought by a company twenty years ago may still be carried on its books at the original purchase price even though it's now worth much more. A totally antiquated factory, on the other hand, may be worth only a fraction of its stated value on the books.

A vitally important question throughout this book is the ability of a company to pay off its bondholders in the case of bankruptcy and liquidation. A quick look at the company's balance sheet gives us some idea of the answer. Assuming that current liabilities will be paid first, we subtract these debts as well as any intangible assets (goodwill isn't very valuable in a bankruptcy proceeding) from total assets to see what is left to bondholder creditors. If what is left is less than the total amount of face-value bonds outstanding, which is usually the case with a troubled company, then the hierarchy of the various classes of bonds becomes important.

Preferred stockholders are in line behind all bondholders in liquidations. Net asset value per share of preferred stock is determined by subtracting long-term liabilities (bonds) as well as current liabilities and intangibles from total assets. Only after all bondholders and preferred stockholders are paid off, would common stockholders receive anything in a corporate liquidation. The net assets behind each share of common stock is what we are usually referring to with the term *book value* or just *book*. The simplest way to arrive at net book value per share of common stock is by subtracting preferred stock and intangibles from stockholders' equity, and dividing the remainder by the number of common shares outstanding.

Remember that the relationship between book value and the current market price of a share of stock varies tremendously from industry to industry because of the way certain assets are valued for the purposes of balance sheet accounting. A stock selling for only half book is not necessarily a bargain; twice book is not necessarily too high. An antiquated steel mill may be worth nothing in a real marketplace, despite its original book value. Prime commercial real estate, on the other hand, may be worth much more than its original value.

4. The total *capitalization* of a company consists of its stockholders' equity (preferred and common stock, capital surplus, and accumulated retained earnings) plus its bonds. The percentage of capitalization that each one of these securities makes up, especially the bonds, is of interest to the securities analyst. Too high a debt (bonds) ratio, for example, can be a warning signal to stockholders.

• THE INCOME STATEMENT •

The balance sheet gave us a look at a typical company's assets and liabilities—what it owns and what it owes—on the last day of its year. Now let's have a look at the typical *income statement*. This statement will tell us how much money the company took in, how much it spent, and what its net profit or loss was, over a full-year period. This information can be even more important to an investor as a factor in determining value.

The first entry on any income statement is *net sales* (sometimes called operating revenues). This is simply the total amount of money received over the year from sales of goods or services.

The second entry tells us what it cost to bring in these

revenues. Depending on the industry they are in, companies may list their *costs of sales and operating expenses* in a variety of ways. *Costs of goods sold* should be the largest category under costs since it includes such major items as labor, operating expenses, supplies, and raw materials. Since companies write off the cost of plant and equipment over a number of years, *depreciation* of these items is taken as an expense each year, just as if it were additional cash being paid out. *Selling and administrative expenses* include advertising, sales commissions, and administrative salaries. If you subtract all the above costs and operating expenses from net sales, the first entry, you get what's called *operating profit*.

From here we have one more income item and two more expense items before we arrive at a net profit or loss figure for the year. If the company has *dividend or interest income* from investments of its own, this item is now added to operating profit, giving us *total income*. The two expense items now deducted are *bond interest* (interest paid out to bondholders of the company) and *federal income taxes*. The final result of all the income and expense items on the income statement is *net profit* or *net income*. This figure is then divided by the number of shares of common stock outstanding to determine the *net earnings per share*.

INTERPRETING THE INCOME STATEMENT

As the balance sheet tells us much about a company's financial health, the income statement is very revealing in areas of profitability and efficiency.

1. You have probably heard the term *profit margin*. Operating margin of profit is simply the percentage of sales (total revenues) that the company's operating profit represents. If a company has $20 million in sales for a year and its operating profit (before paying out taxes and interest on its bonds) was $2 million, then it is said to have had a 10% "margin" that year. Another measurement of profitability is *net profit ratio:* the percentage of sales that is represented by net profits (after taxes and interest). The same company might have net profits of $1 million, which would represent a net profit ratio of 5 percent. This means that the company actually kept only 5¢ on every dollar of revenue it took in. This information is meaningful only if it is used to compare that company to another company in the same industry.

2. A company's ability to pay its fixed expenses of bond interest and preferred stock dividends is of great concern to analysts and investors. A comparison should be made between interest expense and total income (since bond interest is paid before taxes). A company's total income should be several times its interest expense for safe coverage. Then compare preferred dividend expenses to net profit (since dividends are paid out after taxes). This coverage should be even greater for comfort.

3. We ended our discussion of the balance sheet by looking at capitalization ratios: the relationship of a company's various classes of securities (bonds, preferred and common stocks) to its overall makeup (capitalization). A company that has a high proportion of bonds is called highly *leveraged.* A high degree of leverage works well when earnings increase from one year to the next, but a decline in earnings can be dangerous for the company with large fixed interest expenses. Many investors avoid companies with a high percentage of debt.

4. Sometimes a company will have a profit or loss resulting from a particular event which is not apt to occur again. Such an unusual item might be an expense that results from some natural disaster or income that results from the sale of some asset. Since such events are nonrecurring, they are labeled *extraordinary items* and are listed separately on an income statement.

5. The single most important determinant of value for a healthy company's common stock (not so in distress and bankruptcy cases) is *earnings per share:* how much net profit is represented by a single share of stock. Unfortunately, there are two ways to figure earnings. *Primary earnings* per share simply measure the total net profit by the number of common shares currently outstanding. *Fully diluted earnings* per share, however, divide those same profits by not only the current common share, but by all the common shares that could be created by convertible securities, warrants, and stock options. Since the creation of more shares of common stock would "dilute" the company's earnings, considering this measurement is very important.

6. The relationship between the price of a stock and its earnings per share—either primary or fully diluted—is of great concern to most investors. Price divided by earnings gives us a price-earnings ratio, better known as just PE.

• ACCUMULATED RETAINED • EARNINGS STATEMENT

This small but important section of an annual report tells us how much money has been reinvested in a company during the past year. (These funds are then put to use in an attempt to strengthen the company and further increase its earnings.)

To determine the total retained earnings at the end of the year, we must begin with the previous year's total, add the new year's net profit (which is stated just above on the income statement), then subtract all dividends paid on both common and preferred stock. The result is the new year-end figure for the total amount of money that has ever been plowed back into the company.

There are two things that we can learn about the company's common stock dividend from this section of the annual report: how much per share is being paid, and what percentage of net earnings those dividends constitute. To get dividends per share, simply divide the total divi-dend (common) payment by the number of shares outstanding. Then you can divide this figure by the company's earnings per share to find out how much of its earnings are being paid out to stockholders and how much are being retained. Some industries, such as utilities, traditionally pay out most of what they earn each year. Other industries are more growth oriented and pay little or no dividends.

• STATEMENT OF SOURCE AND • APPLICATION OF FUNDS

The final section of a typical balance sheet gives us a brief summary of where the company's money came from and where it went, in the fiscal year that just ended. The company's *cash flow* is considered to be a combination of its net profits (the bottom line of the income statement) and depreciation (an item listed under costs on the income statement). The reason that the depreciation is added back in to determine actual cash flow is that this entry was never a real cash outlay to begin with. Depreciation is simply a bookkeeping entry which represents a decline in value and useful life of fixed assets. Cash flow, then, is the actual amount of money that the company ended up with at the end of the year after all expenses.

This section then tells us where the cash flow went, and how much was left over to increase the company's *working capital* (a balance sheet item). Here the report summarizes the dividend payments for both common and preferred stock, and then tells us how much was invested in new assets. The difference between cash flow and the above expenditures determines the change in working capital.

This change in the year's working capital (current assets minus current liabilities = working capital) is reflected on the balance sheet and summarized in a separate section of the annual report. Here we find out exactly where the company's new working capital was distributed by way of increasing current assets of decreasing current liabilities.

A final corporate measurement that analysts always take in the continuous search for value is called *return on equity*. This equation tells us how hard an investor's money is working in the company: how much profit was made by the company compared to the amount of stockholders' equity which makes up ownership of the company. The average return on equity (often abbreviated as ROE) for major corporations today is about 12%, which means that the company earns twelve cents for every dollar of the owners' equity. Higher ROEs, however, indicate superior management performance, rapid growth, and less dependence on outside financing for future expansion. Investors should compare a company's return not only to other corporations, but also to the returns available on other investment opportunities, such as bonds and money-market instruments.

• AUDITS, FOOTNOTES, AND SUMMARIES •

In the back of every annual report is a certification from some accounting firm that the information in the report is a fair representation of the company's financial condition and that the auditing methods used therein conformed to "generally accepted accounting principles." It's not unusual, however, to find the *auditor's approval* qualified by information pertaining to some of the data presented in the report or to some pending event (i.e., a court case) which could alter parts of the data in the report. Approximately one out of every eight annual reports contains only qualified or contingent auditors' opinions.

In the beginning of this chapter, I mentioned that amateurs read annual reports from front to back and that professionals read them from back to front. Here I might add that the real professional reads them from back to front, starting with the *footnotes*. Footnotes are an integral part of the whole report and usually contain information that is essential to assessing the company accurately. Two major factors that affect a company's reported earnings can be easily interpreted by checking the footnotes: how the company figures its inventory prices and how it depreciates its assets. A conservative accounting practice today attempts to minimize the effect of inflation on inventory profits (for years earnings were artificially increased by inflation) and understates earnings by taking rapid depreciation of its fixed assets. It is easy for a company to inflate its earnings by doing just the opposite, but its reporting methods must be explained in the ever-important footnotes.

Even more important than the current year figures that we find on a balance sheet and income statement are the longer-term trends that can be found in five or ten year *financial summaries*. These abbreviated tables often appear in annual reports; a similar table can be found on the Standard and Poor's report that all stockbrokers provide. Many of the trends and patterns developed over the years are essential to know. Find out what the company's earnings trend looks like, particularly during years of difficulty in its industry. Its profit margin tells us a lot about its management's ability to run the company efficiently. "Summaries," as they are often called, also may show us longer-term patterns of return on equity (ROE), dividend payments, debt structure, book value, net profit, and working capital.

SAMPLE ANNUAL REPORT

Blue Ridge Real Estate Company and Subsidiaries and Big Boulder Corporation

COMBINED BALANCE SHEETS
Through May 31, 1983 and 1982

ASSETS

	1983	1982
Current assets:		
Cash (including interest-bearing amounts of $1,635,616 in 1983 and $1,250,830 in 1982)	$ 1,729,765	$ 1,441,150
Current installments of mortgage notes receivable............	363,617	120,039
Accounts and accrued interest receivable	109,707	61,328
Prepaid expenses	68,002	75,907
Total current assets.........	2,271,091	1,698,424
Mortgage notes receivable, less current installments	281,409	414,624
Properties:		
Land, principally unimproved (1983, 30,482 acres per land ledger)	1,480,485	1,459,161
Land improvements..........	821,809	820,534
Corporate buildings	331,478	282,918
Office buildings leased to others, including land of $333,428 in 1983 and 1982.............	3,629,918	3,615,749
Ski facilities	9,864,327	8,883,620
Equipment	216,165	196,710
Improvements in progress	133,041	258,066
	16,477,223	15,516,758
Less accumulated depreciation.	6,146,846	5,381,315
	10,330,377	10,135,443
	$12,882,877	$12,248,491

LIABILITIES AND SHAREHOLDERS' EQUITY

	1983	1982
Current liabilities:		
Current installments of long-term debt......................	$ 588,829	$ 566,531
Accounts payable	119,838	113,535
Interest and other accrued liabilities...................	298,769	256,653
Accrued income taxes	41,818	361,369
Deferred income taxes	112,900	36,200
Total current liabilities	1,162,154	1,334,288
Long-term debt, less current installments	3,983,183	4,108,458
Deferred income taxes	1,260,865	1,109,465
Combined shareholders' equity:		
Capital stock, without par value, stated value $.30 per combined share. Blue Ridge and Big Boulder each have authorized 3,000,000 shares and each have issued 2,198,148 shares in 1983 and 1982	659,444	659,444
Capital in excess of stated value .	1,461,748	1,461,748
Earnings retained in the business	4,355,483	3,575,088
	6,476,675	5,696,280
	$12,882,877	$12,248,491

COMBINED STATEMENTS OF INCOME

Years ended May 31,	1983	1982*	1981*
Revenues:			
Ski facilities............	$4,086,466	$4,172,165	$3,453,355
Real estate management and rental operations .	1,029,085	904,273	778,206
Disposition of land	1,043,782	618,202	507,400
Land and land improvements, rentals, royalties, etc.................	219,327	202,503	203,913
	6,378,660	5,897,143	4,942,874
Costs and expenses:			
Operating costs........	4,009,530	3,635,390	3,146,132
Cost of properties disposed and related expenses .	171,528	61,260	110,779
General and administrative expenses............	799,578	626,728	519,639
	4,980,636	4,323,378	3,776,550
Income from operations .	1,398,024	1,573,765	1,166,324
Other income (expense):			
Interest and other income..............	220,064	247,254	145,283
Interest expense (less $16,429, $33,540, and $21,599 capitalized in 1983, 1982 and 1981, respectively)	(515,093)	(490,392)	(361,280)
	(295,029)	(243,138)	(215,997)
Income before income taxes	1,102,995	1,330,627	950,327
Provision for income taxes:			
Current	94,500	409,200	285,500
Deferred	228,100	36,900	99,800
	322,600	446,100	385,300
Net income	$ 780,395	$ 884,527	$ 565,027
Earnings per average combined share	$ .36	$ .40	$ .26

COMBINED STATEMENTS OF EARNINGS RETAINED IN THE BUSINESS

Years ended May 31,	1983	1982	1981
Beginning of year	$3,575,088	3,351,243	$2,786,216
Net income	780,395	884,527	565,027
4% stock dividend	—	(660,682)	—
End of year..............	$4,355,483	$3,575,088	$3,351,243

COMBINED STATEMENTS OF CHANGES IN FINANCIAL POSITION

Years ended May 31,	1983	1982	1981
Working capital was provided by: Operations:			
Net income............	$ 780,395	$ 884,527	$ 565,027
Add items not requiring working capital in the current period:			
Depreciation.........	797,685	715,456	596,854
Deferred income taxes	151,400	107,350	99,200
Working capital provided by operations	1,729,480	1,707,333	1,261,081
Dispositions of land	155,796	32,462	68,358
Additional long-term debt .	499,677	1,724,596	1,051,608
Reductions of long-term receivables	210,746	425,312	159,807
Other	—	20,265	—
	2,595,699	3,909,968	2,540,854

Working capital was used for:

Additions to properties, net	1,148,415	2,112,299	1,424,384
Reductions of long-term debt	624,952	1,605,035	573,628
Investment in long-term receivables	77,531	332,594	. 303,875
	1,850,898	4,049,928	2,301,887
Increase (decrease) in working capital	744,801	(139,960)	238,967
Working capital, beginning of year	364,136	504,096	265,129
Working capital, end of year .	$1,108,937	$ 364,136	$ 504,096

Component increases (decreases) in working capital:

Cash	288,615	90,733	631,742
Receivables	291,957	(53,885)	43,103
Prepaid expenses	(7,905)	(4,268)	(48,235)
Current installments of long-term debt	(22,298)	(50,512)	(156,015)
Accounts payable and accrued liabilities	(48,419)	(48,860)	32,230
Accrued and deferred income taxes	242,851	(75,168)	(263,858)
	$ 744,801	$(139,960)	$ 238,967

12

Before You Invest

No investment book is complete without a chapter that connects the specific subject of the book with how that information actually fits the reader's overall financial plans. While this is not a general investment or financial planning book by any means, the integration of a Phoenix portfolio into your total financial plan should be conducted with care.

It has always surprised me—given the level of importance and anxiety that we attach to the subject of money—how little attention most people pay to their own personal money management. Even people who are directly involved with financial matters in their professional lives often neglect to take even the basic steps—such as tax planning and investment planning—toward keeping their hard-earned money working the best it can.

There are only three ways to get richer than you are now: by earning more money, by paying less taxes, and by investing more wisely. Unfortunately, I cannot help you much in the first category (although I am convinced that anyone who wants to can make a lot of money). Neither can I be of much help to you regarding your taxes, although there is no lack of information available on that subject. I do hope, however, that I have been helpful in getting you to *invest* more wisely.

The money that you invest in securities should be money that you can afford to risk and that you don't need for anything else. In the next few pages I will identify the money that you should earmark for Phoenix investing and try to establish the place that these funds should take in your overall financial plans. Before you even think about investing in stocks, you should already have the following needs taken care of:

Savings. Our most basic financial need is to have a certain amount of cash on hand for unexpected expenses as well as for routine living costs. There is now a wide range of places to store cash, all of which are safe and liquid. Bank money funds, broker money funds, and super-NOW accounts each pay competitive rates, have little or no fees and restrictions, and carry check-writing privileges.

How much you need to have completely safe and liquid depends entirely on your own situation. Family expenses, taxes, stability of income, sources of credit, and other factors should all be considered in figuring how much you need "in the bank." If you can't pin it down, stay on the conservative side.

Safe Money. In addition to your cash-on-hand money, you should have some back-up money that's almost as safe and almost as liquid. This is money that you don't expect to ever need, but that you could turn into cash on short notice if you needed to.

You should be able to get a higher interest rate on this money by going with longer-term maturity investments (although I would not exceed about eight years in maturity). For lower tax bracket investors I would recommend six- to eight-year certificates of deposit, treasury bonds, or high grade ("A" or better) NYSE-listed corporate bonds. The CDs can be redeemed at face value at any time (with an interest penalty), and the bonds can be quickly sold on the open market if the money is needed before maturity. The relatively short-term maturity date will help protect your bond principal in case interest rates rise after your purchase. (Twenty and thirty year maturities are much riskier.)

For higher tax bracket investors (40% and up), I would recommend high grade, new issue, municipal bonds from your own home state, also with relatively short maturity dates. New issues save you money on dealer mark-ups and result in a better interest rate. Buying in your own state will make your income free from state taxes, as well as federal. Since tax-free bonds have been paying about three quarters the rate that equal-quality and equal-maturity taxable bonds pay, municipals are really a bargain for higher bracket investors.

Insurance. As boring as the subject is, life insurance is an absolute necessity for most of us. Unfortunately, most people are either covered inadequately or are paying too much to get adequate protection.

"Term" insurance makes much more sense than "whole life." With term insurance, you get nothing but straight coverage; with whole life you also get tied into a low-interest savings plan. Despite what your insurance agent might tell you (whole life is much more profitable for him), whole life is a bad deal: big penalties for discontinuing, much higher costs, much more complicated policies, and very low interest rates.

Save money by buying renewable term insurance (guaranteed to be renewed despite your health), and invest the savings wisely for your later years when insurance costs will be higher. Your own company may have the best rate with a group term policy that you can plug into. A thirty-year-old should be able to buy $100,000 of life insurance for under $185 a year; a forty-year-old for about $260; a fifty-year-old for about $520. Adequate insurance coverage for your family should precede any stock market investments.

IRAs. The opening up of IRA eligibility in 1982 was the

most important change in our retirement system since Social Security started in 1936. The emphasis is now on self-reliance; don't depend on either the government or your employer to provide adequate income for you during your retirement years. An IRA is a great supplement to whatever other retirement plan you might have, and you don't have to pay any fees, take any risks, or have any minimum amount of money to get started.

I predict that IRAs will eventually replace real estate as the main source of personal wealth in this country. With the $2,000 maximum contribution almost sure to be raised (Keoghs have come from $1,250 all the way to $30,000 per year), IRA assets in this country will be immense. Try compounding $100 billion (a $5,000 contribution limit would bring in this amount annually) a year for thirty years. Don't underestimate this opportunity in your tax planning each year; it may be the best shelter and savings deal you'll ever get.

Other Retirement Plans. There are a number of other retirement plans that offer tax-sheltering opportunities that are hard to refuse. Your company may offer you a "salary reduction plan" or a "deferred compensation plan," both of which put some of your income to work for you—tax deferred—until a later date. Many corporations also offer an attractive thrift or savings plan into which a company-matched contribution can be placed directly from your pay check. Even though there are no tax benefits with these plans, most are very generous.

If you are self-employed, you should certainly consider a Keogh plan (with its new $30,000 contribution limit) or your own pension/profit-sharing plan (if you are incorporated).

Keep in mind that with many of these plans—IRAs, Keoghs, pension and profit-sharing accounts—you can invest in stocks and bonds. Many people think that an IRA, for example, is some kind of specific investment itself, such as a stock or a bond or an option. But an IRA, like a Keogh, is simply the *account* into which you may put almost any kind of investment that you choose. There is no reason why you couldn't be a Phoenix investor with tax deferred money.

Credit. Every investor should have an available line of credit before committing money to the market. An unexpected major expense or a sudden rare investment opportunity is no time to have to choose between a lengthy loan procedure and an untimely portfolio liquidation.

To start with, talk to your banker. You can set up a personal line of credit, based on your own financial statement, that you can draw on whenever you need to. Also talk to your broker. Some of the large financial companies are now offering attractive loans against home equity. A typical arrangement is this: an open line of credit for ten years on 70% of your net equity, at a floating interest rate based on prime. Finally, most recovery securities themselves are marginable; your broker will lend against them.

Home. Home ownership has always been a great American dream. But the 1980s have so far proven to be the most difficult time since the Depression for most people to accomplish this goal. With mortgage rates still very high and prices at stratospheric levels after the inflationary 1970s, most first-time buyers (without the help of equity in another house) are just shocked at what it takes to buy the home they want.

Most financial advisers recommend home ownership before stock market investments. As a general rule, this advice is probably still valid. But as an investment, I feel that the value of home ownership in the 1980s is questionable, unless the rate of inflation spirals upward once again. Throughout the 1970s, with high inflation and low interest rates, home ownership was an ideal investment: a leveraged, tax-sheltered, inflation hedge. But today, you should buy a house only for one reason—because you really want to live in it. Don't think of it as a great investment, and don't get in over your head thinking that price appreciation will bail you out; it might not.

I also don't see anything wrong with renters owning securities at this time, for two reasons. First of all, I feel that "financial instruments" will outperform tangible investments in the 1980s. Secondly, it's a lot cheaper to rent than to own these days, and the difference can be put to work more productively in terms of building your own assets. A $200,000 house today will cost you about $40,000 to $50,000 in cash and over $2,000 a month in payments. Depending on the area, the same house might be rented for only $600 to $800 per month, with no cash outlay at all. The difference is significant.

We have briefly reviewed a few of the basic financial priorities that you should feel comfortable with before even considering stocks and bonds. There are exceptions, of course, to each of the items mentioned above.

The Phoenix Approach is by no means a get-rich-quick scheme. The money that you commit to this investment plan should be considered long-term money, not in-and-out money. The Phoenix Approach is concerned with buying value: underpriced assets. Think of this money as the same money that you would use to buy a troubled local business that you feel has tremendous potential and that can be bought for far less than it's really worth.

The purpose of this chapter has been to identify the money that you should earmark for investing in securities —especially of depressed companies—and to get a better feel for where these investments fit into your overall financial picture.

13

The Great Recession (1980–1982)

The battered end of corporate America is the result of the harshest recession this country has seen since the Great Depression. The 1980–1982 economy brought corporate and financial America to the very brink of disaster. There were more corporate bankruptcies in 1982 and 1983, for example, than in any years since the early 1930s (over 50,000 failures in '82 and '83). The number of publicly traded (stock) companies alone that filed for protection under Chapter 11 of the bankruptcy code in 1982 and 1983 stands at a staggering one hundred and fifty-eight. The number of publicly traded companies that reported losses during that same period was, of course, much higher: Two hundred and thirty-four NYSE companies alone operated in the red for a one-year period ending mid-1983.

There have always been opportunities for the astute investor to take advantage of the underpriced, distressed securities of companies that will eventually return to financial good health. What is important to realize, however, is that in 1984 the pickings are greater than ever before because of the economic hardships of the preceding three years. Particularly hard hit were the most highly cyclical industries: airlines, auto and truck manufacturers, home builders, oil refiners, railroads, steel, textiles, agricultural equipment, aluminum, appliances, heavy machinery, iron, metals, rubber, tires and trucking. After discussing an investment strategy that operates in this troubled arena, let's take a look at what created the environment of extreme corporate distress to begin with.

POST-WAR EXPANSION

The financial trauma that most nations felt during the past three years came very close to bringing the world economic system to its knees. The effects in this country alone were devastating: record inflation rates and interest rates in 1980 and 1981 that, in turn, caused record business failures and unemployment in 1982 and 1983. Not since the Depression had we seen such widespread corporate distress: In addition to the 50,000 American companies that filed for bankruptcy in 1982–83, as many 400,000 companies simply went out of business, paying their debts instead of seeking bankruptcy protection.

What went wrong? Every American has been aware of our desperate economic plight over the past several years—especially those unfortunate enough to have been out of work—yet surprisingly few of us have really examined the sociological and political trends of the 1970s that brought about this crisis of the early 1980s.

The 1950 to 1972 era will always be remembered by historians as a period of unprecedented economic stability, expansion, and growing worldwide prosperity. After centuries of only intermittent growth in the Western world, the post-World War II international environment seemed to foster ideal conditions for stable growth. To begin with, energy was cheap everywhere; oil prices, for example, were only $2 a barrel. During this period, most Western nations evolved from an agricultural to an industrial orientation. Food production had grown as a result of advanced agricultural techniques and equipment, and this allowed millions of farm workers to take part in the rapid industrialization of America. These were also the golden years of higher education expansion in this country.

Economic growth took place at a healthy 5% per year throughout the 1950s and 1960s, while interest rates and inflation both stayed very low. (Hardly a concern to anyone, the inflation rate remained in the 2% to 4% range for the entire two decades, while short-term interest rates generally floated between 2% and 6%.) Almost everyone had job security, the unemployment rate seldom rising above 4%. After years of international depression in the 1930s and international war in the 1940s, the world seemed ready for long and compatible economic growth by the 1950s. International trade expanded to new heights for the next twenty years. The standard of living in industrial nations improved dramatically.

THE RISING TIDE OF INFLATION

The American dream of endless economic growth and individual financial security was quickly and unexpectedly dashed in the 1970s by crippling worldwide inflation. It was this very problem of uncontrollable inflation that brought on skyrocketing interest rates (by the end of the '70s), which, in turn, caused the recessionary crisis and business failures of the early 1980s. The cause of the spiraling inflation, in my opinion, was a three-sided attack that this country wasn't prepared for: sudden skyrocketing energy costs, a rapid rise in government spending with subsequent deficits, and the ensuing struggle among American workers and consumers to maintain their standard of living amidst rapidly rising costs.

The first OPEC oil price hikes in 1973 hit the world like a thunderbolt. Hindsight now mocks our wastefulness, and our naïveté about this precious resource, but prior to that time most of us never gave a second thought to the costs or limits of energy. By the end of the decade, world oil prices had risen some seventeen fold (from $2 to $34 per barrel), helping to drive up the U.S. annual inflation rate from 2% to 14%.

American industry and American society were particularly unprepared for what we considered at the time to be energy blackmail. (Most of us suddenly felt that we had some kind of inalienable right to natural resources at a cheap price.) Our whole society was hopelessly hooked on cheap oil: from fuel-wasting cars to inefficient factories and inefficient houses. And the restructuring of both capital equipment and long-ingrained American habits takes a lot of time.

A combination of wage increases and government expansion throughout the '70s continued to fuel the fire that OPEC had ignited. Labor unions demanded cost-of-living raises, which made inflation a self-perpetuating phenomenon. The ensuing panic to maintain our standard of living led to a host of increased government subsidies, such as unemployment insurance, education loans, as well as enormous Social Security benefit increases.

The cost of doing business, especially because of union labor costs, soared throughout the decade. The increase in wages, even after adjusting for inflation, far exceeded increases in productivity. American labor, already less efficient than its foreign counterparts, began to be a drag on corporate investment. Prices for products and services subsequently shot up too, further fueling the inflationary spiral. A great irony in this period lies in the desperate attempt that most of us made to protect ourselves from the effects of inflation, which, of course, only perpetuated the problem further. We became a nation of chronic spenders, convinced that prices for everything could only go higher.

A whole new investment strategy developed, based on leveraging money to the maximum and riding the tidal wave of inflation. Paper investments were out; inflation-based tangible assets were in. A whole generation of young entrepreneurs emerged as millionaires after just a few years of playing the hot new real estate market. The only requirement was a little cash and the decision to get started; inflation took care of the rest. Lack of any business sense at all was usually forgiven by surging prices, as a nation of real estate geniuses grew out of the late '70s—condominiumizing of America.

Meanwhile, most of America fought desperately to stave off the stranglehold of inflation. Government expansion during this period drove up interest rates. Private industry suddenly found itself in the precarious position of competing against the government for the same investor funds. As industry incurred more operating and capital expenses and the government's own debt grew, interest rates began to spiral.

THE HURDLE OF HIGH INTEREST RATES

With record-high interest and inflation rates, escalating labor costs, restrictive government regulatory policies, and a high, counter-productive corporate tax structure, industrial America entered the new decade of the eighties in a totally adverse business climate. Anticipating this environment, most industries had already reduced capital expenditures considerably, delaying much-needed revamping of obsolete, energy-inefficient factories and equipment. (Overall capital investment in this country dropped in half between 1970 and the early 1980s.) These reductions put us at a disadvantage to foreign competitors, putting a further crimp in American industry. (By comparison, Japan's rate of capital investment is four times ours. That country's highly efficient labor force is also much more compatible with goals of total industrial production, readily accepting pay cuts as well as pay raises.)

The inflation rate subsided in the early '80s. Gone were the days of rampant consumer spending ("buy it today because it will only cost more tomorrow"). But interest rates continued to soar between 1979 and 1982 for three reasons: a general fear of reinflation, competition for money because of the growing government deficit, and because the new Federal Reserve Board Chairman, Paul Volker, decided to use high interest rates (tight money policy) as his own way of fighting inflation in the private sector during this period. The year 1981 was peculiar in economic history with its rapidly declining inflation rate coinciding with its rapidly increasing interest rates.

Record high interest rates did succeed in reducing the crippling inflation that plagued us throughout the 1970s, but despite that important accomplishment, the economy looked very sick in the early 1980s: America experienced the worst recession, highest corporate failure rate, and highest unemployment rate since the Great Depression. During the crest of the severe recession in 1982, in fact, many people feared a total economic collapse similar to that of the 1930s.

The self-perpetuation of distress did come dangerously close to catastrophe. The tens of thousands of corporate bankruptcies in 1982 and 1983 had far-reaching effects. Every business failure sets off a chain reaction: The company's lenders, suppliers, supporting and related businesses and employees all suffer. Unemployed workers reduce the number of consumers that support other businesses. Failing businesses can not only hurt their own creditors and bank lenders but sometimes set off a panic in the financial community. Banks that have taken big losses from recent bankruptcies—Braniff, Nucorp, Lionel, AM International, Wickes, Penn Square Bank—often have more difficulty with their own financial requirements, such as the sale of bonds or CDs. Big corporate failures can have particularly far-reaching effects on their own industries. When Braniff filed for bankruptcy in April 1982, the whole industry was hurt by the excess aircraft available on the market. This reduced the value of each airline's assets and consequently diminished their ability to borrow more money, which, in turn, raised their costs for capital improvement and equipment.

The most common problem that recently bankrupt companies had that made them fail was the enormous burden of high interest rates. They were simply paying more in interest than they could earn with the borrowed money, which is a hopelessly losing proposition. Many corporations are still inordinately laden with debt today. Even though interest rates have declined considerably over the past two years, they are still quite high if measured in real terms (compared to the rate of inflation). In more inflationary times, the rising value of inventories combined with a favorable business cycle would often make up for the extra costs of financing. But in recent years, higher interest costs combined with a dramatic business slowdown have substantially cut the margin of error that a borderline company survives by.

OVERREACTION

As bad as it was, corporate distress in 1982–83 was certainly not the same as in 1932–33. The failure rate (where creditors lose money) in the recent recession was 100 out of every 10,000 companies at its worst, which was only half the rate of the Depression. The $3 billion in total liabilities of the six bankrupt companies mentioned above are dwarfed by today's $3 *trillion* economy. Let's take a closer look at some of the casualties of the past few years to see if they were subject to that common syndrome of overreaction by the press and public. How much actual damage did these recent corporate failures do to their industries?

Panic struck in 1982 when the Oklahoma bank, Penn Square, was closed down after a long record of horrible mismanagement of funds. Talks of a national and even international banking collapse prevailed throughout the year. Although many weak banks were merged into stronger banks during the year, a total of only thirty-four actually failed in 1982, compared to a total U.S. bank population of over 14,000. That's only one failure out of every 400 banks, during the very height of our recessionary crisis. In the early 1930s, by comparison, over 5,000 U.S. banks went out of business. Today, banks and bank depositors alike are protected by two federal agencies that have the job of guiding our financial system: the Fed and the FDIC.

Even the huge international loans that our major banks made so freewheelingly in the 1970s were never as unmanageable as most people thought. Many of the Third World loans are backed by U.S. government guarantees, while the nonguaranteed loans are usually distributed among several of the largest international banks.

Farm industry failures in the last recession were also overstated. To begin with, the majority of agricultural bankruptcies are voluntary, a long-standing practice of farmers who retire or leave the agriculture business. Secondly, most farm mortgage loans today are backed by federal agencies: the Federal Land Bank and the Farmers Home Loan Administration. The commercial banks are now usually at risk only for farm equipment loans.

Besides the outstanding investment opportunities that often result from bankrupt companies, there are other redeeming qualities found in corporate failure. In the system of free enterprise, competition naturally breeds both success and failure. Bankruptcy is a great Darwinian weeding-out process. As Frank Borman (whose own company—Eastern Airlines—was once close to failure) is fond of saying, "Capitalism without bankruptcy is like Christianity without hell."

An airline's failure not only might provide bottom fishers with an investment opportunity, but it will ultimately increase the efficiency of the airline industry, which got vastly overextended after it was deregulated. Excess capacity in this type of industry can quickly be reduced by surviving companies. The looming threat of insolvency tends to make the free market system strive for efficiency. And assets, resources, and people often get recycled into better hands within an industry whenever there is a failure, adding strength to the survivors.

INVESTMENT CYCLES

The 1970s were the years for tangible assets; ask any veteran real estate investor. When interest rates are low and the inflation rate is high, it's hard to lose on this kind of investment. But by the end of that decade, just about the time when the marvels of real estate and gold and other tangible collectibles hit the covers of *Time* and *Newsweek*, a funny thing happened: interest rates went up and the inflation rate went down. Just when most of us were beginning to play, that game was over.

From 1979 until mid-1982, we now know, Cash was King. Interest rates went through the roof. Money-market funds exploded from $10 billion in assets to over $230 billion, as their interest rates sometimes exceeded 20%. In this atmosphere of high interest rates and low inflation, the most rewarding investments turned out to be the safest and most liquid ones—"cash instruments." But, once again, just as the last skeptics were finally convinced of the wonders of these new money marvels, the second half of 1982 spoiled it all with dramatic drops in interest rates. Investing started to get more difficult.

Wise investors then turned to the most traditional vehicles—stocks and bonds—for the first time in ten years. These instruments appeared very cheap after years of neglect, and the investment atmosphere finally seemed ideal for their success: low interest rates combined with a low inflation rate. What followed was the greatest rise of prices and activity in Wall Street's history. Most analysts see the renewed interest in the financial markets as the beginning of a new investment era.

The 1982–83 stock market rally was clearly led by the institutional favorites: highly visible, blue chip companies as well as the popular, overpriced technology companies. Still ignored, and perhaps the only real bargains left in the market today, are the out-of-favor, distressed, and even bankrupt companies. Many of these companies, without a doubt, will rise again to financial stardom within the next few years.

BUSINESS FAILURES PER YEAR
(1950 – 1982)

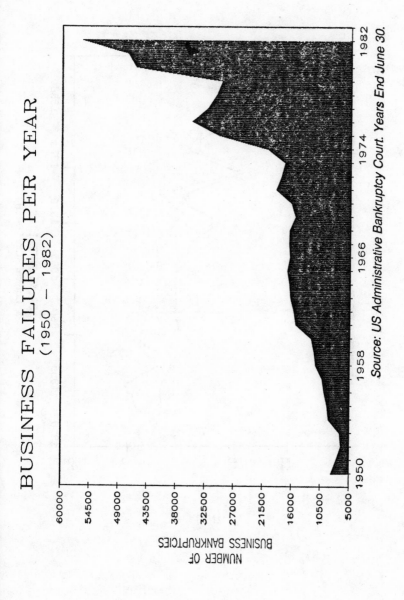

NUMBER OF BUSINESS BANKRUPTCIES

Source: US Administrative Bankruptcy Court. Years End June 30.

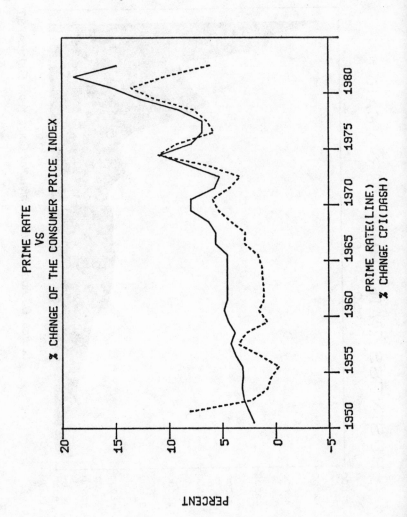

PRIME RATE
VS
% CHANGE OF THE CONSUMER PRICE INDEX

PRIME RATE(LINE)
% CHANGE. CPI(DASH)

PERCENT

Graph courtesy Data Resources, Inc.

14

Price Histories of Bankruptcy Stocks

The following are graphs of the price behavior of several NYSE companies that have filed for Chapter 11 during the 1980s, recorded weekly from six months prior to filing until one year after filing. (Prices and graphing by Data Resources Inc. for this book.)

Four of the companies—Wickes, Braniff, AM International, and Bobbie Brooks—registered significant market rebounds during their first twelve months of trading in bankruptcy. But the others did not, supporting the fact that each Chapter 11 case is unique.

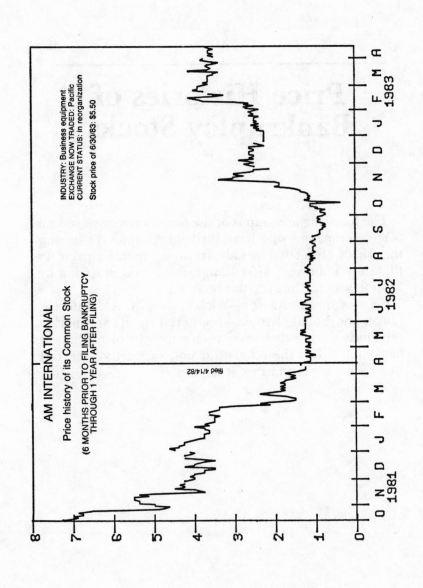

AM INTERNATIONAL

Price history of its Common Stock

(6 MONTHS PRIOR TO FILING BANKRUPTCY
THROUGH 1 YEAR AFTER FILING)

INDUSTRY: Business equipment
EXCHANGE NOW TRADED: Pacific
CURRENT STATUS: in reorganization

Stock price of 6/30/83: $5.50

filed 4/14/82

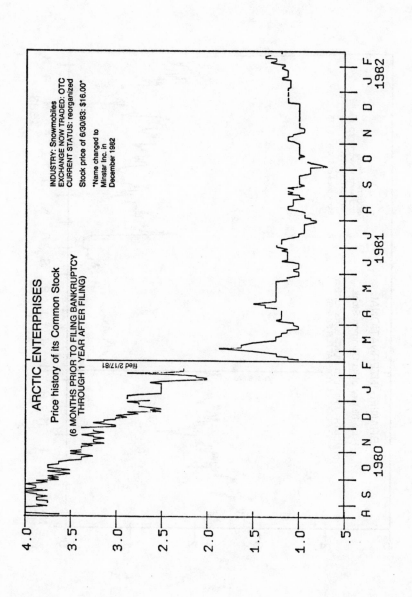

ARCTIC ENTERPRISES

Price history of its Common Stock

(6 MONTHS PRIOR TO FILING BANKRUPTCY
THROUGH 1 YEAR AFTER FILING)

INDUSTRY: Snowmobiles
EXCHANGE NOW TRADED: OTC
CURRENT STATUS: reorganized

Stock price of 6/30/83: $16.00*

*Name changed to
Minstar Inc. in
December 1982

filed 2/17/81

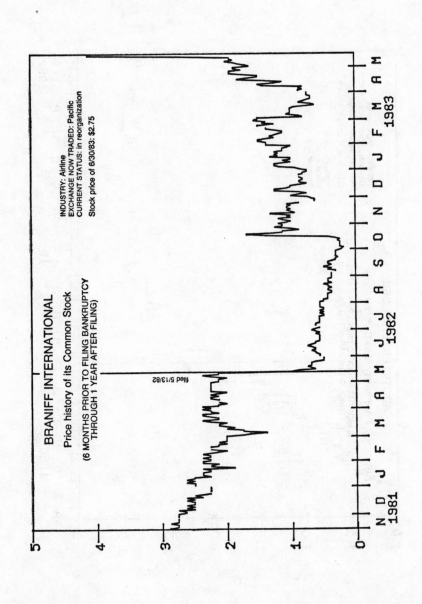

BRANIFF INTERNATIONAL

Price history of its Common Stock

(6 MONTHS PRIOR TO FILING BANKRUPTCY
THROUGH 1 YEAR AFTER FILING)

INDUSTRY: Airline
EXCHANGE NOW TRADED: Pacific
CURRENT STATUS: in reorganization

Stock price of 6/30/83: $2.75

filed 5/13/82

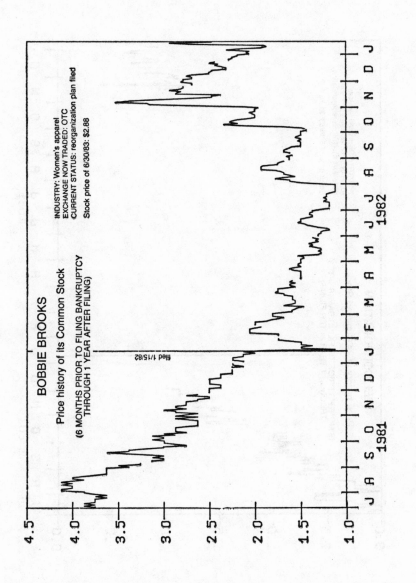

BOBBIE BROOKS

Price history of its Common Stock

(6 MONTHS PRIOR TO FILING BANKRUPTCY
THROUGH 1 YEAR AFTER FILING)

INDUSTRY: Women's apparel
EXCHANGE NOW TRADED: OTC
CURRENT STATUS: reorganization plan filed

Stock price of 6/30/83: $2.88

filed 1/15/82

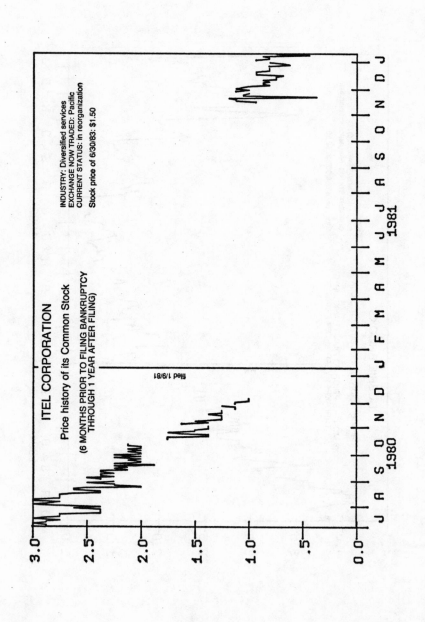

ITEL CORPORATION

Price history of its Common Stock

(6 MONTHS PRIOR TO FILING BANKRUPTCY
THROUGH 1 YEAR AFTER FILING)

INDUSTRY: Diversified services
EXCHANGE NOW TRADED: Pacific
CURRENT STATUS: in reorganization

Stock price of 6/30/83: $1.50

filed 1/9/81

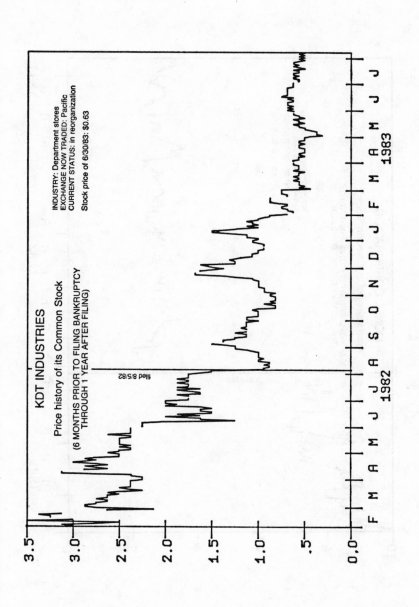

KDT INDUSTRIES

Price history of its Common Stock

(6 MONTHS PRIOR TO FILING BANKRUPTCY
THROUGH 1 YEAR AFTER FILING)

INDUSTRY: Department stores
EXCHANGE NOW TRADED: Pacific
CURRENT STATUS: in reorganization

Stock price of 6/30/83: $0.63

filed 8/5/82

1982   1983

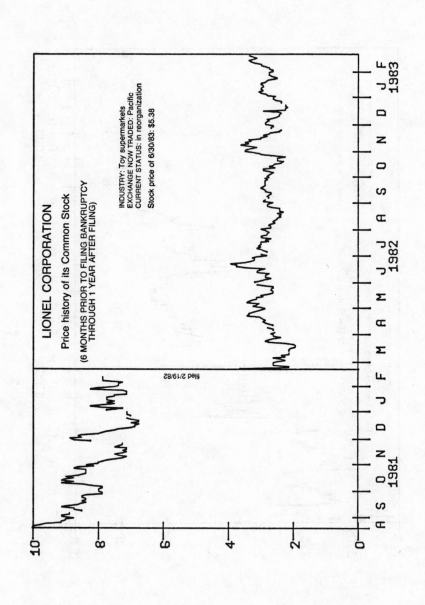

LIONEL CORPORATION

Price history of its Common Stock

(6 MONTHS PRIOR TO FILING BANKRUPTCY
THROUGH 1 YEAR AFTER FILING)

INDUSTRY: Toy supermarkets
EXCHANGE NOW TRADED: Pacific
CURRENT STATUS: in reorganization

Stock price of 6/30/83: $5.38

filed 2/19/82

10

8

6

4

2

0

A S O N D J F   M A M J J A S O N D J F
  1981   1982   1983

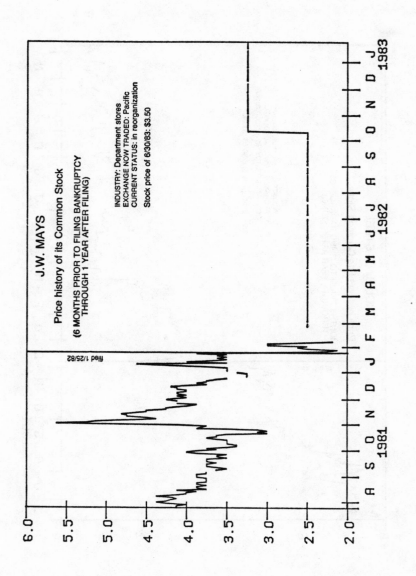

J.W. MAYS

Price history of its Common Stock

(6 MONTHS PRIOR TO FILING BANKRUPTCY
THROUGH 1 YEAR AFTER FILING)

INDUSTRY: Department stores
EXCHANGE NOW TRADED: Pacific
CURRENT STATUS: in reorganization

Stock price of 6/30/83: $3.50

filed 1/25/82

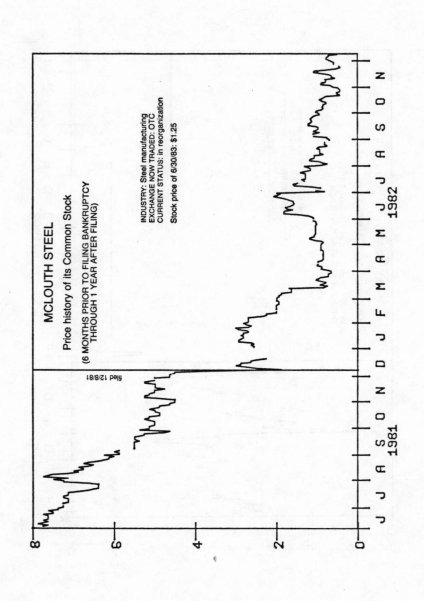

MCLOUTH STEEL

Price history of its Common Stock

(6 MONTHS PRIOR TO FILING BANKRUPTCY THROUGH 1 YEAR AFTER FILING)

INDUSTRY: Steel manufacturing
EXCHANGE NOW TRADED: OTC
CURRENT STATUS: in reorganization

Stock price of 6/30/83: $1.25

filed 12/8/81

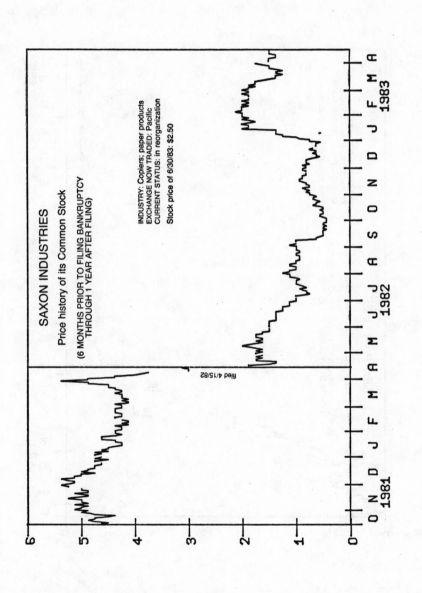

SAXON INDUSTRIES

Price history of its Common Stock

(6 MONTHS PRIOR TO FILING BANKRUPTCY
THROUGH 1 YEAR AFTER FILING)

INDUSTRY: Copiers; paper products
EXCHANGE NOW TRADED: Pacific
CURRENT STATUS: in reorganization

Stock price of 6/30/83: $2.50

filed 4/15/82

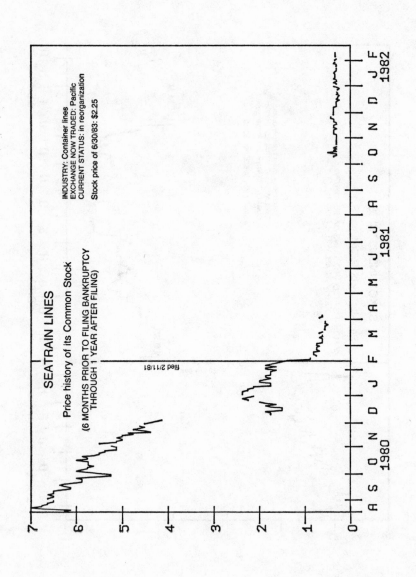

SEATRAIN LINES

Price history of its Common Stock

(6 MONTHS PRIOR TO FILING BANKRUPTCY
THROUGH 1 YEAR AFTER FILING)

INDUSTRY: Container lines
EXCHANGE NOW TRADED: Pacific
CURRENT STATUS: in reorganization

Stock price as of 6/30/83: $2.25

filed 2/11/81

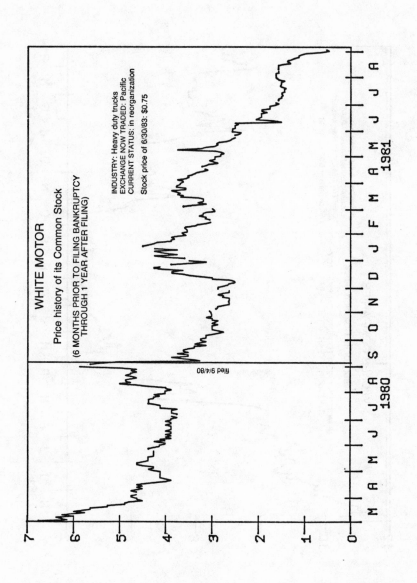

WHITE MOTOR

Price history of its Common Stock

(6 MONTHS PRIOR TO FILING BANKRUPTCY
THROUGH 1 YEAR AFTER FILING)

INDUSTRY: Heavy duty trucks
EXCHANGE NOW TRADED: Pacific
CURRENT STATUS: in reorganization

Stock price of 6/30/83: $0.75

filed 9/4/80

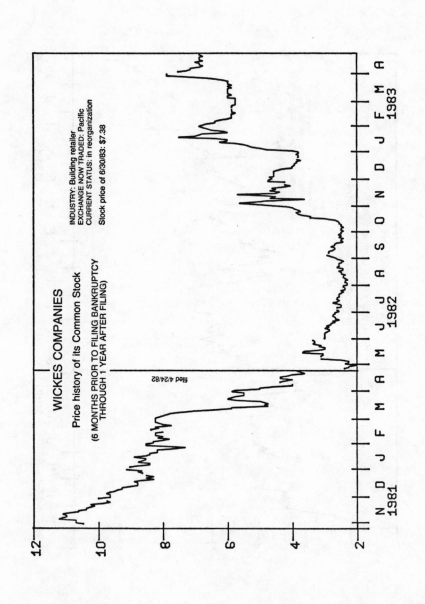

WICKES COMPANIES

Price history of its Common Stock

(6 MONTHS PRIOR TO FILING BANKRUPTCY
THROUGH 1 YEAR AFTER FILING)

INDUSTRY: Building retailer
EXCHANGE NOW TRADED: Pacific
CURRENT STATUS: in reorganization

Stock price of 6/30/83: $7.38

filed 4/24/82

The Phoenix Glossary

The following words and terms have either been used in this book or are applicable to the subjects of the book.

ACCRUED INTEREST: Daily interest that has built up on a bond since the last payment date. A bond buyer normally pays to the seller interest that has accrued to date, then keeps the full interest payment the next time it comes due.

ANNUAL REPORT: The company's yearly financial report to its stockholders. The most important financial information included in an annual report is the balance sheet and income statement (earnings report).

ARBITRAGE: The simultaneous purchase and sale of the same security, or the equivalent of the same security, in order to take advantage of a price difference in two places that it trades.

ASSETS: Everything that a corporation owns. Its most liquid assets are called current assets, and include cash and securities as well as inventories and receivables. Fixed assets include things like buildings and equipment.

BALANCE SHEET: That part of a company's annual report that shows what the company owns and what it owes (assets and liabilities). The difference between the two essentially represents the stockholders' equity in the company.

BANKRUPTCY: An adjudication in which a debtor is protected by the court while creditors are dealt with in an equitable way.

BOND: A debt obligation of a corporation. The company (debtor) borrows money from investors (creditors of the corporation), generally in $1,000 increments, with the promise of specified interest payments and repayment on a predetermined maturity date. The bond itself can be bought and sold in the open market during its life.

BOOK VALUE: The theoretical value of a single share of stock based on the asset values that the company carries on its records. Assets minus liabilities and obligations, divided by the number of common shares outstanding, gives us this value.

CAPITAL STOCK: Any common or preferred stock which makes up ownership of a company.

CAPITALIZATION: The total of all the securities of a company, including its common and preferred stocks as well as all bond issues. While bonds are generally carried on a company's books at face value, stocks are often carried at an arbitrary figure called par value.

CASH FLOW: The total net income of a company plus any special bookkeeping or tax deductions that do not represent an actual outlay of funds, such as depreciation.

COLLATERAL TRUST BOND: A bond that is backed by securities of the debtor company, or by securities owned by that company which are held by a trustee.

COMMON STOCK: One of the two types of securities that represent equity ownership of a corporation. The other, preferred stock, has certain priorities of dividends and asset claims over common stock.

CONGLOMERATE: A corporation that owns or controls a number of other companies in unrelated industries.

CONSOLIDATED STATEMENT: A financial statement that combines the reports of a parent company and its subsidiaries as if they were all one company.

CONVERTIBLE: Usually a bond or preferred stock that can be exchanged for common stock of the same company.

COVERAGE OF FIXED CHARGES: The ratio of a company's pretax earnings to its fixed bond interest. A healthy company should have its interest payments covered several times over.

CREDITOR: An individual or company that is owed money in a bankruptcy case.

CUMULATIVE PREFERRED: A preferred stock that has the company's guarantee that any omitted dividends will be made up to the stockholder of that issue before dividends will be paid on any other of the company's stock issues.

CURRENT ASSETS: A company's most liquid assets, which include securities, cash, receivables, and most inventories.

CURRENT LIABILITIES: A company's most immediate debts. These are usually defined as money due to be paid out within one year.

CURRENT RATIO: Ratio of a company's current assets to its current liabilities.

DEBENTURES: A corporate bond secured only by the company's name and good faith.

DEBTOR: The company that owes money to individuals or other companies in a bankruptcy case.

DEFAULT: Usually refers to the failure of a corporation to meet either an interest or principal payment on a bond.

DEPRECIATION: The devaluation of an asset, for accounting and tax purposes, over the expected useful life of that asset.

DILUTION: Usually refers to the reduction of earnings per share of stock, and the reduction of ownership position by existing stockholders, because of the issuance of more shares.

DISCHARGE: A creditor's claim that has been thrown out by court order in a bankruptcy case. The debtor does not have to pay the claim.

DIVIDEND: A distribution of cash or further shares to stockholders, usually coming from current earnings (although sometimes taken from retained earnings).

DOW THEORY: The theory of Charles Dow that says that when both Dow Jones Averages (Transportation and Industrial) break out of an established price range, a new market trend has been established.

EARNINGS PER SHARE: Total corporate earnings (for three months or a year), minus preferred dividends, divided by the number of common shares outstanding.

EARNINGS REPORT: A statement by a company on how much net profit or loss it had over a given period of time, usually three months or a year.

EQUIPMENT TRUST CERTIFICATE: A bond that is secured by a specific piece of equipment whose title is held by a trustee as collateral against the terms of the bond. This type of security is usually issued by an airline or railroad for the purpose of financing a jetliner or rail car.

EQUITY: Ownership of a company, as represented by common or preferred stock.

FACE VALUE: The amount of money that a company promises to pay bondholders upon maturity. Also called par value, and usually $1,000 per bond, this amount is stated on the face of the bond certificate.

FISCAL YEAR: The twelve-month period that a corporation uses to define its year for bookkeeping and accounting purposes. Because of the various business cycles from industry to industry, many companies use a fiscal year that is different from the calendar year.

FLAT: A bond that trades without accrued interest being added to the price. Bonds in default trade flat.

FUNDED DEBT: The long-term debt obligations of a company, including bonds and bank loans.

GENERAL MORTGAGE BOND: A bond that is backed by a blanket mortgage on the company's property. Other mortgage bonds of the same company might have seniority over the general mortgage bond.

GUARANTEED BOND: A bond whose principal or interest is backed by another company, in addition to the issuer. A guaranteed stock is one whose dividend is similarly backed.

HOLDING COMPANY: Any company that owns a controlling interest in another company or in several other companies.

INCOME BONDS: A bond whose interest payments are contingent upon the company's earnings.

INDENTURE: The original contract for a bond issue, which spells out the exact terms of the bond as well as the rights of the issuer, investors, and trustee.

INSIDER: Someone who is very close to a corporation, such as a director, officer, control person, or even a relative of one of these people.

INSOLVENT: The financial state in which a corporation either cannot pay its current debts or has a negative net worth.

LETTERED STOCK: Unregistered stock which cannot be sold in the open marketplace.

LEVERAGE: The effect that borrowed money has on the net earnings of a company. The extra working capital boosts earnings during profitable times, but fixed interest payments are a drag on earnings during difficult times.

LIABILITIES: Everything that a company owes, such as the principal and interest of bonds and loans, tax obligations, payroll, declared dividends, and any other claims against the company.

LIEN: The claim on a specific piece of property that has been pledged to secure a bond.

LIQUIDATION: The dissolution of a corporation under Chapter 7 of the Federal Bankruptcy Code, whereby the company's assets are sold and the proceeds distributed equitably to creditors and security-holders on a priority basis.

MATURITY: The date that a bond is due to be paid off by the corporation.

MINOR INTEREST: The remaining common stock of a company whose controlling interest is owned by a holding company.

MORTGAGE BOND: A bond that is secured by a mortgage on a specific piece of property.

NONRECURRING ITEM: Any unusual event that creates a particular gain or loss for a company that is not apt to happen again. The selling off of an asset or subsidiary would create an unusual gain, for example, while a natural disaster might create an unusual loss on the company's income statement.

OPEN INDENTURE: A bond indenture that allows additional bonds to be issued in the future under certain conditions.

OPERATING RATIO: The relationship of operating expenses to gross revenues.

OUTSTANDING STOCK: The shares of a company that are

currently held by stockholders. This does not include unissued shares held by the company.

PAR: An arbitrary value assigned to a share of common stock to be carried on the company's balance sheet. In the case of preferred stock, par value is significant because it is the price on which dividend is calculated. Par value for a bond is the original issue price (usually $1,000), as well as the price at which the company promises to repay the bond (also called face value).

PARTICIPATING PREFERRED: A preferred stock which is entitled to extra dividends (based on the amount paid to common stockholders) in addition to its regular fixed dividend.

PHILADELPHIA PLAN: An arrangement used to back equipment obligations in which the chattel is leased to the issuer of the debt by a trustee who holds legal title to the equipment. This plan is commonly used to finance aircraft, buses, locomotives, and other types of transportation equipment.

PREFERENCE: An arrangement made between a creditor and a debtor in a bankruptcy case, in which the creditor ends up with better compensation than other creditors in the same class.

PREFERENCE STOCK: A class of stock sometimes issued by utility companies that pays a fixed dividend and stands between preferred stock and common stock in the hierarchy of security classes.

PREFERRED STOCK: A security that represents equity ownership in a company and is entitled to a fixed dividend that has priority in payment over that of the common stockholders of the company. Preferred stockholders also have a priority claim on the company's assets over common stockholders in a bankruptcy case.

PRICE-EARNINGS RATIO: The current price of a stock in relation to (divided by) the company's earnings per share over the past year. A common measurement of a stock is value; the term is usually called just PE.

PRIOR PREFERRED: A preferred stock that has seniority over other preferreds in its claim on dividends and company assets.

RATIO ANALYSIS: The comparison of a company's various financial figures as an analytical method of determining the health of the company.

RECAPITALIZATION: The retirement of certain classes of a company's securities and replacement of new securities.

RECEIVERSHIP: Commonly used prior to 1933 in cases of insolvency, where a state court appointed a receiver to protect the company's property and operate its business until a solution could be worked out for the company's debts.

REORGANIZATION: A corporate bankruptcy solution where a successor company is formed and new securities are issued to security holders of the bankruptcy company. The purpose of reorganization is to keep the business concern in operation and to avoid liquidation.

SET-OFF: When two parties owe one another money in a bankruptcy case and the debts are deemed by the court to cancel one another.

SINKING FUNDS: A scheduled redemption of bonds or preferred stock that is used to reduce the size of the issue over a period of time.

SUBORDINATED BOND: Generally refers to a debenture that is junior in ranking to another debenture of the same company.

TRUSTEE: In a bankruptcy proceeding, a person appointed by the court to investigate the finances of the debtor, account for the assets of the debtor, and examine the claims of the creditors.

VOTING RIGHT: The right of a stockholder to vote in company issues. Usually common stockholders have one vote per share, while perferred stockholders normally vote only in cases of default.

WARRANT: A certificate which gives the owner the right to purchase securities (usually common shares) of a company at a specific price any time within a stated time period (usually several years).

WORKING CAPITAL: Current assets minus current liabilities, which indicates the amount of liquid funds a company has available at a given time.

About the Author

WILLIAM J. GRACE, JR., vice president of a major Wall Street investment firm, is one of the most important new financial writers in the country. His first book, *The ABCs of IRAs,* is among the most popular investment guides of the 1980s. In the past year, he has completed *The Phoenix Approach,* written for the *Washington Post,* been an active guest speaker, and given numerous financial commentaries for radio and television, including The Larry King Show, The Merv Griffin Show and Good Morning America. A highly successful investor himself, Mr. Grace is located in Washington, D.C., where he advises many of the nation's leaders on their own personal investments.